HOW TO PROVIDE A CONVINCING ALIBI

My name is P.K. Pinkerton & I am a Private Eye operating out of Virginia City, Nevada Territory. At the moment I am in Jail on the charge of Murder.

I am writing this Journal because my lawyer told me to set down my side of the story. He told me to write it as if I was talking to a jury of "12 good men and true" or a kindly, sympathetic Judge with "white hair and twinkling eyes."

He said I should start by putting my name, age & qualifications.

I have already stated my name: P.K. Pinkerton.

I am 12 years old.

I can read & write & I can speak American and Lakota. I can also speak a little Spanish & Chinese & a few words of French.

I am really good at tracking & hunting. My eyes are as sharp as a hawk's & my ears are as keen as a rabbit's & my sense of smell is almost as good as a bear's.

For the sake of honesty, I must confess that I have a Thorn.

My Thorn is that people confound me. I am not good at reading people's faces & sometimes have trouble knowing if they are telling me the truth or lying.

As well as my Thorn, I have some Foibles & Eccentricities.

It is my Foibles & Eccentricities—and my Thorn—that have landed me here in jail today, beneath the shadow of the hangman's noose.

★ ★ ★ ★ ★ ★

OTHER BOOKS YOU MAY ENJOY

P.K. PINKERTON
AND THE
PETRIFIED
MAN

P.K. PINKERTON
AND THE
PETRIFIED MAN

CAROLINE LAWRENCE

PUFFIN BOOKS
An Imprint of Penguin Group (USA)

PUFFIN BOOKS
Published by the Penguin Group
Penguin Group (USA) LLC
375 Hudson Street
New York, New York 10014

USA * Canada * UK * Ireland * Australia
New Zealand * India * South Africa * China

penguin.com
A Penguin Random House Company

First published in Great Britain by Orion Children's Books,
a division of Orion Publishing Group, Ltd., 2012
First published in the United States of America by G. P. Putnam's Sons,
a division of Penguin Young Readers Group, 2013
Published by Puffin Books, an imprint of Penguin Young Readers Group, 2014

THE LIBRARY OF CONGRESS HAS CATALOGED THE G. P. PUTNAM'S SONS EDITION AS FOLLOWS:
Lawrence, Caroline. P.K. Pinkerton and the petrified man / Caroline Lawrence. p. cm.
Summary: "After escaping the ruthless desperados, master-of-disguise P.K. Pinkerton has now
set up a Private Eye business in Virginia City and is ready when a young maid named Martha
approaches him for help in escaping a killer"—Provided by publisher.
ISBN: 978-0-399-25634-9 (hc)
[1. Mystery and detective stories. 2. Disguise—Fiction. 3. Orphans—Fiction.
4. Racially mixed people—Fiction. 5. Nevada—History—19th century—Fiction.] I. Title.
PZ7.L425Pkp 2013
[Fic]—dc23
2012026737

Puffin Books ISBN 978-0-14-751033-4

Printed in the United States of America

1 3 5 7 9 10 8 6 4 2

To Nevada historian and
B Street B & B proprietress Carolyn Eichin,
who introduced me to the journals of Alf Doten,
a vein I can mine for years.

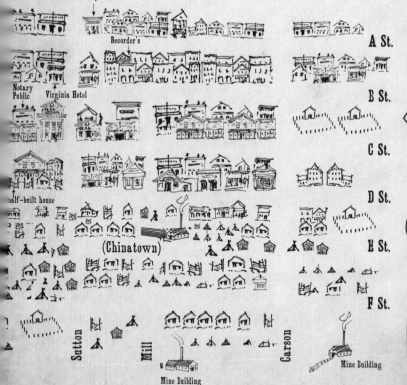

Mount Davidson

towards peak of
Mount Davidson
(uphill)

Mexican
Mine

Territorial
Enterprise

Recorder's

A St.

Notary
Public

Virginia Hotel

B St.

C St.

half-built house

D St.

(Chinatown)

E St.

F St.

Sutton

Mill

Carson

Mine Building

Mine Building

Ledger Sheet 1

MY NAME IS P.K. PINKERTON & I am a Private Eye operating out of Virginia City, Nevada Territory. At the moment I am in Jail on the charge of Murder.

I am writing this Journal because my lawyer told me to set down my side of the story. He told me to write it as if I was talking to a jury of "12 good men and true" or a kindly, sympathetic Judge with "white hair and twinkling eyes."

He said I should start by putting my name, age & qualifications.

I have already stated my name: P.K. Pinkerton.

I am 12 years old.

I can read & write & I can speak American and

Lakota. I can also speak a little Spanish & Chinese & a few words of French.

I am real good at tracking & hunting. My eyes are as sharp as a hawk's & my ears are as keen as a rabbit's & my sense of smell is almost as good as a bear's.

For the sake of honesty, I must confess that I have a Thorn.

My Thorn is that people confound me. I am not good at reading people's faces & sometimes have trouble knowing if they are telling the truth or lying.

As well as my Thorn, I have some Foibles & Eccentricities.

One of my Foibles is that I get the Mulligrubs.

One of my Eccentricities is I like Collecting things.

It is my Foibles & Eccentricities—and my Thorn—that have landed me here in jail today, beneath the shadow of the hangman's noose.

PK PINKERTON
PRIVATE EYE

WE HARDLY EVER SLEEP

Ledger Sheet 2

HERE IS WHAT HAPPENED.

After vanquishing three Deadly Desperados last Monday, I used $300 of the Reward Money to buy premises for my new business.

Mr. Sol Bloomfield was in the process of amalgamating his two small Tobacco Stores into one big Emporium down on C Street. I bought the smallest of his stores, the one on South B Street. Although it is long & narrow it suits me fine because it is located next to a Photographic Studio (where I can get disguises) and the Colombo Restaurant (where I take my meals).

Mr. Bloomfield removed the last of his cigars &

snuff & pipe tobacco from that store on Tuesday evening at 5:00 p.m.

I moved in on Tuesday evening at 6:00 p.m.

I opened my door for business at 9:00 a.m. on Wed October 1.

I had put up a shingle outside my front door with the words: P.K. PINKERTON, PRIVATE EYE. WE HARDLY EVER SLEEP. And I had a big sign in the window of the door that told people I was OPEN.

I had been greatly supported by the townsfolk after vanquishing a deadly desperado a few days before, and I was confident that I would soon get many clients. My foster pa, Emmet, always used to tell me to "strike while the iron is hot."

But all that morning not a single person came in through my door.

Maybe it was because the Washoe Zephyr had been blowing hard since the night before. I had been finishing the account of my first Case and did not notice, but now that I had nothing to do but sit and wait for clients, the powerful wind seemed to taunt me. They call it a "zephyr" but it was howling & moaning & spitting gravel at my shop front. My left arm began to throb where I had been shot two days before by a .22 caliber ball.

I began to feel very low.

By and by I felt so low that I was in danger of getting the Mulligrubs.

The "Mulligrubs" is what my foster ma, Evangeline, called a bad kind of trance that creeps up on me when I feel low. I can stay in those Bad Trances for hours. I rock & moan &

cannot easily be roused. When I come out of those trances, my brain feels thick & wooly, as if my head was stuffed full of cotton balls. Getting the Mulligrubs is another one of my Foibles.

Ma Evangeline—God rest her soul—taught me a way of staving off the Mulligrubs. If I concentrate on ordering a Collection, it distracts me & I forget to be low. When I was living with Ma Evangeline and Pa Emmet down in Temperance, they let me keep a Bug Collection & a Button Collection.

But I did not have either of those collections at my new residence in Virginia City, so I looked about me with an aim to starting a new one.

Mr. Sol Bloomfield had left all the labels on the shelves along with the tobacco crumbs & flakes that gave the place its distinctive smell.

I went back to my desk & found a pack of cigarrito papers & spread them out & copied down the names of all the different tobaccos. Then I went to the shelves and found bits of tobacco & started to put a sample of each tobacco on top of every label.

Using an out-of-date brochure that Mr. Bloomfield left behind, I catalogued over 50 Cuban Cigars, 32 Domestic Cigars, 17 types of Leaf Tobacco, 12 different Plugs & Twists and 6 varieties of Snuff.

So that made over 100 types of smoking, chewing and leaf tobacco. I decided to call it my Big Tobacco Collection so that it would begin with *B* like my other two collections: Bugs & Buttons.

Sometimes I looked up at the door that still admitted no

Clients & I felt kind of queasy in my stomach. But as soon as I returned to my new task I felt better.

In this way I staved off the Mulligrubs & fought the urge to be downcast. Sometimes I even forgot my throbbing arm & the howling wind & the memory of the terrible thing I had seen in my cabin down in Temperance.

It was a little past 5 p.m. and the sun had just dipped behind Mount Davidson when a bearded miner flung open the door to my office. I was so absorbed in ordering flecks of snuff that I almost jumped out of my skin. Some of that Zephyr whirled in and threatened to stir up my Big Tobacco Collection, so I shielded it with my arms & asked the man to shut the door.

He did so & stood there panting.

As I said, I am not good at reading people. It is my Thorn.

Ma Evangeline taught me five facial Expressions to look out for.

No. 1—If someone's mouth curves up & their eyes crinkle, that is a Genuine Smile.

No. 2—If their mouth stretches sideways & their eyes are not crinkled, that is a Fake Smile.

No. 3—If a person turns down their mouth & crinkles up their nose, they are disgusted.

No. 4—If their eyes open real wide, they are probably surprised or scared.

No. 5—If they make their eyes narrow, they are either mad at you or thinking or suspicious.

The eyes of the miner who had just burst into my office were open real wide.

It was definitely Expression No. 4.

He was scared.

I thought, "At last. Someone has brought me a mystery to solve."

Ledger Sheet 3

ARE YOU THE DETECTIVE?" cried the bearded miner, taking a step into my narrow office.

I did not betray my excitement at receiving my first Client.

"Yes," I said in a calm & businesslike tone. "I am P.K. Pinkerton, Private Eye. No problem too big, no case too small."

"Come quick!" panted the miner. "It's gone! It was thar a minute ago and now it's gone! Come see!"

I got up & grabbed my good slouch hat from a peg by the door & flipped my OPEN sign to CLOSED & followed him outside, closing the door as quickly as I could. Out on the blustery boardwalk, the shriek-ing Zephyr tried to snatch the hat from my head & the blue woolen coat from my back. Two other men were standing out there on the boardwalk. The wind was whipping up their slouch hats, beards & flannel shirts, and even the pants tucked into knee-high boots. I deduced from their flapping attire that they were miners, too.

As I locked the door behind me, they were all crying, "It's gone! It's gone!"

"What is gone?" I asked the miners. I had to shout to make myself heard.

"Come on," said the first one. "We'll show you!"

The three miners led the way: north along B Street & then left up Sutton towards A Street, their long brown beards fluttering behind them like pennants.

The wind was so strong that it made the planks of the boardwalk rattle. We had to lean into it at an angle of about 45 degrees just to make headway. That blasting Zephyr had driven most people indoors but a passing woman screamed as it lifted her hoopskirt right over her head to reveal frilly bloomers. A small dog was being pushed down the street in the opposite direction to the one it was heading. Oxen and mules kept their heads down & their eyes squinched & their teeth gritted.

In front of me, the three miners were shouting things like, "Where d'you think it went?" and "Who could of took it?"

"What is gone?" I repeated into the howling wind.

"Thar!" shouted the first miner, pointing. "It was right thar!"

I stopped and stared at the northwest corner of Sutton and A Street. I could not believe my eyes. Through a cloud of dust I could see nothing but a Vacant Lot.

"The Daily Territorial Enterprise Newspaper building," I said. "It is gone."

Two days previously I had been carried to the reporters' sleeping area next to the newspaper's printing office so that I could have a .22 caliber bullet dug out of my arm. Now the wooden building & its lean-to annex had Completely Vanished.

There remained not a single stick of wood. A tumbleweed sped across that Vacant Lot; it was going about a mile a minute.

"It was thar yesterday," Miner No. 2 shouted above the howling wind.

"And now it's gone," shouted Miner No. 3.

"Who could of took it?" shouted the first miner. "You're a Detective. You better look for clews!"

I looked around.

A woman's parasol flew by.

"Lookee here," shouted Miner No. 2. "There might be a clew in this morning's paper." He held it out.

The half-folded newspaper was flapping in the violent wind so I took it & looked where his grubby finger was stabbing & I read the following:

A GALE. *About 7 o'clock Tuesday evening a sudden blast of wind picked up a shooting gallery, two lodging houses and a drug store from their tall wooden stilts and set them*

down again some ten or twelve feet back of their original
location, with such a degree of roughness as to jostle their
insides into a sort of chaos. There were many guests in the
lodging houses at the time of the accident, but it is pleasant
to reflect that they seized their carpet sacks and vacated the
premises. No one hurt.

"Do you think maybe it was the Washoe Zephyr?" said the
first miner above the howling wind. "Do you think this pesky
breeze lifted it right up and set it down elsewheres?"

"That thar wind is a *Scriptural Wind*," shouted another, "on
account of no man knows *whence it cometh.*"

I looked down at the article & then back up to find the
three miners laughing & slapping their thighs & pointing
at me.

"He believed us!" cried one.

"He was looking for clews!" shouted another.

"He calls himself a 'Detective'!" The third one laughed.

That was when I realized the Ugly Truth.

They had not brought me my first case. They were pranking me.

I clenched my fists and considered kicking the nearest
miner hard in the shin. But Pa Emmet had taught me not to
kick people hard in the shin. He taught me to count to ten &
quote Philippians 4:5, "Let your moderation be known to all
men."

So I did not kick any of the miners hard in the shin. Nor
did I draw down on them with the Smith & Wesson's seven-
shooter in my pocket.

Instead I took a deep breath & bowed my head & counted to ten & quoted Philippians 4:5.

"Amen," I said.

As I lifted my head, the wind seemed to die down a little. I saw that the miners had gone & a tall man in a flapping gray suit stood beside me. He had a round face, a dark mustache & clean-shaven chin. He was smoking a cigar. He looked familiar.

"Hello, P.K.," he shouted above the wind. "Are you looking for the Enterprise?"

"Yes," I shouted back. "Some miners told me this wind blew it away. I reckon they were pranking me."

"Yes indeed," he shouted. "We moved down to our fine new premises on C Street yesterday. I guess those Chinese firewood-peddlers have been over this place and picked it clean." He sucked his cigar & blew out & the wind snatched away the smoke. "I came up here to see what still needed doing, but the answer is nary a thing. I could not have hired men to do such a good job."

I pointed at the article in the fluttering newspaper. "They tried to use this article called 'A Gale' to convince me," I said.

The man leant forward and looked at the article.

"Oh, that is just an attempt at humor by Mr. Sam Clemens, our new Local Reporter," he said. "He is still finding his feet, as they say."

Then I recognized the man who was speaking to me. He was Mr. Joe Goodman, one of the co-owners of the Territorial Enterprise Newspaper. He had promised to teach me some Latin phrases.

"You promised to teach some Latin phrases," I said.

"So I did," he replied. "Why don't you come down and visit us one day? You can find us at Twenty-Seven North C Street."

"I will." I folded the newspaper & put it in my coat pocket & turned to go back to my office.

"Oh, P.K.?" he said, shouting against the wind.

I turned back. "Yes?"

"Do not be discouraged. *Fortes fortuna iuvat.*"

"Beg pardon?"

He took out a pencil and wrote it down on the margin of my newspaper.

"That is Latin," he said. "It means 'Fortune favors the brave.'"

Ledger Sheet 4

WHEN I GOT BACK to my office I spread the newspaper out on top of my Big Tobacco Collection & studied the article by Sam Clemens that had inspired the miners to prank me.

It was obviously a passel of lies but there it was in black & white.

That made me mad.

Then I saw some other articles by Sam Clemens, a.k.a. "Josh," that made me even madder. In return for the gift of his seven-shooter, I had given Sam Clemens permission to write an article based on my experience of surviving a wagon-train massacre. When I saw a headline, **INDIAN TROUBLES ON THE OVERLAND ROUTE**, I knew it was his work, too.

As I read it, I got madder and madder. Mr. Sam Clemens had taken my story of being attacked by Indians and multiplied it by 12 or 15. He got many Facts wrong.

For example, he said it was Snake Indians that attacked the wagons. This got me riled because I am half Lakota and our enemies call us "Snake." So that was an Insult. Also, it was Shoshone that attacked us, not Lakota. So that was a Lie.

He then told how those Indians had attacked a "Methodist Train" & how the "whole party knelt down and began to pray as soon as the attack was commenced" but despite this the Snakes killed all the men and carried off the women & children. That was a Lie, too, and an Insult to Methodists.

But what really riled me was his description of wagons "transformed into magnified nutmeg-graters" by all the holes made by arrows. I guess he thought some people might find that funny. But I did not. My ma was killed in such an attack, along with her friend Tommy Three & our Chinese cook, Hang Sung.

I was so mad that I snatched up those center pages of the paper and took them into my back room to the chamber pot, intending to use his article to wipe my bottom.

But as I was sitting there, fuming over his lies, I noticed some illustrated Advertisements on the same page.

Those Ads gave me an idea so good that I forgot to be mad at that Reporter.

I finished my business & went back into my office &

spread out the page of Advertisements & took a blank ledger sheet & carefully wrote upon it:

THE FIRST PRIVATE DETECTIVE AGENCY
IN VIRGINIA CITY
P.K. PINKERTON, PRIVATE EYE,
South B Street nr Taylor
No Job too Small, No Challenge too Big,
Reasonable Rates
Specialties: Tracking Lost Animals,
Solving Mysteries, Shadowing Suspects

Then I drew an open eye and beneath it the words: We Hardly Ever Sleep.

The eye resembled a Potato somewhat, but I was confident the printers would do it better.

Then I braved the howling wind to take my Advertisement to the new offices of the Territorial Enterprise down on C Street. I paid them to put it in the next day's paper & I also bought a three-month subscription including delivery.

Placing that Advertisement had revived my spirits.

My arm had stopped throbbing & my appetite returned.

"*Fortes fortuna iuvat*," I said to myself. "Fortune favors the brave."

I went back up to B Street & had a square meal at the Colombo Restaurant.

That night I slept soundly, certain that the next day would bring me my first real Client and my first real Case.

Little did I dream that Case would spell my Doom.

Ledger Sheet 5

ON MY SECOND DAY of business—Thurs Oct 2—I rose at dawn, said my prayers & cleaned my Smith & Wesson's seven-shooter. Then I went next door to the Colombo Restaurant for a hearty Detective Breakfast of two mutton chops, eggs & buttered toast with marmalade. (I call this a "Detective Breakfast" because it is what Inspector Bucket favors in the novel *Bleak House* by Charles Dickens.)

Titus Jepson let me take a tin pot of coffee & a tin cup back to my office.

It was a fine morning. Yesterday's wind had died & the dust had settled. People were sashaying down the boardwalk and wagons were driving up the street. From some sage bushes on the mountainside a quail called out, "Chicago! Chicago!" That quail was reminding me of my vow that one day I would go to Chicago and work for the National Detective Agency of my uncle Allan.

A new saloon had opened across the way & although it was only 7:30 a.m., I could hear a piano clanging out a song I seemed to hear everywhere. I reckon that if Virginia City had its own anthem it would be "Camptown Races." Some music entrances me but this song had become so familiar that I could hum it with no danger of falling under its spell.

I found Thursday's *Territorial Enterprise* lying on the boardwalk outside my office. I put down the coffeepot & cup for a moment so that I could turn the handle of my office door. (I had not locked it because there was nothing much in there to steal.) I left the door wide-open to encourage business & I put the newspaper under my arm & took the coffeepot & cup inside.

As soon as I came into my office, the little hairs on the back of my neck prickled up.

Every time I step inside I can smell tobacco. But this time, I also caught the faintest whiff of horse manure & ammonia & another sweet smell that I could not identify. Lavender? Cloves? Opium?

"Hello?" I said. "Is anybody here?"

There was no reply.

I sniffed again, but now all I could smell was my Big Tobacco Collection.

Little did I realize that someone was Lying in Wait for me behind the counter at the back of my shop. I should have listened to my instincts, but I was excited by the prospect of seeing my Advertisement, so I shrugged away the prickly premonition & poured myself a cup of coffee & carefully spread out the paper on top of my Big Tobacco Collection & eagerly scanned the pages.

The front page contained news of a great Battle at a place called Antietam back east & of a new "Proclamation" by President Lincoln.

Those things were of little interest to me so I turned over the page.

There was my Advertisement on page three.

They had copied my drawing of an Eye. It still resembled a Potato, but aside from that I thought the Advertisement a good one. I was confident it would bring me my First Client in no time.

Near my Advertisement was a Notice of interest to me. It concerned a shocking crime that had occurred the week before: the Brutal Murder of a Soiled Dove named Miss Sally Sampson.

I do not have the paper in front of me now, but I can replicate most of that notice. You show me something once, I never forget it. It read as follows:

SALE OF PERSONAL PROPERTY
OF SALLY SAMPSON, DECEASED
SEPTEMBER 26TH, A.D. 1862

Notice is hereby given by an order of the Probate Court of the 1st day of October, A.D. 1862, in the matter of the estate of SALLY SAMPSON, a.k.a. "SHORT SALLY," deceased.

The undersigned Administratrix of the estate of said deceased will sell the following items at public auction, to the highest bidder, for cash, on SATURDAY, the 4th day of October, a.d. 1862, at one o'clock p.m. at the auction room of J.C. Currie & Co. in the city of Virginia, viz: Various High-quality dresses, capes, bonnets & parasols; 1 fireman's helmet; 2 whale-bone corsets & assorted undergarments; 1 Double Bedstead; 1 Double Spring Mattress; 1 Parlor Table; 3 Maple Chairs; 1 Mahog Whatnot; 2 white Mares; 1 buggy with red upholstery and black lacquer. (Mares & Buggy may be viewed at the Flora Temple Livery Stable.) Signed Mrs. Zoe BROWN, Administratrix of the Estate of Sally Sampson, deceased.

I had just finished reading this interesting notice when someone came in through my open door.

No, it was not the Client whose case would lead to my Demise. That person was crouching behind the counter at the back of my shop, though I did not discover that until later.

The person who came through my door was Becky "Bee" Bloomfield, the daughter of the man who had sold me my premises. She is 11 years old and claims to be the only girl in her class who has never been kissed. That is all she ever seems to want from me: a kiss.

I am not in the business of giving kisses.

I am in the Detective Business.

"What do you want?" I said without rising. "Shouldn't you be in school?"

"Good morning to you, too, P.K.!" Bee was wearing a green & white calico dress. She had a bonnet on her head and a parcel in her hands. "I am on my way to school now. What is that?" She was looking down at my desk.

"The *Daily Territorial Enterprise*," I said.

"No, underneath. All those pieces of cigarrito paper with writing and tobacco on them."

"That is my Big Tobacco Collection," I replied.

"P.K.," she said, "you are mighty peculiar. But I will still allow you to kiss me."

I folded my arms across my chest & tipped back my chair. "I am not in the Kissing Business," I said. "I am in the Detective Business. Do you have a Mystery for me to solve?"

"No, but I do have a parcel for you," she said. She plunked it on my desk so hard that some of my Big Tobacco Collection jumped onto the floor.

That made me mad & I stood up.

She said quickly, "It was on the boardwalk outside your door. Didn't you see it sitting there?"

The parcel was about the size of a cigar box. It was crudely wrapped in brown paper & twine with the words **FOR THE DETEKTEVE** scrawled in pencil.

I opened the parcel.

It was a wooden cigar box. Inside was a baby made of rocks resting on a bed of sawdust.

Yes. A Baby made of six smooth lumps of gray granite. There was an oval rock for the body, a round one for the head and four longish ones for the arms and legs. You could tell it was meant to be a baby because of the crude face painted on one. The worst thing about it were the blood-red letters painted on its rock belly: **R.I.P.**

"Rest In Peace," said Bee & brought her face close to the rock baby. "Is that *blood*?"

"No," I said. "It is paint. Blood turns brown when it dries."

"Ugh!" Bee shuddered. "It is ghastly."

I nodded. Then I reached down & picked up a small roll of paper lying next to the Stone Baby. It was a Page torn from a book.

"What does it say?" asked Bee as I unrolled it. "Does it say who it's meant for?"

I shook my head. "It is a page torn from a book," I said. "*Rock me to sleep, Mother, rock me to sleep.*"

Bee's forehead smoothed out. "I know that song."

"Song?"

"Yes, it is the chorus from a song about a dying soldier who wishes his mother was there to comfort him." She sang, "*Backward, turn backward, O Time, in your flight, Make me a child again just for tonight; Mother, come back from the echoless shore, Take me again to your heart as of yore.* What do you think it means?" she said.

"I do not know," I replied. "It is a Mystery."

"What if it is not a Mystery?" she said suddenly. "What if it is a *Warning*? Rest in Peace is what they put on *tombstones*." Bee's voice kind of squeaked when she said that last word. "Is there anybody who has it in for you?"

I nodded. "Two Deadly Desperados."

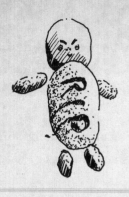

Ledger Sheet 6

TWO DEADLY DESPERADOS are after you?" gasped Bee Bloomfield. "How terrible!" Then she said, "What is a Desperado?"

I said, "A Desperado is a desperate outlaw. They are after me because I vanquished their boss."

"Oh, P.K.!" Bee covered the base of her throat with her hand & lowered her voice. "What do they look like?"

I said, "Boz is short with a squinty left eye and a whiny voice. Extra Dub is tall and scrawny with a big Adam's apple and a raspy voice. I thought they left town but maybe they returned to exact their revenge. They would probably like to gut me," I added.

"Oh, P.K.!" Bee nipped round to my side of the desk & threw her arms around me. I froze. I do not like being touched. Also, my left shoulder was still sore from being shot with that .22 caliber ball.

"You are so brave," said Bee. She pursed her lips & brought them closer & closer. I could smell minty Sozodont tooth powder.

I realized with horror that she was going to kiss me.

I writhed away just in time & ran around the other side of the desk. Bee pursued me.

Thankfully I was saved by the arrival of a man in a blue flannel shirt. He came stamping in through the open door, shouting, "Where is it? What have you done with it, you impudent puppy?"

Bee shrank back and I stepped forward with relief.

It was the new reporter in town, Sam Clemens, a.k.a. "Josh." I recognized him by his muttonchop whiskers and the faint smell of dead-critter tobacco that clung to his person.

He was of medium height & build with dark reddish-brown hair and flashing greenish-blue eyes. Usually he drawled, but today he spoke fast.

"Dang it, Pinky!" he said. "I am mad at you." Sure enough, he was wearing Expression No. 5, with his eyes narrowed.

"I am mad at you, too," I said. "And don't call me Pinky."

At this his expression changed entirely. It went straight from No. 5 to No. 4: Surprise. His eyes opened wide. "*You?* Mad at *me?* Why? And how am I supposed to tell when your expression never changes? You are as inscrutable as the wooden Indian down at Bloomfield's New Tobacco Emporium."

I folded my arms across my chest. "I am mad," I said, "because of two articles you wrote. One called 'A Gale' and one called 'Indian Troubles on the Overland Route.' Both articles contain statements that are Not True."

"Not true?" he said. "Not TRUE?" Then he burst out laughing. "Well of course they ain't true," he said. "It is journalism. I had to fill two columns. I had hoped that one about Indian Troubles would make the front page," he added. "And am bitterly disappointed that I was pushed back to page three."

"You said it was Sioux that attacked our train," I said, "when in fact it was Shoshone."

"Your wagon train was attacked by Indians?" gasped Bee.

I nodded. "Two years ago. They killed my Indian ma and her friend Tommy Three and also our Chinese cook."

"You are half Indian?" said Bee. She had a strange expression on her face. I could not read it.

"Course he is," said Sam Clemens. "Can't you tell by his dusky complexion and snapping black eyes?" He did not wait for her reply but said to me, "Sioux are all the fashion on account of the fact that they butchered about a thousand settlers over in Minnesota last month. I just combined a couple of stories."

"But I thought you were obliged to print the Truth," I protested.

"Ye gods, no!" drawled Sam Clemens. "Our only obligation is to make it interesting. The public wants matters of thrilling interest for breakfast! Mush-and-milk journalism gives me the fantods."

Bee was still staring at me. She had a new expression on

her face now. It was a kind of wide-eyed half smile. I could not read that one neither.

But I could read Sam Clemens. He had now narrowed his eyes into Expression No. 5—Anger or Suspicion.

"So where is it?" he demanded.

"Where is what?"

"An anonymous note was waiting for me at the Enterprise this morning." Sam Clemens rattled the piece of paper in his hand. "It said Virginia's newest Detective had my most precious possession. That's you, if I am not mistaken."

"You are not mistaken," I said. "Let me see that note."

He showed me a crude note. It had these words scrawled on it in pencil. **VURJINEES NEWIST DETEKTEVE HAS YUR MOST PRESHOUS POZESHUN**. It was unsigned.

My deductive skills immediately told me that the same person wrote this and the note on my stone baby.

I said, "I believe the same person wrote this and the note on my stone baby."

"Stone baby?" said Sam Clemens. "What stone baby?"

"That stone baby," I said, pointing to the half-unwrapped cigar box on my desk.

"I found it outside P.K.'s front door a few minutes ago," said Bee. She shivered. "It gives me the fantods. We believe it is a warning message to P.K. from some Deadly Desperados bent on *revenge*." She spoke the last words in a dramatic whisper.

Sam Clemens took a few steps forward & leaned over the cigar box. "Dang my buttons," he drawled, "if it ain't a petrified baby bearing a sinister message."

"Petrified?" said Bee. "What does that mean?"

"It means turned to stone," said Sam Clemens. "There has been a spate of reports of people turned to stone in some of the papers back east."

"It is not a petrified baby," I said. "It is six rocks arranged to look like a baby."

Sam Clemens gave me a look. I could not read it.

"Part of a song came with it," I said, and held out the torn-out page with the words of the song.

Sam Clemens read the note. "Dang it!" he cursed. "I'll bet someone is pranking me. I hate that song."

"How could you hate it?" cried Bee, clasping her hands over her heart. "It is a beautiful song & *so* sentimental."

"That is exactly what I hate about it," said Sam Clemens. He stuck his forefinger in the rock baby's sawdust bed & poked around in there.

"Eureka!" he cried a moment later. "Here it is! My most precious possession."

Ledger Sheet 7

SAM CLEMENS HELD UP an old corncob pipe with a bamboo stem.

"Found it!" he said. "It was buried in the sawdust."

"*That* is your most precious possession?" said Bee, wrinkling her nose in Expression No. 3: Disgust.

"Yes," said Sam Clemens. "The boys at the Enterprise have dubbed it 'The Pipe of a Thousand Smells.'"

"It does smell like the remains of some dead critter," I observed.

"Well, I guess they agree with you there. I

reckon they hid it in this box as a prank against me: Virginia's newest reporter." He looked at me. "And possibly against you, too, being Virginia's newest Private Eye. They probably wanted to kill two birds with one stone baby."

I said, "I reckon I would rather be pranked than threatened."

Sam Clemens narrowed his eyes at the box. "On the other hand," he said. "That is a mighty ghoulish baby. Maybe it *is* a threat. Do we have any enemies?"

I nodded. "Whittlin Walt's pards."

"That's right," he said. "I forgot. I hoped they had vamoosed the ranch."

He opened a muslin pouch of tobacco and pressed some into the bowl of the "Pipe of a Thousand Smells." He struck a match & lit it & puffed thoughtfully. Immediately the smell of dead critter got stronger.

"Ugh!" cried Bee, crinkling her nose into Expression No. 3.

"What kind of tobacco is that?" I asked. "I do not recognize the smell nor appearance."

"Yes," said Bee, tossing her curls. "I would like to know, too. I will warn my papa *never* to stock that brand in our Tobacco Emporium."

"It's called Killickinick," drawled Sam Clemens. "It's an Injun blend. It is composed of equal parts of tobacco stems, chopped straw, old soldiers, oak leaves, dog-fennel, corn-shucks, sunflower petals, outside leaves of the cabbage plant, and any refuse of any description whatever that costs nothing and will burn."

Bee was staring at him openmouthed.

"I know it is rank," added Sam Clemens, "but it summons

fond memories. It reminds me of what I used to smoke when I was a boy in Hannibal, Missouri. That tobacco was so cheap that we used to trade newspapers for it. It was called 'Garth's D-mnedest,'" he added.

"Oh!" cried Bee, covering her ears with her hands. "I refuse to stay and hear such *language*!"

She marched out of the shop, stamping with the heels of her button-up boots.

Sam Clemens watched Becky Bloomfield flounce out of the shop & puffed thoughtfully on his pipe.

"This pipe is special, too," he said. "You will see it is a corn-cob pipe. This pipe and the smell of the tobacco in it are about my only links with my past."

I said, "The smell of Green's Irish Flake always reminds me of Pa Emmet."

"Yes," he said, "the bond of a man and his tobacco is a sacred one. And a man's first tobacco forever holds a special place in his heart. Like his first love."

At this I remained silent. I have never been in love, nor do I intend to be.

Sam Clemens puffed and exhaled the smoke up. "Yes, a man may exchange one wife for another, but rarely is he unfaithful to his tobacco."

He looked at me with a kind of glint in his eye. "Do you smoke, P.K.?"

"No," I said. "But I am interested in different types of tobacco." I removed the newspaper from my desk to show him my hundred or so labels with bits of tobacco on them. "This is my Big Tobacco Collection. Would you like to test me?"

"Beg pardon?"

"I will close my eyes," I said, "and you hold one of these tobacco samples under my nose. I will tell you what brand it is."

He puffed his pipe & shook his head. "P.K., you are a very eccentric person."

"Yes," I agreed. "I have many Foibles and Eccentricities. Plus my Thorn."

He said, "What is your Thorn?"

I said, "I cannot read people easily. Sometimes I do not know whether they are pranking me or not."

"Then let me console you with this." He gave me a pinch of Killickinick and even told me how to spell it.

Then he departed, closing the door behind him.

I duly wrote down *KILLICKINICK* on a cigarrito paper and placed the crumbs he had given me upon it. I had arranged my Collection in Alphabetical order: Killickinick came about halfway between "Aardvark" snuff & "Zepeda" cigars.

Suddenly, a floorboard near the back of my shop creaked. All the little hairs on the back of my neck prickled again and I froze. For all this time, nearly half an hour, someone had been hiding behind my counter and I had not been consciously aware of it. Now I was.

Could it be the person who had left the ghoulish baby?

I leapt from my chair, pulled my Smith & Wesson's seven-shooter from my pocket and whirled to face the back of my shop.

"Come out with your hands high," I commanded. "Or I will fill you full of lead."

Ledger Sheet 8

AT THE BACK OF MY OFFICE are two things.

No. 1—a counter behind which Sol
  Bloomfield used to stand to sell his
  tobacco products.
No. 2—a door leading to a small back
  room, which is now my bedchamber.

Someone was hiding behind that counter. I
reckoned they had come in when I was out to
breakfast. I had nothing to steal so I had not
locked the door. I did not figure someone would
creep in to ambush me.

I thought, "Is it Boz back there?"

Then I thought, "Or Extra Dub?"

And finally, "Or maybe both?"

I heard that floorboard creak again.

I cocked my Smith & Wesson's seven-shooter and repeated my warning. "Drop your weapons. Come out with your hands aloft!"

Although my voice was firm, my heart was batting hard against my ribs.

A head lifted up above the counter for a moment. I saw dark skin & a pale bonnet.

The head dipped down again, real quick. It was enough to show me it was a Negro girl of about my age. Her eyes were wide with terror, an expression even I have no trouble reading.

I uncocked my piece & said, "Do not be afraid. I am putting my revolver away."

I put my revolver back in my pocket.

I was not scared anymore but my hands were still shaky.

"Please come out," I said. "I am sorry I threw down on you. I will not hurt you."

"Are you the detective," came a trembly voice, "what finds lost animals and people and solves mysteries?"

I figured she must have seen my Advertisement.

"That is me," I said. "P.K. Pinkerton, Private Eye. Do not be afraid."

She came out from behind the counter: barefoot & shivering in a thin cotton nightdress & matching night bonnet. She smelled strongly of some kind of pomade made of cloves, lavender & ammonia, and faintly of horse manure & straw.

"You got to help me," said the girl in a whisper. "He killed Miss Sal and now he is gonna kill me, too." Her accent was about the strongest I ever heard, but I could just about understand her.

"What is your name and who is Miss Sal?"

She came a little closer. "Martha," she whispered. "Miss Sal's lady's maid."

I said, "Miss Sal? Do you mean Short Sally, the Soiled Dove who got her throat cut last week?"

Martha frowned. "She wasn't no dove. She was a *Lady*. And she was strangulated, not cut."

I said, "Strangulated? I heard she got her throat cut from ear to ear."

Martha gave a kind of shudder. "Oh no, sir. I was there. I heard him do it. Saw it, too. She was a-choking an' a-gasping." Martha hugged herself. "It was awful. And then he came for me."

"The man who strangled Miss Sally knows you saw him do it?" I said.

She nodded. "He saw me and chased me. But I got away to a place he don't know about. I been laying low for a long time. This morning, early, I hear some men talking about you. They say you're a detective what finds people even though you're just a kid. They say you are up on B Street and you have a Sign supposed to be an Eye. So I come uphill and find that Sign with an Eye but I think he is following so I sneak in and lay low. I can't pay. But I got this." She reached up and undid a clasp at the back of her neck & held out a little black & gold cross on a gold chain. Her hand was shaking. "You got to find him and tell people he done it."

"Don't worry about paying me now," I said. "Just tell me his name."

"I ain't sure," said Martha. "Miss Sal, she call him different things and I can't recall right now." Her lower lip trembled.

Then she caught sight of the cigar box on my desk & her eyes went so wide you could see the white all around them. "What is *that?*" she said.

"Don't take any mind of that ghoulish stone baby," I said, taking the box off my desk and putting it on the floor. "It was just a prank."

But she was not listening. She had seen something else. Something in my oyster-can waste bucket. She put the gold cross on my desk & bent down & pulled out an old brown apple core.

"Ain't you gonna eat this?" she said, holding it up.

"No," I said. "But it is dirty—" Before I could say another word she had devoured it.

"Are you hungry?" I asked.

She nodded. "Powerful hungry," she said. "I ain't had nothing but a little barley and raw oats for days and days."

I said, "Why don't you come along with me to the Colombo Restaurant? I will buy you breakfast. Or lunch. Or both. You can tell me what you know about the killer."

"No," she whispered. "He might see me. Every time I go out I think I see him following me."

"Who?" I said. "The killer?"

She nodded. "When I was trying to find you just now I feel him after me. So I sneak in and I hid back there."

I said, "And you cannot remember his name?"

Martha nodded & chewed her lower lip. "Miss Sal, she call him something. I remembered it yesterday . . . but now I disremember."

"Do not worry," I said. "It will come to you. And you are sure it is the killer who is following you?"

"I ain't sure. I can't see faraway things so good." She shuddered. "But I *feel* it is him. I was laying low for so long I thought he'd of gone. But he hasn't and he is after me, I am sure of it."

She began to cry.

I gave her a handkerchief & said, "*Fortes fortuna iuvat.* That is Latin for 'Fortune favors the brave.'"

She said through her tears. "I'm an orphan and I got nobody now. How can I be brave?"

I said, "I am a double orphan. And I don't have anybody either. That is why we have to be brave."

She looked up at me with wide eyes. I could not read her expression.

I said, "If you can't remember his name, can you maybe tell me what he looks like?"

She nodded. "He was tall and slim, with yellow hair and one of them li'l billy goat beards."

I took out my Detective Notebook and wrote down:

Short Sally's Killer: tall & slim & blond with a billy goat beard.

I was about to ask her what the killer had been wearing when from outside came a sudden volley of gunshots.

Martha doubled forward with a gasp, clutching her stomach.

The world seemed to stand still & I went cold all over.

Short Sally's Killer must have followed Martha here.

And now he had shot her.

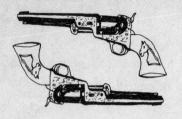

Ledger Sheet 9

WERE THOSE PISTOL SHOTS? asked Martha. Although still doubled over in pain she was looking up at me wide-eyed.

"Yes," I said. "Where are you hit?"

"I ain't hit," she whimpered. "Just hungry. My stomach was asleep but that apple roused it up. Oh!" she gasped again as her stomach cramped.

"Praise be," I said, "but the person who fired might be the man who is after you. Get back behind the counter while I check."

I ran to the door & grabbed my hat & as I opened the front door, Martha called out something about a Forest and a Bear, or maybe a Bar.

"Stay!" I commanded. "I will be right back."

She nodded and sank down out of sight behind the counter.

I went out, closed the door & quickly locked it behind me.

B Street resembled a *Tableau Vivant* with all the carts & wagons & pack animals at a standstill and people staring with open mouths & upraised arms. A cloud of gunsmoke still hung over the scene. As I jumped down off the boardwalk, everybody started to move towards a figure lying in the street.

It was a red-haired, red-bearded man in dark trowsers and a brown & burgundy patterned vest & a rusty black coat. Nearby, his plug hat lay half squashed by a wagon wheel. The man lay on his back, but as I watched, he propped himself up on his elbows & looked down at his patterned vest.

"He shot me," said the man. "He shot me thrice."

"I had no choice." This from a man with 2 smoking revolvers & an English accent.

He was tall & slim & blond with a billy goat beard!

Was he Short Sally's killer? Had he followed Martha here? If so, then why had he shot the red-bearded man?

His next words answered my question. "I was not looking for trouble. You threw down on me." The Englishman holstered his guns, a pair of Navy revolvers with ivory grips.

The lying-down red-haired man had three smoking holes in his patterned vest and I saw that some blood was starting to ooze out. He looked at his chest and then back up at the Englishman.

"You shot me thrice," he repeated. He had an Irish accent

like Mr. O'Malley who had been on Ma & Pa Emmet's Wagon Train. "Did I hit *you* at all? Did I at least crease you?"

"Afraid not," said the Englishman. He removed a pipe from his pocket and tapped it on the bottom of his boot.

"At least tell me I'm shot by the famous Farmer Peel," said the Irishman. "You *are* Farmer Peel? I saw the bullet scar under your eye."

Sure enough, I saw that the Englishman bore the scar of an old bullet hole under his right cheekbone.

"Don't call me 'Farmer,'" he said. "My name is Farner with an *n*. Langford Farner Peel." He was filling his pipe & I saw from the label on the pouch that he smoked Red Lion tobacco. He lit a match and got it going.

"Stand back!" said a voice. "Make way for the doctor."

A man pushed through and knelt down beside the injured man.

It was Doc Pinkerton—no relation—who had mended my arm a few days before.

"Oh joy!" drawled a familiar voice behind me. "A Scoop at last. A duel in the street at high noon." The familiar voice was accompanied by an even more familiar smell of dead critter. Yes, it was Mr. Sam Clemens again.

"It ain't high noon, Sam," said another familiar voice. "It is only eight thirty a.m. and this story is mine."

I turned to see Mr. Dan De Quille had joined us. I recognized him by his long face, dark goatee and sticky-out ears. He smelled of printer's ink.

"What do you mean, it's yours?" said Sam in a low tone. "I was here first."

"That may be," said Dan, "but I got seniority. All shootings are reported by me. Hands off."

Like Sam Clemens, Dan De Quille was a reporter for the Territorial Enterprise, but he had been there longer. I judged he was also about five years older than Clemens.

"That ain't fair!" said Sam Clemens. "I need to fill another two columns today."

"It may seem unfair," replied Dan De Quille, "but there it is. Nothing can change it. If you want some gruesome deaths," he added, "why don't you waltz on down to the Coroner's office?"

"I just might do that," replied Sam Clemens. His eyes were narrowed and he was blowing his pipe smoke down. From that I knew he was riled.

Doc Pinkerton stood up. "This man may live if he gets immediate treatment," he said. "Somebody help me take him inside."

Four men stepped forward and each took an arm or a leg.

"Outch! Outch! Outch!" cried the wounded man as they heaved him aloft.

The four men started to take him into the Shamrock Saloon, which had recently opened across the street from my office.

But a burly man on the boardwalk barred their way. He wore an apron around his waist and Expression No. 5 on his face. "Don't you even think of bringing Murphy in here," he said in an Irish accent. "I won't have him bleeding all over my brand new floor."

"Where, then?" said Doc Pinkerton. "I must get him out of the thoroughfare."

"I say, bring him in here!" said an English-accented voice. "I have a couch."

We all looked up to see my neighbor Isaiah Coffin standing in the open door of the Ambrotype & Photographic Gallery next door to my shop. He was hatless & smoking his meerschaum pipe. I realized that he was also *tall & slim & blond with a billy goat beard!*

Then I looked around the crowd and saw two other men who fit Martha's description of Short Sally's killer.

I thought, "Finding Short Sally's Killer is not going to be as easy as I expected."

Then I thought, "I had better ask Martha what he was wearing."

And finally, "But first I have to get that starving girl some food."

I headed towards the Colombo Restaurant, walking behind the four men carrying Murphy. They were going the same direction as me anyway.

"Outch! Outch! Outch!" cried Murphy as his friends stepped up onto the boardwalk and carried him into Isaiah Coffin's Photographic Gallery.

I lingered for a moment outside the open door, then remembered my mission and hurried on to the Colombo Restaurant. All the customers had come out to see what the shooting was about. Now they were shuffling back inside. Some of them still had napkins tucked into their collars or newspapers under their arms.

Gus, the Mexican waiter, gave me a plate of beans & bacon & still-warm biscuits that a customer had left without touching because the sight of oozing bullet holes had destroyed his appetite. Gus did not even charge me.

Before I went into my office, I peeped through the open doorway of Isaiah Coffin's Photographic Gallery.

They had put Murphy on a buffalo skin on the couch. Doc Pinkerton was sitting on a chair & bent over him. I could see the four friends & Isaiah Coffin & his Chinese assistant, Ping. I wanted to watch, too, but I had a client to attend to.

My first client.

A poor starving girl who was being hunted by a coldblooded killer because she was an Eye Witness to murder.

But when I unlocked the door of my office and went inside, I made a distressing discovery.

My first Genuine Client had disappeared.

Ledger Sheet 10

THE FRONT OF MY OFFICE opens out onto a board-walk and street like a normal building in a normal town.

But Virginia is not a normal town. It is built on such a steep mountain that the fronts of the mountain-facing houses are level with the street they face, but many of their backs are often propped up on stilts. Mine was one of those west-facing buildings, with its backside dangling over thin air.

My office is also peculiar in that it has no rear entrance. In the back room there is only a sash window overlooking the roofs of the buildings on the west side of C Street and that two-story drop between.

When I went back to my bedchamber to search for Martha, I was astounded to see the lower half of the window was wide-open. Had Martha jumped onto the roof of the Washoe Exchange Billiard Saloon? There was a gap of about a yard and a half between the backs of our buildings, but the saloon's wooden roof is also about six feet below my window.

I could not imagine a terrified girl like Martha making such a leap.

But she had not flown away, so she must have jumped.

I took a deep breath and climbed up onto the sill and gripped the sides of the window frame and prepared to leap.

I was just about to launch myself into space when I saw a wooden ladder nailed to the wooden-plank side of the building below my window! I had never noticed it before, probably because I had never stuck my head out so far. I judged it to be some sort of escape in case of fire.

Martha must have skedaddled down that ladder.

Going down that old ladder did not seem much safer than jumping onto the roof of the Washoe Exchange Billiard Saloon, but I did not have a choice. I turned myself around & stuck one leg out of the window & groped with my toes until I found the top rung & eased my weight down on it. I could feel it creak. I am small and skinny, but I wager Martha weighed even less than me. Would the ladder hold my weight? I swung my other leg out of the window & cautiously descended rung by rung. My heart stopped beating when my foot almost went through the cracked fifth rung. Luckily the other rungs held.

As I went down, I got to where I could see underneath the building I shared with the photographic studio. It was a steep, dank slope of earth. Nothing grew there, as the sunshine was blocked by the building backing onto it.

When I finally reached solid ground I heaved a giant sigh of relief. This part was littered with empty bottles & tin cans. I guessed they lived high at the Washoe Saloon, for I saw champagne bottles and tinned peaches.

Among the cans and bottles, I spotted the fresh print of a small bare foot. Despite the gloom, it did not take any of my special Indian tracking skills to follow Martha's trail. It went past an outhouse to an alley leading down between two saloons onto C Street. After those dim back passages, it was good to emerge onto the bright & warm & lively street. But I soon lost Martha's trail on the boardwalk.

Not trusting the ladder & window route back, I returned to that alley and found a path back up the steep slope between buildings to B Street. I emerged onto the boardwalk and returned to my office via the front door.

Once inside, I sat at my desk & picked up the black & gold cross on a chain & stared at it.

My first Genuine Client had finally appeared & hired me to solve the biggest mystery in Virginia City. I reckoned she had given me her most precious possession to do this.

And now she was gone.

There had been only one set of prints going from the

bottom of that ladder to C Street. So I knew she had not been killed or captured, just frightened.

Something must have spooked her while I was out. Had someone knocked at the door? Or tried to open it, despite the CLOSED sign? Or did she just panic?

I was pondering these questions when I was roused from my reverie by a bloodcurdling scream from next door.

Ledger Sheet 11

MY OFFICE SHARES PART of a sky window and all of one dividing wall with the Ambrotype Studio. Usually I cannot hear what goes on next door but that scream seemed to fill the whole street.

I guessed it was thrice-shot Murphy, being operated on by Doc Pinkerton.

I hurried next door to investigate this theory.

I was right.

Murphy lay on the buffalo-skin-draped couch, surrounded by four standing men and one prostrate one. The man on the floor was Isaiah Coffin.

"What happened to Mr. Coffin?" I asked, closing the door behind me.

"He fainted," snapped Ping, who was holding a teacup with a metal ball in it. "Here," said Ping. "You hold. I try to revive him."

I took the cup and moved closer to Murphy.

As Ping gently slapped Isaiah Coffin's face, I watched the doctor work.

It was fascinating. Doc Pinkerton was seated on the edge of a fringed armchair and leaning over his patient. He had cut into the wounds to make them bigger & he was using an instrument to hold one wound open so that he could get at the ball.

"Aaaaaah!" screamed Murphy.

"For God's sake," muttered Doc Pinkerton. "I can't work with all that noise. Here. Bite on this bullet." He put something in Murphy's mouth.

I came closer and knelt down beside the chair, so I could see better. I held the teacup ready for when Doc Pinkerton extracted the second ball.

"These are .36 caliber balls, ain't they?" I asked, as it went into my teacup with a clink.

"Yes, indeed," said Doc Pinkerton. "Thirty-six caliber Navy balls." For the first time he seemed to notice me. "Why, hello, P.K.," he said. "How are you? How is your arm coming along?"

"I am tolerable," I said. "My arm aches a little and has recently started to itch."

"Itching is good," grunted Doc Pinkerton. "That means it's healing. Just resist the urge to scratch it. Can you reach me the long tweezers from my black bag?" he added. "This last ball has gone in deep."

"Yes, sir," I said. I put down the china teacup & fetched out his long tweezers.

I handed them over.

Murphy had stopped screaming. He had gone very still. His eyes were closed.

"Is he dead?" I asked.

"Just passed out, I hope," said the doctor. "Probably best for all concerned. It is lucky for him that I heard those shots."

"I think he swallowed that bullet he was biting on," I said.

Doc Pinkerton did not reply. He was intent on his work.

"If someone punched him hard in the stomach," I said, "would the bullet go off?"

Doc Pinkerton smiled. "Only if he swallowed powder and a lit match," he said. "I gave him a lead ball to bite on, not a cartridge."

I nodded. My own Smith & Wesson's seven-shooter has cartridges with the cap & ball & powder all encased in a single shell but most gunmen here in Virginia have to combine those separate ingredients in the chambers of their revolvers.

I watched Doc Pinkerton probe with the tweezers for a while.

Ping had revived Isaiah Coffin & was now standing just behind me & holding a sponge floating in a bowl of water.

"Doggone it!" said Doc Pinkerton. "That sky window provides excellent light but my spectacles are badly scratched and befogged. I am waiting for a new pair to arrive from San Francisco. P.K., can you see the ball in there?"

"I see it," I said. "It is kind of a silver glint among all the red slimy bits."

"Here," said Doc Pinkerton, handing me the long tweezers. "I will hold the sides of the wound open. See if you can fetch it out. Be careful not to pierce any throbbing veins or vital organs."

I stood up & bent over the wound & probed for the ball.

A moment later I held up the ball, held fast by the long tweezers.

Doc Pinkerton squinted at it. "Is the ball whole?" he said. "That is to say, in one piece?"

"Yes, sir," I said.

"Well done, P.K.," said he. "Ping? Hand me that sponge. Let's clean him up before we bandage him."

I put the ball in the teacup with the two others. I had enjoyed helping Doc Pinkerton. Concentrating like that made me forget everything else. I reckoned operating on a person was almost as good as ordering a Collection for staving off the Mulligrubs.

Doc Pinkerton showed me how to pack the wounds with lint and bind them with bandages. As he was finishing, I heard footsteps come into the shop & I smelled cigar smoke.

"Doc," said a man's voice.

Doc Pinkerton glanced up. "Hello, Deputy Marshal," he said.

I looked at the Deputy Marshal with interest. He was a short man with a coffee-colored plug hat on his head, a thin cheroot in his mouth & a big Colt's Army stuck into his belt. He had a thick black mustache & matching eyebrows & a squashed nose.

I had not yet met any of the lawmen here in Virginia.

Maybe this Deputy Marshal could help me find Sally's Killer and protect Martha.

I do not like touching people but I stood up and politely extended my hand.

"My name is P.K. Pinkerton, Private Eye," I said. "We are both fighting for Justice and Truth."

The Deputy Marshal turned his gaze on me.

The eyes beneath the heavy eyebrows were unblinking. They reminded me of Snake Eyes.

I withdrew my hand as he made no move to shake it but just stared at me.

His gaze made me feel cold inside.

At last he removed the cheroot from his mouth. "P.K. Pinkerton?" he said in a growl. "You the one whose foster parents was scalped and murdered down in Temperance last week?"

"Yes, sir," I replied.

The Deputy Marshal did not offer his commiserations. Instead he jabbed his cheroot at the unconscious Murphy. "If that man dies, it is your dam fault."

Go to scene of Crime
Look for Clews
Interview Witnesses
List Suspects
Motive & Means
Aliki?

Ledger Sheet 12

THE DEPUTY MARSHAL of Virginia City was regarding me with Expression No. 3: Disgust.

"That is your dam fault!" he repeated.

Doc Pinkerton rose frowning from his chair. "Are you saying P.K. was the cause of the shooting affray in which this man was injured?"

"That is exactly what I am saying." He sucked hard at his cigar & blew the smoke down. "He kilt that Whittlin Walt and upset the balance. Now every young Rough is trying to fill the vacancy Walt left. They all want to be Chief."

"Chief?" said Doc Pinkerton.

"Chief of the Desperados," said the Deputy

Marshal. "That Farmer Peel, for example. He's been here in Virginia for over a month." He jabbed his cheroot at me. "He was no trouble at all until your heroics last week. It is that Dam Domino Effect."

I said, "What is the Dam Domino Effect?"

Ping came into the studio. He had been disposing of Murphy's bloody shirt. "I know dam domino effect," he said. "Stand up dominoes like customers in line. Push one. All others fall down. Bam, bam, bam, bam, bam."

"Durn right," said the Deputy Marshal. "One galldarn action sets a passel of events in motion." He turned his unblinking gaze on me. "Who gave you leave to start killing off this town's citizens, anyway?" he growled.

"I did not kill Whittlin Walt on purpose," I said. "It was self-defense."

"And who gave you leave to call yourself a Detective?"

Before I could think of an answer he growled, "I don't like Injuns, I don't like Detectives and I don't like *you*. I ain't sure it is even legal for a brat like you to set up as a Private Eye. You cause any trouble & I will have you thrown in jail or even hanged." He threw down his dead cigar, turned on his heel and departed.

As I gazed after him, I said, "I guess that means I should not expect much help from the Law in my investigation of the murder of Short Sally."

"You are going to investigate the murder of that Nymph of the Night?" said Isaiah Coffin.

I nodded & picked up the Marshal's discarded cigar butt &

examined it. I was pretty sure it was a Long Nine. Long Nine cigars are pencil thin and nine inches long. This one had been smoked down to one inch, but it was pencil thin and matched the description in the catalogue. I saved it for further examination.

Doc Pinkerton looked over his spectacles at me & lowered his voice. "Be careful of Jack Williams. He is little more than a desperado himself. It is said that he has sometimes drawn his revolver and demanded money contributions from the citizens of Virginia at dead of night. Not long ago he shot a man dead over a game of billiards."

I nodded to show him I had understood.

Doc Pinkerton took out his own pipe and lit it. "Deputy Marshal Williams is right about one thing," he said. "You are far too young to be a Detective."

"That may be," I said, "but I have a client who needs me."

I did not mention that I had failed to protect my client who was now lying low or on the run.

I went next door to my office & unlocked the door & went in & locked it behind me & left the CLOSED sign showing. I needed to think.

I reached into my pocket and pulled out some cigar butts and my Pinkerton Detective Button. I put the butts on my desk but held on to my pa's button. It was the only thing of his I had.

It reminded me that I had Detective blood flowing through my veins.

It reminded me that my aim was to learn detective skills

and then join my uncle Allan Pinkerton at his Detective Agency in Chicago.

It reminded me that my pa might still be alive, and that I wanted him to be proud of me.

I put the button back & took out my Detective Notebook and wrote down everything Martha had said.

I am good at remembering things I see but not so much things I hear. So I need to make notes.

When I had finished, I looked at the last few words she had called out to me.

The Forest

and

Bear or Bar?

I reckoned she had been trying to tell me where she was hiding out. It was obviously a Bear Cave in a Forest.

I reckoned she would be safe there, as long as the bear did not return, but I had to find the Killer before she starved to death.

I turned to a new page in my Detective Notebook & chewed the stub of my pencil & tried to recall how Mr. Bucket and other literary detectives solved murders.

The first thing they usually did was go to the Scene of the Crime & look for Clews. After that they would Interview Witnesses & come up with a list of Suspects.

I wrote down

Go to Scene of Crime
Look for Clews
Interview Witnesses
Suspects

I knew Detectives also looked for Motive & Means. Motive is why the culprit committed the crime & Means is how they did it. If a Suspect is able to prove he was somewhere else when the crime occurred, that is called an Alibi.

I wrote down

Motive & Means
Alibi?

I looked at my list. The first letter of each step spelled GLISMA.

That would help me remember to Go to the scene of the crime & Look for clews & Interview witnesses & list the Suspects who had Motive & Means. Then I would find out which of those Suspects had Alibis and cross them off my list. When I had crossed off all the Suspects but one, I would have the Culprit.

It seemed fairly straightforward to me.

But something Martha had said was niggling at me. Before I went down to the Scene of the Crime, I thought I had better interview one of the people who had first told me of Short Sally's Murder, a gambler named Poker Face Jace.

Jace is probably the wisest man in Virginia City.

I thought I might find him at the Fashion Saloon on North B Street.

I was right.

Ledger Sheet 13

THE FASHION SALOON IS a One-Bit Bar with swinging wood-slat doors & bare plank tables & sawdust on the floor & a big window with a 100-mile view. It is bright & quiet & has a safe & cozy feel. I like it there, apart from the rank smell of tobacco-tinted saliva. But you get that smell nearly everywhere in this place.

On that day it did not smell too bad as fresh sawdust had recently been sprinkled over the floor.

Jason Francis Montgomery, a.k.a. Poker Face Jace, was sitting at his usual table with his back to the wall beside a window with a 100-mile view. He was in the middle of a card game. I knew better than to disturb him, so I went up to the bar & stepped up on the brass foot rail to make myself a little taller.

Jace did not even look my way but I knew he had seen me. He sees everything.

Jace is real clever. He is the one who taught me that while a man's face and mouth may lie, his body always tells the truth.

At the end of the bar near the back of the saloon stood Jace's friend & bodyguard, Stonewall. He is a big, ugly man with eyes that point in different directions. He packs a big Le Mat's pistol & keeps an eye out for trouble. He is partial to sucking lemon wedges like his hero, Stonewall Jackson.

I turned to face the long mirror behind the bar.

It showed a boy with an expressionless face beneath a black slouch hat. The boy wore a faded red (not pink) flannel shirt & blue woolen coat with brass buttons. That boy was me & yet not me. I looked at the reflection of Jace in the mirror. I like watching people when they do not know I am watching them.

"Morning, P.K.," said Mr. Leahigh, the barkeeper, in his low voice. He knew I was a friend of Jace's. Mr. Leahigh is tall & thin with a head so narrow it makes me think of an axe. I like people with faces like that. I do not confuse them with other people.

I would have recognized his axe-head face even had he not been standing behind the bar with his apron and wiping cloth.

"Good morning, Lee," I said politely. (That is what everyone calls him: Lee.)

"What'll it be?" he said. "Whiskey? Tarantula Juice? Pink Gin?"

People here in Virginia like to josh you. But they often do it with nary a wink nor smile & sometimes it is hard to tell.

I was not sure if he was joshing me or not, so I replied politely, "It was my ma's dying wish that I never kill nor gamble nor drink hard liquor. Have you got any 'soft' drinks?"

"I got soda water," he said. "You can have it plain or with syrup."

"What flavor syrup do you have?" I asked.

"Vanilla, ginger and sarsaparilla," he said. "I recommend the sarsaparilla. It is good for purifying the blood in this thin air."

"Give me a sarsaparilla soda then, please."

He nodded & turned & got a four-sided blue-green bottle from the shelf below the mirror. It said Dr. Townsend's Sarsaparilla on the side. He put a shot of syrup in the bottom of a glass mug & then topped up the mug with fizzing soda from a spigot. He left the blue-green bottle on the bar so I could see it was the Genuine Article, imported from faraway New York.

"That'll be a short bit," he said.

I put down a dime & sipped my sarsaparilla soda.

It was sweet & spicy & prickly all at the same time. It made my throat & stomach tingle in a nice way.

As I turned to watch Jace, a man in a brown bowler hat came to stand beside me. He ordered whiskey & then whistled a little tune under his breath. I did not pay attention to him because I was looking at Jace.

Jace was one of the main reasons I had decided to stay in Virginia City. When I realized he knew how to read people, I wanted his knowledge more than I had ever wanted anything. He agreed to teach me, in exchange for my help.

Jace was playing poker with three other men.

Unlike Mr. Leahigh, the men all looked pretty much the same to me. They all had mustaches & hats & wore dark clothes. In fact, they all looked a bit like Jace, who also has a mustache & hat & wears dark clothes. But there is something about Jace that makes him stand out from the crowd. He has a kind of stillness. All the other men were fidgeting or tapping their fingers or shuffling their feet. But he just sat there, his face in shadow because of the window behind him, occasionally taking a puff from his cigar.

Two of the other men were smoking cigars, too, and a cloud of blue smoke hung over their table. The fourth man was a tobacco chewer. I could tell by the lump in his left cheek.

Jace had taught me how to tell what a person is thinking by looking at their feet. I could tell that the tobacco chewer had a good hand. The toe of his right foot was pointing up. But the man opposite probably had a better hand. His feet were doing a little dance under the table.

I took a sip of my sarsaparilla soda, and set down my glass mug on the bar so that the handle pointed towards the man with the dancing feet.

Jace folded up his fanned-out cards. "I'm out," he said.

"Me, too," said the man across from him. They both put their cards facedown and sat back.

The tobacco chewer put a gold coin into a pile of coins. Then he turned his head and spat into a brass spittoon on the floor beside him.

"How is pecking for corn like chewing tobacco?" said the man in the brown bowler hat who was standing beside me. He had a pleasant Southern accent a little like Jace's.

I turned and looked at him.

He was tall & slim & blond with a billy goat beard!

I wondered if he was the Killer and if he had followed me here.

"It is a conundrum," said the possible Killer of Short Sally. "A riddle with a pun for an answer. I repeat: How is pecking for corn like chewing tobacco?"

"I do not know," said I. "How is pecking for corn like chewing tobacco?"

The man smiled & took out a pipe. "Because it is a foul habit." He looked at me as if he was expecting a response. "Did you catch the pun?" he said. "'Fowl' with a *w* sounds just like 'Foul' with a *u*. A *fowl* habit. Chickens peck for corn and they are fowl."

I nodded. I liked that. It was a bit like a mystery in one sentence.

"I like that," I said. "It is a bit like a mystery in one sentence."

"If you like it, then you are supposed to laugh," said he.

"I never laugh," I said. "Nor cry, neither."

"Oh," he said, and took a sip of whiskey.

He puffed his pipe, and the scent of it sent a strange pang to my heart. He was smoking the same brand of tobacco as my foster pa, who had been murdered the week before. My throat felt tight & my vision got blurry. It must have been the smoke because I never cry.

I blinked and everything got clearer.

"Is that Green's Irish Flake tobacco?" I asked him.

"Why, yes," he drawled. "Would you like some?"

"No, thank you," I said. "I do not smoke or chew. I believe them to be *foul* habits."

He chuckled & puffed away.

"But I like the smell of that one," I admitted. "My dead foster pa used to smoke it."

He nodded. "It reminds me of home, too." He put the briar pipe in his mouth and extended his hand. "Absalom Smith," he said. "Actor and Professional Punster."

"P.K. Pinkerton," I replied, shaking his hand. "Private Eye."

Ma Evangeline taught me a Trick to remembering people's names and faces. She said to make a picture of that name and link it to something I can imagine in my head and then put the person in it. Absalom was a person from the Bible. He was King David's favorite son, but his vanity betrayed him and he was caught in low-lying tree branches by his long hair and died. Absalom Smith had short hair as far as his bowler hat let me see, so I pictured him sitting on the branch from which King David's favorite son dangled.

"Are you a Pinkerton Detective?" he repeated. "I did not realize they made them so small."

"I am a Pinkerton, and a Detective," I said, "but I am not employed by the Pinkerton Detective Agency, *per se*. I am a Private Eye."

"What does every detective, no matter how smart, overlook?" he said.

"I do not know."

He removed his pipe. "His nose." He paused to see if I would laugh.

I did not laugh & he said, "Are you working on a detective job now?"

"Yes," I replied. "We call them 'cases.'" Caution prevented me saying more.

At a table near Jace's a man gave an almighty sneeze. He put some snuff in his nostril and sneezed again.

"What would contain all the snuff in the world?" said Mr. Absalom Smith, and as I was puzzling this out, he said, "No one knows." He repeated this, tapping his nose & I realized he had said, "No one *NOSE*."

I said, "That was another conundrum."

"It was. And I believe *that* one almost made you smile."

I was about to deny this when the jingly sound of spurs made me turn around real fast. That sound makes me jumpy because two of my mortal enemies wear spurs: Boz & Extra Dub.

But it was not Boz or Extra Dub.

It was only a smiling youth of about 17 or 18 years old with a dainty little slouch hat tipped over his left eye. I turned away in relief and then turned back.

He was tall & slim & blond with a billy goat beard!

Actually, he was of medium height. But perhaps to Martha he might seem tall. And his mustache & beard were almost invisible, being mainly fluff. But under his small hat, his hair was the yellowest I had seen.

He was very dusty but you could tell he was good-looking underneath. He had about the whitest teeth I ever saw & the biggest silver spurs, too.

He also had two revolvers. The flaps of the holsters were undone & I could see the walnut grips of those guns.

He turned his brilliant smile towards the bar but as soon as he saw me his smile faded. He put on Expression No. 5 & took up a gunfighter's stance. "You!" he said. "Draw!"

Ledger Sheet 14

WHEN THE BLOND YOUTH said *Draw!* all conversation in the saloon instantly ceased. Out of the corner of my eye I saw Mr. Leahigh slowly sink down behind the bar. Jace and the other poker players had stopped in mid-deal.

"Draw!" The youth tipped his head back so that his jaunty slouch hat did not block his vision. "I ain't afraid of you."

A pipe clattered to the floor, and I realized the dusty young man was not looking at me, but at the man standing beside me.

Mr. Absalom Smith did not rise to the bait nor

make the slightest move. Was he petrified with fear? Or cool as a radish?

"I see that piece in your pocket," said the blond gunman.

I glanced over at Absalom Smith's right-hand trowser pocket. Sure enough, it was bulging, and I was close enough to see the brass trigger guard of an Augusta Revolver, which some folk called the "Confederate Colt."

(Although I do not have a Gun Collection, I know a lot about firearms.)

"I see your piece," repeated the blond youth, "so I know you're heeled. Now draw!"

Absalom Smith made no reply.

"What is wrong with you?" said the young man. "Why won't you draw? Ain't you Farmer Peel? Chief of the Desperados?"

Absalom Smith still made no reply.

I spoke up. "He ain't Farner Peel," I said. "His name is Absalom Smith."

The young gunman's eyes flickered towards me. They were very blue, with thick eyelashes. "You keep out of this, kid!" But after a moment his eyes flicked back. "You sure it ain't him? He fits the description."

I looked at Absalom Smith. It was true: he did look a bit like Peel, but no more than the dusty gunman himself. And of course he did not have the scar of a bullet below his right cheekbone.

I said, "Farner Peel has a bullet scar below his right cheek-bone. That is how you can tell them apart."

Absalom Smith finally spoke. His voice was shaky. "The boy's right," he said in his Southern accent. "I am not Farmer

Peel. I admit I carry a gun, but so does everyone in this place."

"Whew!" The young man exhaled & took off his hat & ran his hand through his dusty hair. Then he flashed his white teeth in a broad grin. "I'm mighty sorry about that. Don't I look a fool?"

People in the saloon started moving again.

The gunman stepped towards Absalom Smith with his right hand extended. "My name is John Dennis," he said. "But you can call me El Dorado Johnny. Let me buy you a whiskey." He turned to Mr. Leahigh, who had resumed his standing position. "Two whiskeys," he said, replacing his hat at its rakish angle. "And a drink for the little Indian, too." He shone his smile on me. "What's that you're drinking, kid?"

"It is soda water with sarsaparilla syrup," I said.

I bent over & picked up the briar pipe & handed it to Absalom Smith, Actor and Professional Punster.

"Thank you, P.K.," he said. He took the pipe with a shaky hand.

"What brings you to Virginia, Johnny?" asked Mr. Leahigh, as he put down a new whiskey glass.

"Oh, I ain't new to these parts," said Mr. El Dorado Johnny. "I got me a placer mine in Flowery Canyon, about two miles from here. I just heard you got a position vacant here in Virginia." He looked around to make sure everybody was listening.

"What position might that be?" asked Mr. Leahigh, filling his glass.

"Chief of the Desperados," announced the youth. He was

smiling again & showing his pearly teeth. "Yes, I aim to be Chief of the Desperados hereabouts."

Some people laughed at that. But not Jace, nor Mr. Leahigh neither.

El Dorado Johnny knocked back his whiskey and put the small glass back on the bar. Then he turned and faced the people in the saloon, who were still watching him with interest.

"Can any of you recommend a good bath house and barber?" he said in a carrying voice. "I intend to call out Farmer Peel today or tomorrow at the latest. If he kills me, I want to make a Good-Looking Corpse."

Some more people laughed & this seemed to please El Dorado Johnny.

"That's right," he said, hooking his thumbs in his gun belt & looking around with a grin. "I aim to be either Chief of the Comstock or a Good-Looking Corpse."

There was more laughter.

Mr. Leahigh filled Johnny up again. "Your best bet for a bath and barber," he said, "is Selfridge & Bach's just a few doors down. They will make you look real pretty."

El Dorado Johnny knocked back his second whiskey, put a silver dollar on the bar, touched the brim of the dainty slouch hat with his finger & clanked out of the saloon in the direction of the bath house.

"By God, I need another whiskey, too," said Absalom Smith.

Mr. Leahigh poured it & Mr. Absalom Smith took it with trembling hand. "What is the difference between roast beef and pea soup?" he asked us.

Before we could answer, he downed his whiskey in one. "Anyone can roast beef," he said & hurried out the back door of the saloon.

Mr. Leahigh gave a rare chuckle.

Then his smile faded & he shook his head. "I sure hope that durn fool El Dorado Johnny don't end up a good-looking corpse."

The card players at Jace's table had finished their hand. They were all rising to depart, shaking hands with Jace and each other.

Jace saw me looking at him and he tipped his head towards the back of the saloon.

I was not sure what he meant at first, but when he disappeared out the back a few minutes later, I followed.

I had not seen him for nearly two whole days. I hoped he did not think I was ignoring him.

I went out the saloon's back door and down some wooden stairs to the steep slope. When I reached the bottom, I could see no sign of him. Apart from some woodpiles & heaps of garbage, there were only a couple of privies out there: the one with a moon cut in the door for women & the star one, for men.

Then I smelled Jace's Cuban cigar & saw a wisp of smoke emerge from the star hole in the door of the right hand privy. Jace smokes a brand called "Mascara," which means "mask" in Spanish. This is fitting, as his face is usually a mask.

I went over to the outhouses & squeezed between them so that unless you were standing right in front of them or right behind them you would not see me.

"Jace?" I said, in a low voice. "You in there?"

"Yeah," came his voice from within. "I'm in here. You did the right thing back there when you spoke up. Defused a nasty situation. But I been thinking ... Might be better for our partnership if we ain't seen together in public. How about you join me and Stonewall for dinner this evening about eight? After dinner you can help me play a few hands of poker over at the Virginia City Saloon. All right?"

"All right," I said. I glanced around. "Can I just ask you something?"

"Ask away," came his voice after a moment. "But make it quick."

Ledger Sheet 15

I HAVE BEEN HIRED to find the Murderer of Short Sally," I told Poker Face Jace through the wall of the privy out back of the Fashion Saloon. "My client says Sally was strangled but you told me her throat was cut."

His voice emerged through cracks in the planks along with wisps of cigar smoke. "You sure you want to take on the biggest mystery in Virginia?" he said. "Ain't the Law investigating?"

I said, "If I can solve this mystery then people will respect me and stop pranking me. Who told you her throat was cut?"

"Don't recall. Heard it in a saloon."

I said, "How can I find out if my client is telling the truth or not?"

Jace's answer came along with another wisp of smoke. "Ask the Coroner. He operates out back of a saloon down on South C Street."

I knew a Coroner was an official who investigated deaths, but I had never heard of one operating out back of a saloon.

"Which saloon?" I asked.

"The Washoe Exchange Billiard Saloon. There is a kind of vault built into the mountain there," explained Jace. "Sometimes they use it as a morgue."

I was surprised to learn there was a coroner's office and a morgue out back of the Washoe Saloon. I figured they must be right underneath my bedroom window.

"P.K.?" said Jace.

"Yes, sir?"

"You take on this case you better be careful not to cross the Coroner or the Deputy Marshal. I do not think they would be favorably disposed towards you."

"Yes, sir," I said. "That is good advice."

"Now skedaddle," said Jace. "I got business to attend to."

I left Jace to finish his business.

It was now past noon and I was hungry.

On my way to see the Coroner, I stopped by the Colombo Restaurant & asked Titus Jepson if he had any old copies of the *Daily Territorial Enterprise* newspaper with reports of Short Sally's murder. He sent Gus to look and he brought a plate of cheese & crackers to my usual table along with a glass of sarsaparilla—my new favorite drink. By and by, Gus brought over a three-day-old, grease-stained newspaper, dated Monday September 29.

It contained a short notice of Sally Sampson's death:

BRUTAL MURDER!
WOMAN KILLED IN HER BED.

On Saturday morning a sporting woman known as "Short" Sally Sampson was found murdered in her crib on D Street. There was no evidence of robbery and the motive remains a mystery. Her ten-year-old servant girl is missing but is not considered dangerous as neighbors said she "would not hurt a fly." Hundreds of men turned out for Miss Sampson's funeral yesterday, including all three Volunteer Fire Companies and a brass band. Most mines shut down for a few hours as a mark of respect. The Reverend Samuel B. Rooney gave his final eulogy before leaving this Territory. He spoke most eloquently of Sally's bravery and compassion. Virginia City and this newspaper eagerly await the results of the inquest. Crimes such as this one should not go unpunished.

That brief report did not say whether Sally had been cut or throttled. But at least it seemed accurate. If Mr. Sam Clemens had written it, he probably would have subjected Short Sally to death by a thousand arrows from marauding Shoshone, or had her peppered with balls like a "nutmeg-grater." I closed the paper & finished my sarsaparilla & thanked Mr. Titus Jepson and Gus, too.

Then I headed down to the Coroner's office at the back of

the Washoe Exchange Billiard Saloon. I decided to take the normal route even though the ladder below my back window could have taken me directly there.

I went down Taylor and turned right and sure enough, there it was: the Washoe Exchange Billiard Saloon, a sturdy building in fireproof brick. As I stood there looking at it, I noticed a big, red-faced man with bushy brown whiskers & a silver-tipped walking stick go down the alley I had used several times. He was unlocking a door. As I came closer, I saw the words G.T. SEWALL, CORONER painted on it. I had been following Martha's footprints with my nose down, which is why I had not noticed the sign before.

The man with the walking stick left the door ajar, so I followed him inside. The office consisted of an unplastered brick room with a large desk & a couple of chairs & some books on a shelf. In one corner of this room was an open door to another room from which wafted a dank breeze carrying nose-prickling traces of mysterious chemicals.

The man turned to put his stovepipe hat on a peg. He did not appear to notice me so I kept on going towards the room with the strange smell.

It was so cool & clammy in there that it made my skin crawl. There were a couple of narrow wooden tables lined up. On one of them lay the body of a dead person under a sheet. I could tell he was dead because the feet sticking out were bloodless & very still.

I thought, "This must be the morgue Jace told me about."

It was the strangest room I had ever seen for it had curved walls made partly of brick and partly of rock, as well as a roof two stories high. I tipped my head back and looked up. I could see threads of light where sunshine showed gaps in the planks. That roof was not very sturdy. If I had jumped onto it from my window, I might have crashed right through & fallen two stories & landed on one of the corpses.

I looked at the body more closely.

There was something not quite right about the corpse beneath its sheet. I tilted my head to one side, to try to figure out what.

Then I had it: the body seemed to be in two parts.

I went over to it & lifted the sheet to make sure.

The man had been cut in two at the waist. The division was straight, but not a neat cut such as a saw would make. It was messy. I reckoned the poor man had been run over by the wheel of a Quartz Wagon or a Stagecoach.

"What the h-ll are you doing in my morgue?" A man's angry voice made me jump & I whirled to see the man with the bushy whiskers & the walking stick. "Who the h-ll are you?" he said.

"My name is P.K. Pinkerton," I said. "Are you Mr. G.T. Sewall, Coroner? If so, I would like to see the report of the inquest on Miss Sally Sampson. I want to know if she was strangulated or cut."

He stared at me goggle-eyed, opening and closing his mouth like a trout. I reckoned that was Expression No. 4: Surprise.

Getting no reply, I said, "I am a Private Eye. I have been hired to find the Killer of Sally Sampson."

"What?" he spluttered. "A Private Eye? By God! I'll bet that dam varmint Clemens put you up to this, didn't he?" He strode out of the morgue & went to the window of his office & peered out into the alley. "I told him not to show his face again. Is he lurking out there?" He returned to the morgue & raised his walking stick. "Where is he? Tell me or I'll thrash you!"

"Mr. Sam Clemens had nothing to do with this," I said.

"Then how the h-ll do you know that varmint's Christian name?" he cried. He drew back his silver-tipped walking stick & swung for me hard.

I ducked & heard the cane whistle through the air only inches above my head.

The Coroner was between me and the door, blocking my escape. I had no choice but to retreat. I ducked down under the table with the two-part corpse & then shrank back as his cane came down again.

CRACK!

He gave the table leg a blow so violent that one of the corpse's arms slipped down. The hand dangled only a few inches before my eyes. I could see that the fingernails were ragged & grimy. I deduced the dead man had been a miner, or maybe a prospector.

CRACK!

No time to ponder details such as dirty fingernails now. I feinted to the right, then scrambled around to the left. I am sorry to say I jostled the table a little & in so doing I made the top half of the corpse fall onto the floor with a splat.

The Coroner leapt back & let loose with a torrent of profanities unfit for publication.

I ran out of the morgue & tore through the outer room & into the bright October morning & down the alley to the C Street boardwalk with its welcome tinkle of piano music & the faint thudding of Quartz Mill Stamps.

I stopped to take a deep breath of the sage-scented air & glanced behind me, just to make sure the Coroner was not in hot pursuit.

He was.

Ledger Sheet 16

COME BACK, YOU scallywag!" bellowed the Coroner, Mr. G.T. Sewall. "I am going to thrash you!"

As I fled through the crowds of people, I felt the Coroner's heavy, jarring footsteps behind me. They caused the whole boardwalk to bounce. His bellowed profanities made the crowds part before us like the Red Sea before Moses. I jumped down from the boardwalk & flew down steep Taylor to D Street & made a sharp left. Here I slowed to a fast walk & clamped my arms to my sides & made myself narrow as I wove among the crowds of bankers, miners, etc. When I spotted a break in traffic, I nipped across D Street.

This was a bold thing to do, considering the two-part body I had just seen, but I knew a well-delivered blow from that silver-headed walking stick could kill me as surely as being run over by a Quartz Wagon.

Up ahead, the spire of the Methodist Episcopal Church seemed to beckon me on. I reckoned the blaspheming Coroner would not follow me inside that safe haven.

The church doors were wide-open, but instead of going inside I quickly squeezed behind one of the wide-open doors. Sandwiched between the raw planks of the outside wall & the white-painted door, I listened with all my might for the sound of pursuing footsteps & cussing. But all I could hear was my heart pounding & my breath coming in rasps.

By and by, I peeked out of that narrow place.

"I believe the coast is clear," came a man's voice to my right.

A man in a vest & shirtsleeves was kneeling in the small garden in front of the church. Apart from him, the "coast" did indeed look "clear," so I emerged from my hiding place.

"Are you praying?" I said.

"No, I am gardening. Planting rose bushes. They say no flowers bloom here and no green things gladden the eye, but I am determined to prove them wrong." He put down his trowel & stood up & dusted off his knees.

He was tall & slim & blond with a billy goat beard!

It seemed such men were everywhere.

"If I am not mistaken," said the fair-haired gardener, "you are Virginia City's newest detective."

"Yes, sir," I said.

"And I am Virginia City's newest Methodist pastor." He

stepped forward and held out his hand. "Charles Volney Anthony."

Although he resembled a hundred other men in Virginia, I reckoned the Methodist pastor (& possible murder suspect) was someone whose name and face I should make a special effort to remember. So I used the trick Ma Evangeline taught me. In my mind's eye I imagined him sitting down, with a vole on one knee & a big ant on the other: vole-nee ant-on-ee.

I allowed him to shake my hand & said, "I am P.K. Pinkerton."

"Yes," he said. "I know that, too."

"How do you know who I am?"

"A certain Miss Feather in my congregation—a school-marm—is concerned about you. She described you to me and told me something of your history. There are not too many half-Indian children running about Virginia dressed in fringed buckskin trowsers, pink flannel shirts and slouch hats," he said.

"My shirt is faded red," said I. "Not pink."

He gave me a keen look. "Are you fleeing someone? Is there anything I can do to help?"

"The Coroner was after me," I said. "He thought I was pranking him."

"Ah," said C.V. Anthony. "I have not met the Coroner but I can see it might be hard for some people to credit a young-ster would set up as a Pinkerton Detective."

"My pa was a Pinkerton," I said. "I hope to follow in his footsteps."

"Your father must be the non-Indian half," he said.

"Yes, sir. My ma was Lakota."

"Are you working on a case now?"

"Yes," I said. "A Murder."

"A Murder?" he said. "Surely you jest."

"No, sir," I said. "I never jest. I am trying to find out who killed Miss Sally Sampson. The first step of my investigation is to go to the Scene of the Crime and look for Clews. Do you happen to know where her crib is?"

I did not mention Martha because I was not sure yet if I could trust him. Although he was a Methodist preacher, he fit the description of the Killer.

His smile faded. "Ah. Poor Sally." He stared down at the ground. "Although I have not been here long, I did know Sally. She was a devoted and generous member of this congregation." He pointed north. "She lived about half a block up on this side of the street. The crib with the yellow door. That is the scene of the crime."

"Thank you, Reverend." I replaced my slouch hat & touched the brim politely.

"P.K.," he said.

I turned. "Yes?"

"I presided at your foster parents' funeral last Sunday."

"Oh," I said. "Thank you. I was not there."

"I know," said the Reverend C.V. Anthony. "I gather you were trapped down a mine shaft with three desperados on your trail. But like Daniel you emerged unscathed from the Den." He looked down at his rose bushes. "I intended to visit your foster pa and pay my respects. But alas! I tarried and thus missed my chance. I regret that."

I did not know what to say, so I said nothing.

He cleared his throat. "Do you share your foster parents' faith?"

"Yes, sir," I said. Then I remembered how I promised my dying foster ma never to kill a man nor drink nor gamble, but did all three within three days of her death. So I added, "Although I might have backslid a little."

"Oh?" said he. "But would you call yourself a Methodist?"

"Yes, sir," I replied. "I may be half Lakota, but I am one hundred percent Methodist."

The Reverend C.V. Anthony nodded. "In that case, you should probably not be frequenting D Street Cribs."

"Thank you for your advice, sir, but I must pursue this investigation. I have set my heart on Being a Detective."

"Why?" he said. "Why that particular career?"

"Three reasons," I said. "First, it is a noble calling: a Detective is someone who uncovers the Truth & brings Justice. Second, being a Detective will help me understand people and the things they do. Third, I hope one day to work alongside my father at the Pinkerton Detective Agency in Chicago that was founded by my uncle Allan. That is why I have set up shop as a Private Eye here in Virginia," I added. "To hone my Detective Skills."

"Well, P.K.," he said. "I cannot argue with your motives. I can only pray that you will not be corrupted by the lower elements of this place and thus come to grief."

"'Unto the pure, all things pure,'" I said, quoting Saint Paul's letter to Titus.

But maybe I should have recollected Proverbs 12 & verse 15:

"The way of a fool is right in his own eyes: but he that hearkeneth unto counsel is wise."

If I had hearkened to the Reverend's counsel, maybe I would not be writing this account in jail beneath the shadow of the hangman's noose.

Ledger Sheet 17

I LEFT THE REVEREND C.V. Anthony to his rose bushes & made my way to Short Sally's crib at No. 8 North D Street. The yellow door was locked, but the right-hand window was open a crack. Peering through the glass, I could see a long & narrow room with a door at the far end. There was no furniture and even the walls were bare.

I put my ear to the crack of the window and listened. I have ears as sharp as a rabbit's but I could hear nothing. I put my nose to the window & sniffed. I caught a faint whiff of lemon oil & tobacco juice. I needed to get in, to make a proper investigation.

The sash window in its frame was warped, but with a bit of wiggling, I managed to raise it enough so that I could squirm through.

I was favoring my wounded left arm, which had started to throb, so I did not land in a symmetrical fashion. I tumbled awkwardly onto the floor & banged my nose hard enough to bring tears but not blood.

I blinked a few times and my vision cleared.

I now saw a stove on the other side of the door but nothing else apart from a Brussels Carpet over most of the floor & lace curtains on the windows & over against the far wall some little drifts of fine dust & fluff & other trash. The carpet was slightly faded from where the sun had shone on it, so I could see faint geometric shapes where there had been a rectangular couch & round table and at the back a big square bed. The only piece of furniture remaining was that cast-iron potbelly stove in the front corner near the door.

I remembered the Notice in the newspaper said that Sally's possessions were to be auctioned on Saturday at Currie's Auctioneers, up on B Street. That must be where everything had been taken.

My heart sank.

There were no clews to be found.

I crossed the empty room & opened the door there to find a narrow closet at the back of the crib. There were wooden pegs on the inner wall & another door in the outer wall & also a dustpan & broom. It was even smaller than the room at the back of my office. I could smell Martha's hair oil and I reckoned this closet must be where she slept.

I closed the closet door & looked back into the main room through the latch hole, which was bigger & cruder than a keyhole. Even though the bed was over on the right, I reckon Martha could just about have witnessed the dastardly deed.

I wondered if Martha had stifled a cry or a sob when she saw the killer strangulating her mistress.

I wondered if that noise had made him turn his gaze towards her hiding place.

Martha must have been terrified as he started for the door. Terrified enough to flee barefoot in nothing but her nightdress and night bonnet.

A single step took me to the back door. I opened it & almost tumbled out but caught myself. Then I saw that the back of the crib was on stilts with a ladder going down to the steep slope.

My nose told me that was where people emptied their chamber pots. I did not want to go down there. There was other rubbish down there, including lots of tin cans. Farther down the slope was a lumberyard and beyond that the outskirts of Chinatown.

I went back into the front room & I looked around at the Scene of the Crime.

"Show me, Lord," I prayed. "Give me a sign."

Immediately the terrible image of my own murdered foster parents rose before my eyes. I tried to push it away.

Then I had a Thought.

In tracking animals, sometimes the Lack of Sign can be as important as the Presence of Spoor. I went over to the brighter square of carpet that had been hidden under the bed. Neither the Brussels Carpet nor any of the floorboards by the wall carried even the faintest stain of blood. If Sally's throat had been cut, the room would not be this clean. Even if the bedding had soaked up most of the blood there would have been drops from the blade. There would be a big old bloodstain right there. Even if it had been scrubbed there would be a mark.

I sniffed the air. No lingering scent of blood. Only the faint smell of Sally's lemon perfume mixed with the rank undertone of tobacco-tinted spit, which was pretty much everywhere in Virginia City.

Short Sally must surely have been strangulated, not cut. My client had told me the truth.

I reached into my pocket to get out my notebook, in order to record this Important Revelation.

But before I could, I heard the door behind me open & a raspy voice said, "Make one move and it will be your last!"

Ledger Sheet 18

I FROZE RIGHT THERE with my Detective Note-book half out of my pocket. I could smell cigar smoke mixed with a flowery undertone.

"Who are you?" said the raspy voice behind me. "And what are you doing in my place?"

At first I had thought the raspy voice belonged to one of my mortal enemies: Dubois "Extra Dub" Donahue. But now it sounded like a woman's. Only I had never heard of a cigar-smoking woman. I started to turn my head.

Something like a rifle barrel poked me hard between my shoulder blades. "I said don't move!" said the voice. "What is your name and what are you doing here?"

I was now certain that the voice belonged to a woman.

But I did not relax. I had learned the hard way that women are just as dangerous as men in Virginia City.

I said, "My name is P.K. Pinkerton, Private Eye. I am investigating the Murder of Miss Sally Sampson. I thought this was her crib."

I felt the rifle barrel withdraw. "All right. Turn around."

I turned to see a stout woman in brown and lavender. She was holding a broom in her hands. I had mistaken it for a rifle barrel. I felt mighty foolish.

"This ain't Sally's crib," said the woman in her raspy voice. She had a small, thin cigar in her mouth. "It is mine. She rented it from me. And that still does not explain what you are doing here."

"I am looking for clews," I said. "I am a Detective. I have been hired to find the man who killed Miss Sally Sampson. I am hoping to compile a list of Suspects."

The woman gave a kind of snort. She was about as wide as she was tall. Her tightly done-up dark hair was streaked with gray. Her lips and cheeks were stained with rouge. She sported a top hat of the sort ladies wear while riding: brown with a lavender scarf around it.

"Why, you is just a puppy," she rasped, taking the little cigar from her mouth and blowing the smoke forcefully in my direction. "Half Injun, too, by the looks of you."

"Yes, ma'am," I said politely. "I am half Lakota, but one hundred percent Methodist."

She snorted again & shook her head. "Short Sally's things are all up at Currie's, waiting to be auctioned day after tomorrow. You will not find any clews around here." She took another deep drag. "Who hired you, anyway?"

I opened my mouth to speak, but then hesitated. I guessed Martha might be a runaway slave, even though she called herself a lady's maid. "Someone whose life is in danger," I replied.

"All our lives are in danger," said the woman. "There is a man in this town murdering helpless women & the Law is doing nothing about it. I suppose I should be glad someone is looking into this, even if it is just a child."

"Sometimes," I said, "a child can go where other people can't."

"True," she said. "Very true." She smiled & put the little cigar in her mouth & stepped forward & held out her hand. "My name is Gertrude Holmes, but everybody calls me Big Gussie. I own the Boarding House next door." She was breathing heavily but I learned later that was just her way. I decided she was more wheezy than raspy. "What did you say your name was again?" she said.

"P.K. Pinkerton," I replied. "Everybody calls me P.K."

I do not like people touching me but I stretched out my hand politely. She nearly crushed it with her gloved hand.

"Well, P.K.," she said in her wheezy voice, "I could use a stiff drink. How about you?"

"I am partial to black coffee," I said, shaking the blood back into my hand. "I also like soda water with sarsaparilla syrup. It purifies the blood."

She said. "I find whiskey purifies my blood just fine." She dropped the butt of her slender cigar & shmooshed it out with the toe of her boot.

I bent over and picked up the stub end of the small cigar.

"What is this?" I asked. "I have never seen one like this."

"That? That there's a cigarrito. I buy mine by the dozen up at Bloomfield's Tobacco Emporium."

"What brand?" I said.

"It's called 'Lady Lilac,'" she said. "I love lilac."

I sniffed the stub. Sure enough, the tobacco did have a tincture of lilac to it. I put it in my pocket.

Big Gussie was watching me with narrowed eyes & her head tilted to one side. "Why did you do that?"

"I am starting a Tobacco Collection," I said. "A Big Tobacco Collection."

She said, "You are a very peculiar person."

I did not know what to say to that so I said nothing.

She looked at me and I looked at her.

"I reckon I can sweep up later," she said. "Why don't you come on over and take some refreshment with me and my girls? I have information that might be of use to you, including the names of about two dozen possible Suspects."

I studied her posture. Her feet were pointed straight towards me and she did not show any signs of lying or deception.

I said, "Thank you, ma'am. Anything you could tell me about Suspects in this case would be mighty useful."

Ledger Sheet 19

NORTH D STREET HAS lots of small whitewashed, pointy-roofed houses called *cribs*. Each has a door & window & a little porch with an overhang so the Ladies can sit outside in fine weather. Some of the cribs lean a little to the left or right.

Big Gussie called her place the "Brick House." It was two stories tall & made of red brick & it stood smack dab in the middle of those cribs. It reminded me of a mother hen with all her little chicks lined up either side, some of them leaning over to be near her.

It was even nicer inside. She led me into a big,

bright parlor with a flowery Brussels Carpet & a high ceiling. On the facing wall was a big mirror that reflected back light & seemed to double the size of the room as well as the plump couches & dark wood furniture. There were four little polished tables with lace doilies & vases full of flowers & china ornaments & fancy ashtrays & cut-glass decanters.

There was a piano against one wall & a fiddle on top.

At a big, long table in the middle sat four women playing a Card Game & drinking coffee. It was past 3 p.m., but they were still in their undergarments.

"Girls," said Big Gussie, "say howdy to P.K. Pinkerton, Virginia's smallest detective."

"Howdy, P.K.," said the four girls. I touched my hat, then remembered myself and removed it.

"P.K. is investigating the death of poor Sal," explained Big Gussie, as she placed two china teacups full of coffee on one end of the polished table. She gestured for me to sit. "Sally used to take her meals here," added Gussie, "until we disagreed about runaways. She had no truck with them."

"Runaways?" I said, thinking of Martha. "Do you mean runaway slaves?"

"Bless my stockings, no! I mean Leg Cases. Skedaddlers. Absquatulaters. Runaway Rebs."

"Beg pardon?" I said, as mystified as ever.

Gussie rolled her eyes. "Deserters," she said. "Especially Confederate deserters. We been getting quite a few of them recently. I reckon we'll get more over the next few weeks on account of that terrible battle back east. Sally said we should turn them cowards in. But I believe most of them just crave the company of soft and gentle women after all that blood and killing."

Big Gussie did not look soft *or* gentle but I nodded for politeness.

"After our disagreement Sal stopped eating with us. Then she seceded from our profession, too."

I got out my Detective Notebook and pencil. "Can you tell me the names and descriptions of her Gentlemen Callers?" I said. "For my list of Suspects?"

"Well," said Gussie, taking a deep pull on her cigarrito, "as I just said, she hadn't had none for a while. She was setting up to be a seamstress."

"You mean she stopped having Gentlemen Callers?" said I.

"That is exactly what I mean," said Gussie.

"But she used to have some?"

"Up till about a month ago."

"I believe one of those Gentlemen Callers killed her," I said. "Can you tell me any of their names?"

"Sure I can," said Big Gussie. "You gals can help, right?"

One of the girls at the other end of the table said, "Sure. We knew most of 'em."

Big Gussie introduced me to the four girls.

One girl was called Irish Rose. She had freckles and reddish-brown hair and an Irish accent. So her name was easy to remember.

Big Mouth Annie had a little rosebud mouth so that was easy to remember for her being the opposite of her name.

The one they called Spring Chicken did not look like a chicken but her corset was grass-green and she was young with fluffy yellow hair, so I thought of a baby chick in the springtime grass.

Honey Pie was plump & had honey-colored hair so I made a picture in my head of her eating pie filled with honey & remembered her that way.

They all gave me names & descriptions & as much other information as they could remember. I wrote them all down in my Detective Notebook.

At the end of our first session I had 23 Suspects, all men who were known to have visited Short Sally up till about a month ago.

23 Suspects! I had to narrow it down some.

Although Martha was short-sighted, she had been able to give me a basic description of the Killer: tall & slim & blond with a billy goat beard. With the help of Big Gussie and her Girls, I crossed off the names of all the men who did not fit that description.

That left me with only eight names.

Then I asked if they knew whether any of the men had been out of town or busy elsewhere on the night when Short Sally was killed, viz: Friday September 26.

One man was known to have gone to Carson City for two days. Another had been in a drunken stupor all night in an upstairs room right there at the Boarding House. So we crossed off two more names.

That left me with a list of six likely suspects in the Murder of Short Sally.

SUSPECTS IN THE MURDER OF
SALLY SAMPSON
(Tall, Slim Men with Fair Hair & Smallish Beards Known to Have Frequented Sally)

1. Ludwig Hamm, barkeeper, German
2. Pierre Forote, barber, French
3. John Dennis, miner, American
4. Yuri Ivanovich, telegraph operator, Russian
5. Isaac E. Brokaw, policeman, American
6. Isaiah Coffin, photographer, English

I was surprised to hear Isaiah Coffin's name come up as a Gentleman Caller of Sally's, but I am pretty sure I did not show it. My face rarely betrays what I am feeling.

One of the other names sounded vaguely familiar.

I am good at remembering names if I see them written down, but not so good if I only hear them.

"John Dennis?" I said. "Where have I heard the name John Dennis?"

"He likes to put on airs," said Big Gussie. "Sometimes calls himself El Dorado Johnny."

Then I remembered. He was the yellow-haired, white-toothed, silver-spurred youth who wanted to be either Chief of the Comstock or a Good-Looking Corpse.

Big Gussie took a fresh Lady Lilac cigarrito out of a silver box. "Of course," she said, "the man who killed Sally might have been a Gentleman Caller we did not know about. One not on the list."

I nodded. "Would anyone else know anything?" I asked.

"Her best friend, Zoe, might," said Gussie, blowing out smoke.

I remembered the Notice in the paper. The Administratrix of Sally's estate had been named as Mrs. Zoe Brown.

"Mrs. Zoe Brown?" I asked. "The Administratrix of Sally's estate?"

They all laughed. "You're the only one who can get right through that word," explained Gussie, tapping her ash. "None of us can get our tongue round it."

"What does that long word mean, anyways?" asked the girl they called Spring Chicken. She was sucking her thumb.

"Means she got named in Sally's will and will get proceeds from the sale," said Gussie. She got up and went to a table & brought back the morning's copy of the *Daily Territorial Enterprise*. It was folded open at the Notice of the Sale of Sally's goods. The Girls looked at it, all except the thumb sucker.

I remembered that a few of the items on the list had puzzled me.

"What is a 'Mahog Whatnot'?" I asked.

Gussie pointed to a kind of triangular table that fit neatly into one corner of the parlor. It had three shelves & was made of dark polished wood.

"That is a Whatnot," she said. "And I guess 'Mahog' is short for mahogany."

"That is a kind of wood," said Big Mouth Annie. "Expensive, like black walnut."

I said, "So Zoe Brown inherited all Sally's property?"

"No idea," said Big Gussie, tapping ash into a little silver ashtray. "You have to ask Zoe."

I made a note of that.

I said, "Was her jewelry stolen? I noticed there was no jewelry on the list of items to be auctioned."

Honey Pie—the plump one—looked up from the newspaper. "He's right," she said. "Sally had that topaz necklace and some pearls, too."

Spring Chicken removed her thumb from her mouth. "And a real tortoiseshell hair comb," she said. "That ain't mentioned neither."

"You'd best ask Zoe about the missing jewelry, too," said Big Gussie.

I said, "Where can I find this Zoe Brown?"

"Zoe lives down there at Number Thirty," said Honey Pie. "Little white crib with a red door."

Big Gussie tipped her head to one side and regarded me with an expression I could not read. "I thought you would of knowed that. Warn't she the one who hired you?"

"I cannot tell you who hired me, but thank you very much for the coffee and the information," I said politely. I closed my Detective Notebook & stood up.

"You ain't going yet, are you?" rasped Big Gussie, and her eyebrows went up. "Don't you want to hear how I found the body?"

I sat down again. "Yes," I said. "Please tell me how you found the body."

Ledger Sheet 20

BIG GUSSIE TOOK a deep pull of her cigarrito. "Short Sally used to board here," she said. "Breakfast and dinner. Like I told you."

"Why?" I asked.

Big Gussie shrugged. "No kitchens in them little cribs. Anyways, Sally was high class. Exclusive. Expensive. She usually only entertained one man per night. She would give them her undivided attention. She served them pastries, along with rum or brandy. She would sing and tell stories and be charming. They paid her ten dollars for the night."

"Ten dollars?" I said. That was a lot of money.

"Yes," said Gussie, taking another drag. "She had

to pay for the spiritous liquors and sweets herself, but even so, she was doing very well. Recently she bought that team of horses and the gig."

"Sissy and Sassy," said Big Mouth Annie.

"Those were the names of the horses," said Spring Chicken, without taking her thumb from her mouth.

"She kept them up at the Flora Temple Livery Stable," said Honey Pie.

"She was going to drive that team over the mountains to San Francisco before the winter snows," said Big Mouth Annie. "It was her dream."

"Not a very practical dream," said Gussie. "It takes about four days with your own gig and those steep mountains tire out the horses something awful. Plus there's the ferry from Sacramento. Sally would have done better to sell the gig and team and buy passage on a stagecoach."

Honey Pie said, "She told me once she had a vision of driving that pretty white pair right into Frisco and everybody would stare at her all admiring like."

"We all have our dreams," said Big Mouth Annie. "Don't mean they'll ever come true."

"After Sally stopped taking her meals here," said Gussie, "she had a Chinaman deliver breakfast every morning along with her wood. I heard she started dining up at Barnum's Restaurant and brought the leftovers back to Martha. So we had not seen her in a while. Only sometimes driving by in that new gig of hers, with or without Martha."

Big Gussie stubbed out her cigarrito & continued her account. "Saturday morning early, the Chinaman banged at my door. He said he had brought the breakfast and wood as usual but the door was open and Martha was nowhar and Miss Sally would not stir from bed. So I went over there. Sure enough, the front door was ajar. So I went on in."

"I heard Gussie scream," said Big Mouth Annie. "It was horrible. Made my blood run cold as snowmelt."

Big Gussie said, "Poor Sal was stone dead, staring bug-eyed at the ceiling with her mouth open. She was real beautiful but she did not make a good-looking corpse." Gussie stared at the table for a moment and then gave herself a little shake. "Course once I closed her eyes and tied her jaw shut with a handkerchief she looked more peaceful."

"At first, we thought Martha might of done it," said Big Mouth Annie.

"Because she didn't come to us for help or nothing, just run off . . . ," said Irish Rose.

"Li'l Martha was her slave girl," said Honey Pie.

"She warn't no slave girl," said Big Mouth Annie. "You ain't allowed no slaves in the Territory. That's why she came here. She told me that once."

Spring Chicken took her thumb out of her mouth. "That true?"

"Yep," said Big Mouth Annie. "Short Sally rescued her. Poor little runaway orphan slave girl."

"Treated her harsh, though," said Honey Pie.

"Not that harsh." Irish Rose turned to me. "Made her do chores, like sweeping the crib every morning till it was speckless. But sometimes Sal took her for rides in the gig. Wish someone would take me for a ride."

"Anyhow," said Big Gussie. "It wasn't little Martha that strangled Sally. That little gal wouldn't hurt a fly. Plus Doc Green said the marks on Sally's neck showed it must of been a man. I reckon Martha saw him do the deed and skedaddled."

I said, "Doc Green saw the body?"

"Yes," said Gussie. "He comes round to see us regular. He said she must have been kilt the night before I found her, because she was cold as yesterday's porridge. But none of us heard any noise, did we?" She looked round at her Girls. They all shook their heads & stared at the table.

"Where does Doc Green live?" I asked.

"South D Street." Gussie sipped her coffee. "Other side of the church. He told us it would all come out at the inquest," she said.

I said, "What did the Coroner say when you told him this? Or the Marshal?"

Big Gussie looked at the girls, then at me. "Nobody ever asked us," she said. "They never held no investigation nor inquest."

"Why not?" I asked.

Gussie shrugged. "Last week we was 'between' Coroners. The Marshal was sick and that Deputy Marshal don't like our kind. He is often tight."

"That old Coroner was usually tight, too," said Big Mouth Annie. "Better no inquest than one by him."

"What is 'tight'?" I asked.

"Means 'drunk,'" she replied.

"The new Coroner ain't much better," said Gussie. "I had

words with him t'other day and find him to be a son of a—"
She looked at me and caught herself just in time. "Well, he
ain't a kindly man. So I, for one, am mighty glad to have someone fighting on our side." Here Gussie lifted her coffee cup
towards me in a toast. "Even if it is just a pint-sized Private
Eye like P.K. here. If ever you need anything," she added, "you
just call on Big Gussie and her gals. We will be there for you."

I thanked her and the four girls & stood up & put my hat
on my head.

Back outside I saw that the sun was dropping down towards Mount Davidson. I judged it to be a quarter past
4 o'clock. I turned right & found Zoe Brown's crib with no
trouble.

It was one of the nicer ones: not too crooked, with a
cherry-red door & the No. 30 painted on it.

I knocked on that door.

There was no reply at first but then I saw a curtain twitch
& a few moments later the door opened up.

I guessed Mrs. Zoe Brown had some Negro blood. She had
big brown eyes with long eyelashes. Her skin was the color
of milky coffee. Her dark hair was soft & curly. Her features
were very symmetrical & she smelled like honeysuckle.

"Can I help you?" she asked in a pleasant accent that I
recognized as Southern.

"My name is P.K. Pinkerton," I said. "I am a Private Eye investigating the brutal Murder of Sally Sampson. Will you
help me?"

"You're investigating Sally's murder? Why, you're just a

child." She was wearing a brown & white calico dress that was faded but clean. It had a lacy cream-colored collar and cuffs.

"I am twelve years old," I said. "I am just small for my age."

She gave a quick glance over her shoulder towards someone in the room behind her. I could not see who it was. "I have company at the moment," she said, "but he is going soon. Can you wait?"

I said that I would wait.

I went and stood across the street in the shadows behind a barrel at the back of a saloon that had its main entrance up on C Street. I took some antelope jerky from my pocket because I had only eaten some cheese & crackers for lunch.

While I chewed the jerky, I opened my notebook and added some suspects:

SUSPECTS IN THE MURDER OF
SALLY SAMPSON
(Tall, Slim Men with Fair Hair & Smallish Beards
Known to Have Frequented Sally)

1. Ludwig Hamm, barkeeper, German
2. Pierre Forote, barber, French
3. John Dennis, miner, American
4. Yuri Ivanovich, telegraph operator, Russian
5. Isaac E. Brokaw, policeman, American
6. Isaiah Coffin, photographer, English

Others who fit the description but were not
known to have visited her

7. Farner Peel, shootist, English

8. Absalom Smith, actor and punster, American

9. C.V. Anthony, reverend, American

After a while the cherry-red door opened and a man came out.

He was a man known to me.

It was Mr. Isaiah Coffin, my neighbor, the photographer.

He was also Suspect No. 6 on my list.

I waited until Isaiah Coffin was out of sight & then ran up to the red door with the No. 30 & pounded hard.

Would I find the beautiful Zoe Brown lying strangulated in her crib & staring bug-eyed at the ceiling with her mouth open?

Ledger Sheet 21

WHEN MRS. ZOE BROWN opened the door her eyes *were* staring a little, but I reckon that was because of my urgent knocking.

"Oh, it is you," she said, and darted glances up and down the street. "I am sorry but I am so nervous since Sally got killed . . . Do please come in," she added in her Southern accent.

Zoe Brown's crib was the same layout as Sally's & almost as bare. Instead of a Brussels Carpet, there were only raw planks. Instead of plaster, the walls were "papered" with cotton flour sacks all stitched together & stuck up in rows. Instead of lace curtains, hung more flour sacks. The only furniture was a narrow bed, a sagging couch, a potbelly stove & a traveling trunk being used as a table. Her being so pretty, I was surprised that she did not have lots of nice vases & doilies & mahog whatnots like Big Gussie.

And yet there was a hat rack along one wall with about six of the fanciest hats I had ever seen.

I deduced from this that she spent all her money on hats.

I could smell coffee. I also caught a whiff of Isaiah Coffin's tobacco. He smoked St. James Blend in his meerschaum pipe. I noticed a few shreds of tobacco on the plank floor.

I said, "In the newspaper it names you as Mrs. Zoe Brown. Are you married?"

"I am a widow," said Mrs. Zoe Brown in her softly accented voice. "I live alone."

I nodded. Back in Dayton there were some women who called themselves "Mrs." so as to seem more respectable.

She poured me a cup of coffee, then gestured for me to sit on the couch. "Have you found out anything about who might of killed poor Sally?" she asked.

I said, "I have just been to Big Gussie's and the girls told me that Sally had lots of jewelry. But the Notice of Auction does not list a single piece. Do you think Sally might have come home that night and startled a thief and he strangled her to silence her? Maybe that was the motive."

"No," said Zoe Brown. "Sally sold all her jewelry a month ago so's she could buy that sweet buggy and pair of horses. She had little at home for a thief to take."

"If the motive was not robbery," I said, "then do you have any notion of why she was killed?"

"She chose a dangerous profession," said Zoe Brown. "Men easily get drunk or jealous or angry. But there was something about Sally that made it more likely that she'd get herself hurt. Her tongue was as tart as an acidulated drop. I did warn her..."

I said, "What is an acidulated drop?"

Zoe Brown said, "It is a type of candy, half sweet and half sour." She got up from the sofa & went to the trunk-which-served-as-a-table & fetched a striped paper bag from on top & brought it back & held it out to me. Inside were some pale-yellow, marble-sized pieces of hard candy.

"Here," she said, extending the bag. "Have one."

I took one of the yellow marbles and put it in my mouth. It was sweet but also so tart that it made my jawbone wince.

"Just like Sally," said Zoe Brown. "She had a tart tongue and was not shy to use it. Some men did not take kindly to being told what she thought of them."

I wrote that down in my Detective Notebook. "Do you have any idea who killed her?" I said.

"I believe it was an old friend," said Zoe Brown. "But I do not know his name. Sally stopped by here the night she died. It was late, about eleven thirty p.m. I was working on a hat and she must have seen my light. I invited her in. She was real excited. Her cheeks were pink & she was talking fast. She told me she had been to Topliffe's—"

I said, "Do you mean the Melodeon on C Street across from the International Hotel?"

She said, "Yes. It is called Topliffe's Theatre. They asked her to sit in the balcony with the other Soiled Doves instead of down on the floor with the Respectable Ladies. They would not even let her enter by the front door. She said she almost came home in a huff, but ended up swallowing her pride & going in the side entrance, the one for Actors and Doves, and she ran into an old friend there. She told me he was going to visit her after the show. That is a clew, I think," she added. "I tried to tell the Deputy Marshal but he would not listen."

"That is useful," I said, making a note. "Do you know the name of this 'old friend' or anything else about him?"

"No," said Zoe. "All I know is that he must have been the one as killed her. You see, she had not entertained any men in over a month. She was turning over a New Leaf."

I flipped back to my list of suspects.

I said, "Could the 'old friend' have been one of her former Gentlemen Callers?"

"I suppose," replied Zoe Brown, "but when she said an 'old friend' I thought she meant someone from her hometown in Alabama."

I watched her carefully as she answered. She did not show any signs of lying and her feet were pointed straight towards me. I felt she was telling the truth.

"What New Leaf was she turning over?" I asked.

Zoe Brown stood up & went to the window & pulled back one of the flour-sack curtains & looked out.

"Sally was fixing to go to California with Martha. She had saved up her money, sold her jewels and bought a pair of horses and rig to take them. She was going to set up as a seamstress with little Martha as her helper. She planned to leave for San Francisco on the first day of October. That was yesterday. If she had come home in a huff that night instead of staying at the Melodeon, she and Martha might be on their way by now."

"What happened to Martha?" I asked carefully.

"I don't rightly know. She used to sleep in that little back room and she must have witnessed the deed. I hope she is hiding somewhere safe. She is a dear little girl."

Even though she had her back to me, I noticed that she was pressing her right hand to the base of her throat. Jace told me women often did that when they were trying to hide something. But they also did it when upset or frightened, so I could not be sure she was lying.

All the same, I made a note in my Detective Notebook.

"Who gets the money from the Auction of Sally's things?" I asked.

"I do," said Zoe Brown. "She left me all her possessions in a Will and made me ward of Martha. But because she still owed the final payment on the horses and gig, I cannot collect any of it until the goods have been sold and the Auctioneers have taken their commission. There are also some bills to be paid: the liquor bill, the doctor and the funeral. Also, the funeral cost me nearly two hundred dollars."

I said, "Is that why so many people came to her funeral? Is that why some of the mines even shut down?"

Zoe Brown turned to look at me and I could see her eyes were brimming with tears. "No," she said. "People came to her funeral because Sally was much loved in this town. There was a mine tunnel cave-in last year. Sally was very brave.

She helped care for the men as they brought them out. The miners loved her for that."

I closed my Detective Notebook & put it in my pocket along with my pencil stub. "I have one more question for you," I said.

She looked at me with her big brown eyes, the thick lashes all sparkly with her tears. "Yes?"

"I noticed a fire helmet on the list of Short Sally's possessions. Do you know why she owned such a thing?"

"Why, yes," said Zoe Brown. "Sally loved men in uniforms and she had a special soft spot for firemen. She admired courage above all things. She made banners for all three companies and she was even an honorary member of the Young America Engine Company." She looked up suddenly. "Perhaps you should investigate Mr. Ludwig Hamm."

I flipped my Detective Notebook back to the list of suspects.

Mr. Ludwig Hamm was the first name on my list.

"But he is a barkeeper," I said, "not a fireman."

"All the firemen in Virginia are volunteers," she said. "I believe he is with the Young America Engine Company."

"Why should I investigate Mr. Ludwig Hamm?"

"Because he was in love with poor Sally. And love can make you do crazy things."

Ledger Sheet 22

AS I AM SURE YOU KNOW, the Young America Engine Company No. 2 is located on South C Street. It shares a building with the Metropolitan Livery Stable between the Young America Saloon & a Gunsmith.

When I got there I went through a prodigious doorway beneath a sign reading **YOUNG AMERICA NO. 2** to find a room containing in its center a strange & colorful contraption on wheels.

It looked like a covered vat on a wagon with some levered handles on either side. It was painted red & blue & gold.

Decorating the plank walls of the big room were a dozen colored prints showing "The Life of a Fireman" & some silk banners & hanging oil lamps. I also saw a shelf holding two trumpets & three heavy leather helmets with No. 2 on the front shield.

"What do you want?" said a gruff voice. "Come to report a fire? Or are you pranking us?"

It was a white-bearded man in a red shirt with canvas pants tucked into his boots. He had been polishing some sticking-out handles on the wheeled contraption. One side of his face was badly burned so that he looked as if he was winking at me. He had a chaw of tobacco in his other cheek.

I removed my hat and said, "I have not come to report a fire. Nor am I pranking you. I am hoping to speak to one of your firemen."

I could not take my eyes from his face.

"What are you staring at, boy?"

"I am staring at your face," I said. "Was it burnt in a fire?"

The man stared at me for a moment. Then he said, "Well, yes, it was. Bad fire in the Bowery in '38."

"Does it hurt?"

"Hurts every danged minute of every danged day." He spat some tobacco juice on the floor.

"I am sorry," I said.

He shrugged. "Most people ignore it," he said. "Pretend not to see it. But I'm proud of it. I wear it like a medal. Fire is like war, you bet. You got to battle it hard and stand by your companions and not give in to Fear."

"*Fortes fortuna iuvat*," I said. "Fortune favors the brave."

"You said it, boy! I may be half crispy but I am the president of the Young America Engine Company Number Two."

I said, "Where is the Young America Engine Company Number One?"

"Ain't no Young America Engine Company Number One." The old fireman spat again. "Our rivals are the Virginia Engine Company Number One. They were here first. But we have a bigger enjine." He pronounced the word as if it was spelled e-n-j-i-n-e so that the last part rhymed with "fine."

I said, "You are rivals?"

He said, "Our enjine comes all the way from Frisco. It was built at a cost of six thousand dollars and it is the largest and most powerful enjine in the Territory. It is a fine machine." He pronounced the last word as if it was spelled m-a-s-h-e-e-n.

He cut himself a chaw of tobacco. "Who you looking for, anyways?"

"Mr. Ludwig Hamm."

"Well, you are in luck." The old fireman popped the chaw in his mouth. "He just happens to work in the Young America Saloon right next door."

"Thank you," I said and turned to go.

"Wait," said the old fireman. He went to the wall and gave a complicated knock on it. It was something like four quick taps, then two quick taps, then a scrape and a tap & finally two scrapes and two quick taps. I wondered if it was Morse code.

Then he put his finger to his lips & pressed his ear to the wall.

While he listened to the wall, I walked around the colorful vat on wheels. Was this the engine?

I examined its levers & fixtures & fittings, trying to figure out how it might work.

I could not do it.

I heard a faint knocking from the other side of the wall.

The old fireman pulled back from the wall and gave me a smile. I could not tell if it was a genuine smile or false, due to its lopsided nature. "He will be over directly," he said.

I pointed at the four-wheeled contraption. "Is that the enjine?" I imitated his pronunciation. "I have never seen one like that."

The old fireman puffed up his chest in the manner of a pigeon. "Why, yes, that is our 'Big Six.'"

I said, "How does it work? Do you put the water in that covered vat?"

"No, the water goes *through* the tank. Pistons pump water out of the ground and into the hoses. Did you know there are cisterns beneath the boardwalks of Virginia?"

"What is a cistern?"

"It is a pit full of water."

He pointed to one side of the box. "You attach this suction pipe here and put one end into one of them water cisterns. Then you attach some long hoses to the other side of the tank and point their nozzles towards the flames. When you got six strong men pumping the brakes, that is to say, these handles, the enjine sucks the water up out of the cistern and squirts it out of them hoses. We can sometimes get a jet of water higher than the flagpole on the International Hotel."

I said, "Do horses pull this enjine? Is that why you are here in a livery stable?"

"Horses don't pull it. We do."

"On account of horses are scared of fire?"

"That, but mostly on account of we need at least eight men there to pump the enjine and point the hose, so we might as well tote it up there ourselves."

Suddenly he stood up a little straighter. "Newt Winton," he said, introducing himself. "President of the Young America Engine Company Number Two." He held out his right hand. I noticed it was burnt, too, and the flesh all mottled and puckered.

I put my hat under my left arm & tried not to shudder as I shook his hand. "P.K. Pinkerton, Private Eye."

"Pinkerton!" he said. "I saw your Advertisement in the newspaper. You solve mysteries, don't you?"

"That's right," I said. "I am investigating the Murder of Miss Sally Sampson last Friday evening."

"Poor Miss Sally," said Newt. "See that Marker?" He pointed to one of the silk banners on the wall. "She sewed that for us all herself. Paid for that silver and gold thread herself, too."

A man in a white apron came in through the open door of the engine house.

He was tall & slim & blond with a billy goat beard!

"What you want, Winton?" he asked. "I am working." When he spoke he made his *w*'s sound like *v*'s. From that I could tell he was German. We had traveled behind a family of Germans on the wagon train west.

"Sorry, Ludwig," said Newt Winton. "This here's that new Detective the boys was talking about. His name is P.K. Pinkerton. He is looking into the murder of Short Sally. Wanted to ask you a few questions. I thought you'd rather do it private like."

Mr. Ludwig Hamm narrowed his eyes at me. It was Expression No. 5: Suspicion or Anger. Or maybe both.

I tried Ma Evangeline's Trick to remembering his name and face. Ludwig was Beethoven's first name so I imagined this man playing a joint of ham instead of a piano: Ludwig + Ham = Ludwig Hamm.

"What you want to know?" he growled. He came up so close that I took a step back.

I looked up at him & said, "I understand that you were one of Sally's Gentlemen Callers. You also match an eye witness description of the Murderer. I would like to know if you have an alibi for last Friday night."

"Impudent whelp!" said Mr. Ludwig Hamm. He took a deep breath, and cuffed my ear. I had to sit down.

"Ludwig!" cried Newt. "What you doing? Why, he's only a porch baby."

Hamm stalked out of the firehouse without replying.

Newt came over to me and helped me stand up.

Something like bright gnats seemed to be floating around between my eyes and his horridly burnt face.

"Don't be mad at Ludwig for knocking you down," said old Newt. "You see, he was mighty fond of Miss Sally Sampson. He used to ask her to marry him pretty near every day of the week, but by gum, she just would not have him."

I felt swimmy-headed & sick.

But I was also happy.

I was about 95 percent certain that I had solved the mystery of who had strangulated Miss Short Sally Sampson.

Ledger Sheet 23

Ludwig Hamm's name had just gone to the top of my list of Suspects for three reasons.

> No. 1—He was crazy in love with Short Sally.
> No. 2—She had a sharp tongue & had already rejected him more than once.
> No. 3—He had a fiery temper & violent disposition.

People confound me & I do not generally understand why they behave as they do, but those three things seemed to add up to a good motive for murder.

Still, I needed to be sure.

If he had been the "old friend" Sally saw at Topliffe's Theatre the night she was killed then I reckoned I had solved the crime.

That was why I decided to leave those other suspects for later and go straight to Topliffe's Theatre to confirm my suspicions.

The double front doors of Topliffe's were firmly closed but I found a door unlocked on the north side of the building. When I opened the door, I could hear banjo music coming from inside. I found myself in a dark area with more doors and stairs. I followed the sound of the music and opened another door into a big, high-ceilinged room with a stage at my end and a bar down at the other.

I was astonished to find four men disguised as Negroes singing & playing & swaying on stage.

They had darkened their faces with something but they did not look very convincing. The black was too shiny and you could see some of the white skin on their ears and neck. The two men in the middle played banjo & fiddle. The man on the far end was jangling a tambourine and the one near me was clacking what appeared to be pieces of polished rib bones. All four had garish pants & floppy bow ties. They were singing a bouncy song called "I's Gwine to de Shuckin."

In the area right in front of the stage on ground level a man played a piano. He had not painted his face with bootblack.

As the men finished and the last notes died away, a female voice spoke behind me, "Hello, P.K. What brings you here?"

I thrust my hand in my pocket & whirled, my seven-shooter cocked & ready. I had recognized the voice of Miss Belle Donne, a Soiled Dove, who had betrayed me a couple of times the week before.

Sure enough, it was Belle.

"Put away your piece, P.K.," she said, with her throaty laugh. "I do not intend to rob you today. Or tie you up neither. I have become an Actress!"

I put my gun back in my pocket & studied her attire. She was wearing a shiny pale blue dress with a puffy skirt & cinched-in bodice that exposed all her shoulders & most of her bosom.

"Oh, P.K.," she said. "I am up soon. I am *so* nervous! Please stay and listen to me?"

The piano player had gone up onstage to give the black-face men some instructions. He went back down to ground level and they started singing a sad song called "Lucy Neal" about a slave girl who dies.

"Why are those men in disguise as Negroes?" I asked Belle over the sound of the music.

Belle rolled her eyes. "They ain't in disguise," she said. "They are blackface Minstrel Singers. Ain't you ever seen a blackface Minstrel Singer?" She was talking to me, but watching the men.

"I have seen some Shakespeare," I said, "but the players did not paint their faces black."

"Ooh! Shakespeare!" she said. "Ain't you high-tone!"

The Minstrel Singers finished their sad song and started playing a jolly piece called "Ring, Ring de Banjo."

It employed all four instruments & had a catchy tune.

I tried not to get entranced by it.

I tapped Belle on the shoulder. "Who is in charge here?" I asked.

She waved me away as if I was a vexatious bug. She was watching the blackface Minstrel Singers.

I looked around to see if there was anyone else who might have seen my prime suspect in the audience the night of Sally's murder. The theater was a big, high-ceilinged room with five round tables up close to the stage and chairs laid out in rows behind them, stretching back to where I stood.

There was something like balconies either side of the stage. I was used to seeing balconies outside a building, not inside.

At the back of the room was a bar with liquor & food for sale. A big blackboard announced that you could buy delicacies such as Pig's Trotters, Pickled Tongue, Oysters & Ham Sandwiches. The blackboard suggested washing these treats down with Champagne, Beer or Cider.

There were posters on the walls with information about interesting acts like "Martin the Wizard" & "Madame Samantha the Seeress" & "Miss Lola and Her Acrobatic Dog."

One of the posters was for the evening of my 12th birthday. The very night Miss Sally Sampson had died!

I went over to look at it. It was pink and half falling off the wall. I did not think anyone would mind me taking it so I pulled it off and folded it up and stuck it in my pocket. I am placing it here in the pages of my account.

TOPLIFFE'S THEATRE!

GRAND COMPLIMENTARY BENEFIT

TENDERED BY THE CITIZENS OF VIRGINIA CITY TO

⤷ MRS. W.H. LEIGHTON ⤶

FRIDAY EVENING,———SEPT. 26, 1862,

ALL THAT GLITTERS IS NOT GOLD.

Stephen Plum . . . A.R. Phelps

Jasper Plum . . . D.C. Anderson

Martha Gibbs . . . Mrs. W.H. Leighton

Harris . . . Mr. Woodhull

Toby Twinkle . . . Yankee Locke

Lady Leatherbridge . . . Mrs. H.A. Perry

Lady Valerin . . . Mrs. G.E. Locke

———

Comic Song . . . Mr. Woodhull

———

To be followed by the One-Act Comedy of

THE WINDMILL!

———

Fancy Dance———Mrs. H.A. Perry

———

To conclude with the Laughable Farce of

THE FOOL OF THE FAMILY!

———

POSITIVELY THE LAST APPEARANCE OF
LEIGHTON'S COMPANY IN THIS CITY

———

DOORS OPEN AT HALF-PAST SEVEN–CURTAIN RISES AT EIGHT

ADMISSION: $1.00

Up on stage, the song had turned into "Old Folks at Home." The banjo player was sitting on a chair playing his banjo while the other three blackface Minstrels swayed behind him. I noticed I was swaying, too, and had to stop myself. Finally they finished and went off behind a curtain.

Belle ascended to the stage.

The piano set off all soft & tinkling, and Belle sang sweet & high. She was singing a song called "Virginia Belle." That song started out sweet & pure. By and by, Belle made her voice lower & rougher, while the piano man played more vigorously. She began swinging her arms & stomping around & pointing out towards the empty chairs & benches.

Belle finished by putting her thumb to her nose and wiggling the four remaining fingers at the imaginary audience. Ma Evangeline always told me that "thumbing your nose"—that is, "cocking a snook"—was rude, but Belle did it with a smiling face, as if it was a salute. The four blackface minstrels had come down to watch & did not seem to be offended. They applauded loudly & so did the piano player. I clapped, too. Belle's cheeks were pink & her eyes were glittery.

As Belle came down from the stage, four Ladies danced onto the stage from two different directions. Two had a small pretend fire engine like the one I had just seen over at the Young America Engine Company. Two had something like a big spool with a hose on it. All four dancers were wearing oversized, red flannel firemen's shirts cinched in tight with black patent-leather belts. They wore tall leather fire helmets with the No. 1 on them & also little black boots, but they appeared to have forgotten their skirts. Looking closer, I saw they were wearing flesh-colored tights. The minstrel singers stood to one side of the stage, playing music while the four Dancing Girls sang a song about "Putting Out Your Fire."

Belle appeared beside me. "How was I?" she asked. Her chest was still rising and falling from the exertion.

I said, "It was very energetic."

"But didn't you like it?"

"I prefer that banjo music," I said, nodding towards the stage. The blackface minstrels were playing faster and faster. They were clipping along a mile a minute with their banjo & fiddle & tambourine & clacking bones. Two of the Dancing Girls were vigorously pumping the lever on the "engine"— one on either side—while the other two pointed a hose at the blackface Minstrel Singers. The hose suddenly squirted out some blue paper streamers. I guessed the Dancing Girls were pretending to "put out" the four singers as they would a fire.

"P.K.!" said Belle Donne.

"What?" I replied, coming to my senses. I had almost got entranced.

"I asked why you came here?"

I said, "I am investigating last week's brutal murder of Short Sally. I have come to see if my lead Suspect was here last Friday. His name is Ludwig Hamm and he is a volunteer fireman at the Young America Engine Company."

"Ludwig?" said Belle Donne. "Sure. She knew him. Everybody knew he was sweet on Sal. He wanted to marry her but she was too high and mighty for him."

"Do you know if he was here that night?" I asked.

"How would I know that?" said Belle, her cheeks still flushed. "Tonight is my first time onstage. Last week I was just another girl with a crib down on D Street. Today I am a solo artiste performing along with a famous troupe: the Sagebrush Minstrels. Ain't it bully?"

I barely heard her, for a man had just come up onstage carrying a Skull.

He was tall & slim & blond with a billy goat beard!

He was dressed in black tights & big puffy bloomers & a white ruffled collar. I knew this was Shakespearian getup.

"Who is that man?" I asked Belle.

"That is Absalom Smith," she said. "He told me he stood in for someone last week and Major Topliffe asked him to be a regular item here at the Music Hall. I am hoping the Major will invite me, too."

I looked closer at the man in the puffy black bloomers. If Belle had not told me, I would not have recognized Mr. Absalom Smith in this new getup, even though I had imagined him sitting on a tree branch just that morning.

I often make that blunder. Sometimes I do not know a person I have met before if they are wearing something new. I moved closer & looked for a feature that might distinguish him from other tall, slim men with billy goat beards. I noticed his eyebrows were straight & dark & that they almost met above his nose.

"Watch out, P.K.!" cried Belle.

I had been looking so intently at his face that I had not noticed Mr. Absalom Smith taking an old dueling pistol out of his puffy bloomers. He cocked it & aimed it at me & pulled the trigger.

BANG!

Ledger Sheet 24

I HIT THE FLOOR at the same moment the gun went off.

As the loud report of the gun died away, I heard a smattering of laughter echo in the high-ceilinged room & I cautiously raised my head.

Absalom Smith was looking at his gun with a comical expression. A bunch of flowers had popped out of the barrel.

"Oh, P.K.!" laughed Belle. "You fell for that!"

She held out a hand to help me to my feet but I pushed it away.

I do not like to be touched.

"Apologies," said Mr. Absalom Smith in a loud &

carrying voice, "to any of you I might have startled. But the sound of gunshots is so common in this place that I did not think it would alarm anyone."

I was on my feet again & dusting myself off.

He put the thumb of his left hand on his chin & pulled down his lower eyelid with the forefinger of the same hand & tucked his chin under & looked at me from under his eyebrows.

Belle Donne said, "That gesture means he was just pranking you."

I glared back at him. I do not like being pranked.

Mr. Absalom Smith shrugged. "Why is a Springtime Meadow even more dangerous than Virginia City?" he asked the echoing room in a loud voice. Then he answered his own question. "Because in a Springtime Meadow, the grass has blades, the flowers have pistils & the leaves shoot!"

At this, he tossed the gun aside & it went off with another *BANG!* as it hit the floor & everybody laughed but me.

"I was in the Fashion Saloon yesterday," said Absalom Smith, "when a three-legged dog walked in. The dog limped up to the bar and announced, 'I'm looking for the man who shot my paw.'"

Belle & the Minstrels & the piano player & the Dancing Firegirls all laughed.

"The other day," said Mr. Absalom Smith, "a young woman fell down a mine shaft. Her brother was there but was unable to help her out. Why not? Because, you see, he could not be a brother and *assist her*, too!"

More laughter. And some groans.

"But hold!" He stopped and struck a dramatic pose. "I am a Shakespearian Ac-tor. Enough of these foolish conundrums."

"No!" cried the four Minstrels. "We want mo!"

"I shall compromise then," said Mr. Absalom Smith. He held out the Skull at arm's length. "To be or not to be," he said. "That is the question. Whether 'tis nobler in the mind to suffer the slings and arrows of outrageous fortune—" He looked out towards the audience. "Speaking of arrows," he said, "I was shot at by Indians on the way out of Carson City. Luckily"—here he paused—"I had a narrow escape!"

Nobody laughed.

He leant forward and pulled down his eye again and repeated, "I had an *arrow* escape."

Everybody laughed.

Absalom Smith tossed the Skull behind him & it bounced & this made folk laugh harder than ever.

A sharp tug on my coat sleeve brought my attention from the stage to Belle.

She said, "If you want to know whether or not Ludwig Hamm was here last Friday, you could always ask the Boss, Major Topliffe. He is coming our way. And he don't look happy."

Ledger Sheet 25

THE OWNER OF TOPLIFFES THEATRE, Major G.W. Topliffe, a sallow-faced man with gray hair over his ears & a monocle, was coming towards me with purpose and intent. He wore a military jacket & Expression No. 5: Suspicion or Anger. Or both.

"Who is this whelp, Belle? And what is he doing here? If he ain't in the show, he should not be here." The Major thumped his walking stick on the wooden floorboards for emphasis.

Belle took me by the shoulders & turned me

towards the exit. "He is nobody," she said. "He is just leaving." She gave me a little shove.

But I turned back & planted my moccasins firmly on the ground. "My name is P.K. Pinkerton, Private Eye," I said.

He turned the eye with the monocle towards me. "You look part Indian," he observed. "Say, can you fire an arrow with accuracy or throw a tomahawk?"

"I am a Detective," I said. "I would like to ask you a few questions concerning the brutal Murder of Miss Sally Sampson."

Major G.W. Topliffe's monocle fell out & dangled from a chain. "You are a Detective?"

"Yes, sir. I have been hired to find Sally's killer. The Coroner has no interest in seeking Justice, nor does the Deputy Marshal." Remembering my manners, I took off my hat & said, "I have come to see if any of the suspects in the murder were here last Friday the twenty-sixth day of September. My chief suspect is Ludwig Hamm, a volunteer fireman at the Young America Engine Company. But I have some other suspects, too."

"Ooh," said Belle. "Let me see the suspects." Before I could stop her, she snatched the Detective Notebook from my hand. She began to read out loud, slowly and haltingly, "Tall, slim men with fair hair and smallish beards known to have—" Then a Name must have caught her eye. She looked at me, white faced. "Isaiah is a Suspect?" she said. "He frequented Sally Sampson?"

Too late, I remembered that Miss Belle Donne and Mr.

Isaiah Coffin were engaged to be married. I snatched back my notebook.

"Dang Isaiah!" cried Belle. "Dang him to the fiery place!" She then let loose a stream of actress profanities.

"My performance cannot be that bad," said Absalom Smith from the stage.

Belle stamped out of the room.

The Major chuckled. "I like that girl. She has spirit. I might just take her on." He peered through his monocle at my notebook. "Those three were all here at the theater last Friday evening."

"Who?" I asked.

Major G.W. Topliffe stabbed at my notebook with a thick forefinger. "The Frenchman, the German and the Russian," he said. "Danged foreigners. Come to think of it, the Englishman might have been here, too."

At first I was disappointed that he could not narrow down my list of suspects.

Then I felt a gleam of hope.

The way he had described my Suspects made me realize something about them for the first time.

One was German, one French, four of them were American, one was Russian and two were English.

It occurred to me that if Martha had heard the Killer speak, she might be able to say whether he was German, French, English, Russian or even a Confederate, from one of the Southern states. That would narrow it down a lot. But Martha was hiding in a Bear Cave in a Forest somewhere.

"Where is the nearest Forest?" I asked Major G.W. Topliffe.

"Forest?" he blustered. "There ain't no forest within fifteen miles of here. This county is almost entirely destitute of timber. They have used up about every stick of wood within sight to build this town."

I pondered this information. Could Martha have traveled 15 miles on bare feet? It seemed unlikely. That meant she was not hiding in a forest after all.

Up onstage, the four minstrels were back for an encore of "Camptown Races."

De Camptown ladies sing dis song,
Doo-dah! doo-dah!
De Camptown racetrack five miles long,
Oh, doo-dah day!
I come down dere wid my hat caved in,
Doo-dah! doo-dah!
I go back home wid a pocket full of tin,
Oh, doo-dah day!
Gwine to run all night! Gwine to run all day!
I bet my money on de bobtail nag,
somebody bet on de bay.

Beside me, Major G.W. Topliffe chuckled and tapped his cane to the music. I looked up to see that the dancing girls had returned as pantomime horses. (I could tell it was them by their flesh-colored legs & their boots.) One of the horses had the letters FLORA TEMPLE on its side. The other one was BROWN JIM. These bogus horses were comically jostling the Minstrel Singers.

"Why do those bogus horses have names written on their sides?" I asked Major G.W. Topliffe.

He stopped tapping his walking stick in time to the music. "Why, they are the famous horses from the song. Flora Temple is the name of the 'bobtail nag' and Brown Jim is 'the bay.'"

I stared at him.

In my mind, something slipped into place, like the missing letter in a typesetter's tray.

"What is it?" he said. "Do you know who committed the crime?"

"No," I replied, "but I think I know where the Eye Witness is hiding."

Just to make sure my reasoning was logical, I opened my Detective Notebook, took out my pencil stub & wrote,

Clews as to Martha's Whereabouts

Clew No. 1—She had not bathed.
Clew No. 2—She smelled of horse manure.
Clew No. 3—She had straw in her night bonnet.
Clew No. 4—She said she had nothing to eat but some "barley & raw oats."

Then I wrote,

Martha must be hiding somewhere closer than a forest, because she came to me within an hour of my Advertisement being published.

Then I wrote,

She might be in a location where she could have over-heard people reading my Advertisement.

And finally,

She must be somewhere here in Virginia City.

Yes, I reckoned I knew where Martha was hiding.

Ledger Sheet 26

I HAD FINALLY FIGURED OUT where Martha was hiding. All the clews had been there. But I had been too dull to put them together.

Martha was not hiding in a Bear Cave in a Forest 15 miles away.

Martha was hiding in a Livery Stable right here in Virginia.

And which one?

"The Flora Temple Livery Stable!" cried Major G.W. Topliffe, who had been looking over my shoulder. "That must be where your Eye Witness is hiding!"

I glanced around to see if anybody had heard his cry, but everyone seemed to be entranced by the music. I nodded & put my finger to my lips.

The Flora Temple Livery Stable was where Sally had kept a fine rig and a pair of white mares to pull it. It had been named in the Notice in this morning's paper. Also, one of Gussie's girls had mentioned it.

Martha had probably gone there with Short Sally from time to time, or at least heard of it. I knew Miss Sally had a pair of white mares. Perhaps Martha was fond of the horses and counted them among her friends.

During my week in Virginia City I must have gone past the Flora Temple Livery Stable a dozen times. It was just a block away from where I now stood.

I thanked the Major for his help & left Topliffe's the same way I had come in.

The sun had sunk behind Mount Davidson about one hour before. The mountain's shadow may fall like a coffin lid, but dusk lasts a fair time in Virginia City.

I hurried along to the west side of C Street near Sutton Avenue. Sure enough, there was the big sign saying **FLORA TEMPLE LIVERY STABLE**. It was hanging over big, wide-open stable doors.

As I headed for the entrance, I saw two stable hands standing there. I did not want to attract attention so I turned around & pretended to go back the way I had come, but secretly hid behind a barrel and waited till they turned to talk to a high-tone man and a woman. Then I snuck in.

Although it was dusk, nobody had lit any lamps in the stable so that it was dim & warm inside. I could smell horses & sweet hay & leather. I like horses & I like that smell.

Short Sally's two white mares were right at the back in a corner stall. I could see their heads, like ghosts in the gloom.

As I made my way silently towards Sissy and Sassy, a soft nickering to my right brought me up short. I turned to see a mustang pony looking at me over the door of his stall. I went over and stroked his nose.

His hide was the exact color of my buckskin trowsers but his mane and eyes were as dark as chocolate. He reminded me of the ponies I had known in the Black Hills, so I greeted him in Lakota. I was surprised to see his ears prick forward. Had he once been an Indian pony?

As a test, I whispered, "Stand!" in Lakota. To my astonishment he reared up a little.

He came back down with a thud & gave a soft snort, as if to say, "See! I understand you perfectly."

I stroked his neck and noticed that his coat was rough. He was well fed, but nobody had groomed him in a long time.

"Who is your rider, boy?" I said in Lakota.

He dipped his head & snorted sadly, as if to say, "My rider has not visited me in a long time."

"I will come back and find out," I said. "But right now I have to find a runaway girl. You don't know if she is hiding around here, do you?"

The pony gave a soft snort & a nod & his ears pricked towards the corner stall, the stall of Sissy and Sassy. You can tell where a horse is looking by the direction their ears are pointed.

"Thank you," I said in Lakota.

He nuzzled my neck.

I do not like being touched by people. But I do not mind being touched by horses. His breath was sweet. I blew into his nostril, so he could get my scent, then I gave him one last stroke and went deeper into the gloom, to the stall in the corner.

Like the buckskin mustang, Sissy & Sassy had not been brushed in a while, but they were well fed. They had oats & a trough for water & plenty of hay piled up at the back.

I sniffed the air.

Sure enough, I thought I detected the scent of Martha's ammonia, clove and lavender pomade.

I opened the door to the stall.

The mares nickered softly. I moved forward and stroked their necks & got to know them a little.

One of the mares kept turning her ears towards a pile of hay in the corner.

I went over to the pile of hay.

Most people would not suspect anyone could be hiding in there, but my keen sense of smell & the horses' ears were powerful clews as to Martha's whereabouts.

Sure enough, as I pulled some of the hay away, I found Martha all curled up like a wood louse in the straw. She was wearing her pale nightdress & night bonnet, but no coat or shawl. The light was so dim that had I not been looking, I would never have seen her.

"Martha?" I whispered. "Martha! Wake up!"

There was no reply. She was lying awful still.

"Martha?" I reached out to touch her shoulder, expecting to feel the cold chill of death. But she was not dead & cold. Beneath the thin cotton, she was burning with fever.

In his nearby stall, the mustang gave a whinny of alarm.

I peeped over Sissy & Sassy's stall door & saw a hatless man in a cloak silhouetted against the square of pale dusk formed by the big open doors of the Livery Stable. As he looked left and right, I caught a glimpse of his profile. *He was tall & slim with a billy goat beard.* Was it Short Sally's Killer? Had he followed me?

If so, I had led him straight to Martha.

Ledger Sheet 27

I QUICKLY TOSSED SOME HAY over Martha and scrouched down behind the water trough. I had promised my foster ma Evangeline never to kill a man but that did not stop me getting out my Smith & Wesson's seven-shooter. If that man came back into the stable and tried to hurt Martha, I would throw down on him.

I sat there on the straw-littered beaten-earth floor, with my back against the rough, wooden water trough so nobody passing by would see me. Then I listened as hard as I could.

I heard the cloaked man's footsteps come closer and closer, pause, then hurry away as another pair of footsteps came through a squeaky door at the back of the stables. I reckoned the second footsteps belonged to a stable boy; I heard him go into the next-door stall and lead out a horse. The cloaked man had already gone quickly back the way he had come.

A few minutes later it was quiet, with only the snuffling of horses and faint sound of a fiddle from a nearby saloon and the deep steady thumping of the Quartz Mill Stamps, a sound that never ceased in Virginia.

When I was sure the coast was clear, I went to Martha and uncovered her.

"Come on, Martha," I whispered. "I think the Killer followed me here. I have got to get you to safety."

She neither stirred nor moaned.

I gently slapped her cheek & pinched her arm, but I could not rouse her.

So I covered her up with straw again & quickly went out of the stall to look around.

At the back of the stables was a small wooden door. The stable boy had bolted it from inside. I unbolted it and it opened with a squeak. I looked out upon the steep mountainside & the backs of some buildings on B Street up above. It was getting dark now, but I could see a woodpile & a few privies & a big pile of horse manure.

That gave me an idea.

I went back in and pulled Martha out of her hay burrow.

I tried to get her to walk but she was as limp as a sack of turnips. So I eased her onto the ground & grabbed her wrists & dragged her out the stall door. There I saw a gunnysack of feed that was almost empty. I took it & emptied it into a bucket & went to Martha & managed to cram her inside the bag. Then I dragged the bag with Martha in it across the hay-littered earthen floor of the stable & out the back door & up the slope to the far side of the manure pile. Standing back, I tried to see it with a Stranger's eyes.

In the dusky light, it looked like an old rubbish sack behind the manure pile.

I thought, "She will be safe there for a while, until I can get her to a Safe Haven."

Then I thought, "But where can I take her?"

Doc Pinkerton might help, but he was ten minutes away, even if I ran, and there was no guarantee he would be in.

Then I had an idea of someone soft-hearted & kind who might take Martha in. The only problem was that I might have to submit to a kiss.

I scrambled up the slope between a bath house & a saloon to B Street, and carefully crossed at a break in traffic & then went up the next part of the slope between buildings to A Street. I had come this way once before when I had been chased down the mountain by some boys from the dump of the Mexican Mine. There was no sign of them today and I was glad.

Five minutes later I reached a big wooden house up on A Street. It had a white picket fence & gate. Lights shining through the windows & the sound of someone practicing piano made it seem cozy and welcoming.

I was breathing hard from the speed of my ascent & the thin air, but also from anxiety. I opened the gate & went up the path & mounted four steps & crossed the porch & knocked on the door.

The piano stopped and a moment later the door opened.

"Why, hello, P.K.," said Bee Bloomfield. "What a pleasure it is to see you. We will soon sit down to dinner. Shall I ask my ma if you may join us?"

"That is a kind invitation, but I have a favor to ask of you. Can you step outside for a moment?"

She tilted her head to one side. "Are you finally going to give me that kiss?"

"Do not josh me," I said. "This is important."

"P.K.," she said, "are you in *danger*?"

"I am not in danger, but my client is. She is a poor ex–slave girl about your age. Can you take her in? Can you protect and care for her?"

"Just let me ask Pa," said Bee. She turned away and then turned back. "P.K.," she said, "did you say she was an ex–slave girl? Is she a . . . Negro?"

"Yes," I said. "She witnessed the murder of a Soiled Dove and now the Killer is after her."

"Oh," said Bee. She made no move to go, but hung her head and stared at her feet.

"Ain't you going to ask your pa?" I said.

"I already know what he will say. He hates Negroes and he hates Soiled Doves. I am sorry, P.K., but we cannot help you."

I gazed at her for a moment, then turned away.

There was no time for me to indulge in disappointment. I had to find someone to help Martha.

I went down the stairs & through the gate.

I heard a loud bell start clanging somewhere farther down the slope & at the same moment I smelled the smoke.

Bee was calling something after me and I thought I heard her father's deep German-accented voice, too.

But I did not really hear what they were saying. I was staring at a thick plume of smoke, darker than the twilit sky, rising up from C Street below me. Even before I heard the frightened screams of the horses, I knew the building on fire was the Flora Temple Livery Stable.

Ledger Sheet 28

I RAN BACK DOWN the steep mountainside between buildings, the way I had come.

When I got to the manure pile behind the Flora Temple Livery Stable I saw that Martha was still safe in her barley sack. But smoke was pouring up & flames were licking at the roof of the stable & I could hear horses whinny inside. Those two pretty white mares were in danger. And that buckskin mustang, too.

Without pausing for thought, I ran to the little back door o f the stable, the one I had left unbolted.

I opened it & a blast of heat nearly knocked me

back. But the flames had not quite reached the rear stalls. I saw Sissy & Sassy rearing up and pawing the air in terror.

I ran to them & undid the latch on their stall door & opened it & stood back. They thundered past me through the narrow door into the scent of fresh night air. I heard shouting and saw figures through the smoke, leading horses out through the front. Only one other horse remained in the stables. It was the buckskin mustang. He screamed with fear & reared up. The heat was almost too much to bear, but I ran forward at a crouch & quickly tried to undo the latch on his stall door. It was so hot that it burned my fingers, but finally the door flew open. I fell back as the terrified mustang charged after the mares. I did not blame him. Horses hate fire above all things. It makes them crazy.

I had just struggled to my feet, choking for air & blinking against the sting of smoke when something knocked me down. It was a powerful waterfall coming from the heavens above. I lay gasping like a fish out of water until it passed.

For a brief moment I saw stars where the roof should have been, then I saw a great arc of glassy orange rise up and come crashing down upon me. It was a stream of water so strong that it pushed me across the slippery earth floor for a good three feet. Once again it passed, moving to my left, and I took this chance to scramble through the open back door of the stables.

For a moment I stood panting & drenched. Then I saw the three horses were still back there, neighing & rearing & trying to scrabble up the steep slope of the mountainside. One of the mares had become tangled in some sort of clothes line and was rearing up perilously close to Martha in her gunnysack by the manure pile. I fumbled for my flint knife and got it out and severed the rope. Then I stroked the mare's neck and calmed her using tricks my Indian ma had taught me.

The fire seemed to be out, but I could see the great arc of water from the fire hose still rising up into the sky and crashing down onto the charred roof of the stables. If it went any higher it might pass beyond the stables & thunder down upon the spot where I stood with the horses & spook them & then they might trample Martha in her gunnysack.

I needed to get them out from behind the stable.

The mustang was the shortest of the horses. I dug my fingers into his dark mane & pulled myself up onto his back. Then I spoke softly in his ear & urged him forward. We emerged from behind the stable and reached the small corral on its northern side. As I had hoped, the two mares followed close behind.

The night air was cool on my face. I could smell the pungent aroma of scorched, wet wood.

There were fourteen horses swirling around in an outside pen. Now that the fire was almost out, they were excited but not panicked.

In the street, on the other side of the corral, men were clustered around a fire engine. But it was not the one I had seen at the Young America Engine Company. This engine must belong to their rivals, the Virginia Engine Company No. 1.

It was over twice as long as the No. 2 engine & had eight men on either side, pumping up & down like the Devil. When 16 arms rose up on one side, 16 went down on the other. Two more men held the hose, which was still throwing up a strong jet of water. They reminded me of the Dancing Girls at Topliffe's Theatre. But this was not comedy. This was life and death.

"STOP PUMPING!" cried a voice louder than God's. I could see a man in a leather fire helmet with No. 1 on it. He held a silver trumpet to his lips. He was not blowing the trumpet. He was giving orders through it. I reckoned he was the foreman of the Virginia Engine Company No. 1.

"WE HAVE DONE IT!" boomed his voice. "THE FIRE IS OUT!"

The exhausted firemen collapsed over their engine while everybody cheered and patted them on their backs. I slid off the buckskin mustang & opened the wooden gate of the corral & slapped his rump. He obediently went in, followed by Sally Sampson's two white mares.

I had just closed the gate behind me when one of the stable hands shouted, "There he is! That boy started the fire!"

"Get him!" cried a man in a plug hat. I reckoned he was the proprietor, Mr. Joseph H. Gardiner.

I started to run, but they soon had me surrounded. The big stable hand gripped me tight & hoisted me aloft.

I do not like being touched & I hate being hoisted aloft.

"Lynch him!" cried a man's voice.

"No!" said another. "Let's soak him in coal oil and set him on fire!"

"Yeah!" said the one holding me. He threw me to the ground with such force that the wind was knocked from my lungs.

"Why, he's just a boy!" cried a woman's voice. I reckoned it was Mrs. Gardiner, the proprietor's wife.

"Boys is the worst!" said the smaller stable hand, hardly more than a boy himself. "They gotta be taught!"

"Burn him!" screeched someone. "Burn him alive! That'll learn him."

I saw the little stable hand coming towards me with a tin can of kerosene.

The big one held a lit match.

BANG!

An upward flash of powder & the report of a gunshot stopped the two youths.

"Get away from him!" cried a man's voice. "Get right away!"

The Rev. C.V. Anthony was pointing a .41 caliber single-shot Deringer towards the sky & glaring at the crowd. Everybody backed off.

The Reverend pocketed his still-smoking piece & helped me to my feet. "Tell me you did not set that fire, P.K.," he said in a low voice.

"I did not set that fire," I gasped, only now getting my breath back. "I had nothing to do with it."

"He's lying!" said the first stable boy. "Shandy and me saw him lurking by the back stall where the fire started!"

"I was trying to help a girl hiding out in the stables. I rescued your horses," I said. "I did not set the fire."

"Then who did?" asked Mr. Joseph H. Gardiner.

I said, "It was a hatless man wearing a cloak!"

"What hatless man?"

"I do not know. But he was tall and slim with a billy goat beard."

"A likely story!" cried Mr. Joseph H. Gardiner.

"I say we lynch him!" cried a new voice.

"I got a piece of rope!" cried another.

Some C Street spectators had come over to join my persecutors.

"For shame!" cried the Rev. in his preacher's voice. "Attempting to lynch a poor child without even a trial. I will take him to the Marshal's where he will await fair justice."

Once again I felt myself lifted bodily up into the air but this time I was folded over a Christian shoulder. As he pushed through the crowd, I had to hold on to my slouch hat lest it fall off. I heard angry voices shouting & I even felt a few fists pummel my back until the Rev. C.V. Anthony quoted John 8:7 in his preacher's voice, "'He that is without sin among you, let him first cast a stone'!"

At this the crowds parted and allowed him to hurry south along C Street and then turn uphill on Sutton. It was almost deserted there. I guess everybody in town had congregated by the burnt stable.

Now that we were away from the bloodthirsty mob, I started to struggle. "Let me go!" I said. "There is a girl I have to help. Do not take me to the Deputy Marshal!"

The Rev. C.V. Anthony stopped & I felt myself swung down. The sloping road slammed the soles of my feet through my thin moccasins. My sore shoulder throbbed as he gripped it hard.

"What girl?" he said. "What are you talking about?"

"There was an Eye Witness to Short Sally's murder," I said. "And the Killer is out to get her."

"Who is this Eye Witness?" the Rev. asked me.

"A Negro girl. A lady's maid," I said. "About ten years old, wearing a nightdress and bonnet. I can prove I am not lying." I pointed to a narrow space I had discovered earlier that day. "We can go through that alley, past the outhouses of the Fashion Saloon and between the backs of some other buildings."

"I remember Sally's little serving girl," said the Rev. "You say she witnessed the deed? She knows the identity of the killer?"

"Yes, sir," I said. "But she has a fever and might die if we do not get her to a doctor. Please will you help me?"

Ledger Sheet 29

I COUNTED MYSELF LUCKY on three counts that evening.

First, that the Methodist pastor, C.V. Anthony, happened to be present at the scene of the fire & saved me from a mob intent on burning and/or lynching me.

Second, that although of a slim build, he was strong enough to carry Martha in her barley sack down to Doc Pinkerton's.

Third, that Doc Pinkerton agreed to care for Martha, even though she reeked of urine, sweat and horse manure. I know now that he is a good Christian.

We took Martha upstairs, and once again, I gently pinched her cheeks to wake her. I was eager to know if the Killer spoke with a German accent so that I could confirm it was Ludwig Hamm. Of the nine Suspects on my list, he was the only German.

But Martha was still burning up with fever & would not be roused. Doc Pinkerton left her in Mrs. Pinkerton's care & walked us downstairs & told me to come back around 10:00 a.m. the following day to see if her fever might have broken.

The Rev. C.V. Anthony headed downhill to his own dinner while I set off through the crowds along C Street towards the International Hotel and my appointment with Jace. But I had not taken three steps along the boardwalk when a thought struck me.

It was a thought so terrible that my innards seemed to fall right down into my legs.

Charles Volney Anthony was No. 9 on my list of suspects. If my short time in Virginia had taught me one thing, it was this: do not trust anybody!

I thought, "Sally ran into an old friend the night she was killed and the Reverend is a new arrival in town!"

I also thought, "What was the Rev. doing at the scene of the fire?"

And finally, "What if he set the fire, discarded his cloak & pretended to save me so I would trust him and tell him where Martha was hiding?"

The Methodist pastor, C.V. Anthony, now knew where

she was, and even which room she was in, for he had carried her upstairs.

If the Rev. *was* the Killer, he could simply sneak back at the dead of night with a ladder, open the window & strangle her at his leisure.

I needed to move Martha one more time.

I needed to find an even safer place than Doc Pinkerton's.

Do not trust anybody. But I had to trust someone.

My first thought was Big Gussie. I was pretty sure I could trust her, but would the killer think to look for Martha there? I needed someone I could trust who was not too obvious.

I closed my eyes & fired a prayer like an arrow up to the Lord. I had barely whispered "Amen" before a name fell into my head.

It was a surprising name but upon reflection I reckoned it was my best bet.

I turned & went back to Doc Pinkerton's & knocked on the door & when he opened it, I quickly explained the problem. He was not convinced that Martha was in danger, but I insisted. At last, he agreed to send her on to a safer place.

I told him how to recognize this person when he came to collect Martha, and I shared my simple plan.

"All right," said Doc Pinkerton at last. "Mrs. Pinkerton is giving Martha a sponge bath so at least she will be clean. And if you give me the address of your Safe Haven I will check on her tomorrow morning."

(You may think I am being Mysterious in my description of these events, but I do not want to confide Martha's whereabouts even to these pages, lest the Killer get hold of them.)

All I can say is this: I ran as fast as I could to the place where I hoped to find my ally & sure enough he was there. As I expected, he agreed to help. I even followed him back to Doc Pinkerton's & watched from the shadows as he took delivery of a "pile of dirty laundry" & wheeled it away in a wheelbarrow. Only when I was sure that nobody was shadowing *him* did I make my way back to my office.

I knew it was well past 8:00 p.m. and that I was going to be sorely late for my dinner appointment with Poker Face Jace, but there was no helping it.

It was lively up on B Street with music spilling out of saloons & people crowding the boardwalk. I went into my office & lit a lamp & locked the door behind me. I did not pull down the blind so that if someone was spying they would see me take the lamp into my back room & think I had retired for the night.

But I did not retire for the night. I peeled off my still-damp coat & changed into a disguise.

I have four disguises, viz:

1. Blanket Indian Disguise—old Paiute blanket, dusty slouch hat & tin begging cup
2. Chinese Boy Disguise—blue pajamas, clogs & flat straw hat with false pigtail
3. Prim Girl Disguise—pink calico dress, bonnet & white button-up boots

4. Rich Boy Disguise—coat, waistcoat, black brogans
   & plug hat

Nos. 2, 3 & 4 were next door in the clothing cupboard of
Mr. Isaiah Coffin's Ambrotype & Photographic Gallery.

However, Disguise No. 1 was hanging from one of the pegs
on the wall.

I pulled it down & wrapped the Paiute blanket around me.
Then I tugged the shapeless felt hat down low & grabbed my
tin coffee cup.

I could not risk going out the front door of my office
dressed as a Paiute, so I offered up a prayer, put the tin cup
inside my shirt, slid out of my window & descended by means
of that rickety ladder. My foot almost went through the fifth
rung.

I thought, "I must buy a new ladder."

And also, "I better remember not to empty my chamber
pot out here anymore."

When I reached the bottom, I waited for my eyes to adjust
to the darkness. Then I picked my way through tin cans and
other worse things to the Coroner's alley. Emerging onto C
Street, I turned left onto the busy boardwalk & made my way
to a nondescript entrance of the International Hotel. This
plain white door is used by tradesmen and delivery boys. You
may have walked past it a thousand times without realizing
that it is another way into the International Hotel. Bare
wooden stairs carry you up to a plush carpeted hallway that
leads to luxury rooms.

When I got to the door with the brass No. 3 on it, I looked up and down the hall to make sure nobody saw a grubby Blanket Indian going into Jace's Rooms. I gave the secret knock on the door and when I heard Stonewall's grunt I went in.

"Where you been?" said Jace. He was standing by the fireplace near Stonewall, who was seated.

"It is almost nine," said Jace. "We been waiting for you."

Jace is good at hiding his emotions, but I could tell he was riled because he blew his cigar smoke strongly down. That was something he himself had taught me.

I said, "Sorry I am late. I got delayed by that fire over at the Flora Temple Livery Stable."

"You got to allow extra time for traffic," said Jace. "Virginia is getting busier every day."

"It was not just the traffic," I said. "The proprietor and two stable hands accused me of setting that fire. I nearly got burned alive and also lynched."

Jace asked me to tell what happened & I did so over dinner. They had already eaten, but there was a kind of tin hat over my plate and the food was almost warm. They sat drinking coffee while I ate a hearty meal of pork chops, greens and corn on the cob. I was hungry and it was good.

Through mouthfuls of food I told them everything that had happened so far that day from the rock baby in the parcel to finding Martha in the stables and getting her to safety.

Finally Jace said, "So you think the man you saw in the stables—the hatless man in the cloak—was Short Sally's Killer?"

"It might have been the Rev. C.V. Anthony," I replied. "And I am also suspicious of Mr. Isaiah Coffin. But my number one suspect is the fireman I was telling you about: the barkeeper over at the Young America Saloon, Mr. Ludwig Hamm."

"What makes you think Hamm is the killer?"

I said, "He was crazy in love with Short Sally. She had a sharp tongue and had already rejected him more than once. Also, he has a fiery temper."

Jace finished his coffee and took a Mascara brand cigar from his breast pocket. "A fiery temper don't make someone a killer," he said, striking a match on the bottom of the table. "Though Sally's manner of death does suggest a crime of passion."

"What do you mean?"

Jace held the flame to the end of the cigar and puffed, turning it to get it burning even. "Like I told you," he said, "when Short Sally was murdered last week, the first rumor was that she'd had her throat cut. Cutting someone's throat is messy, but more importantly it is coldhearted. The killer usually does it because it is quick and silent and he needs something."

I nodded.

Jace puffed some more. "Strangling, on the other hand, is usually a hot-blooded crime."

I thought about my main suspect in the murder of Miss Sally Sampson, the hot-tempered Mr. Ludwig Hamm, and I rubbed my ear, still sore from his boxing it.

"To strangle someone," continued Jace, "you have to get

your hands directly on that person's throat and squeeze. It takes a while to get the job done," he added. "It requires a different frame of mind from the other."

His voice sounded kind of thick & I looked at him hard. He was blowing smoke slowly down, a thing people do when they are sad.

"Have you ever strangled a man or cut his throat?" I asked.

"Yes," said Poker Face Jace, without meeting my gaze. "I have done both those things."

Ledger Sheet 30

YOU STRANGLED A MAN *and* cut a throat?" I asked Jace.

Jace nodded. "It was wartime."

"The war back east?" I said.

He shook his head. "The Mexican War. Fifteen years ago."

I waited in case he had anything more to add.

He examined his cigar.

"I had to cut a sentry's throat once," he said, "in order to keep him quiet. A few weeks later I found myself in a pitched battle. I was out of ammunition and my rifle was gone. We were fighting hand to hand. A man went for me. It was either me or him . . ." Jace trailed off & looked down at the table. "The first method is cold-blooded. The second is hot-blooded." He glanced over at Stonewall, who had been sitting silently throughout the meal. "Neither is pleasant. It is an awful thing to kill a man."

I nodded. "Even in self-defense," I said.

I remembered the face of the man I had killed. I also remembered how easy it had been to pull out my seven-shooter and point it at Belle Donne when she startled me over at Topliffe's.

"What about a gun?" I asked. "What frame of mind do you have to be in to shoot someone?"

Jace shrugged. "Scared, angry, butterfingered," he said. "But I'll wager most shootings in this town are done by men in the grip of alcohol." He rubbed his forehead, then looked up at me. "What I am trying to say is that it appears Sally's murder was a crime of passion or anger. If someone had been planning to rob her, I reckon he would have used a quicker method. She either said something or did something to make a man crazy with rage."

I nodded. "That is what I think. I think Mr. Ludwig Hamm proposed marriage and she laughed at him and maybe said something hurtful. So he strangled her. Then he saw Martha and he knew he had to kill her, too, because she had witnessed the crime and might tell. He chanced to see her this morning when she came to me for help. I reckon he has been shadowing me ever since. That is why he set the stable on fire. To make it seem accidental."

"You think he followed you to the stable?"

"Yes, sir."

"I thought you said he tended bar."

"I did."

"Then how could he loiter for hours in the street shadowing you?"

I had no answer for that. But Jace had planted a Seed of Doubt in my mind.

Jace examined his cigar. "Were you followed here?"

"No, sir. I snuck out my back window and kept to the darkest shadows. Plus I am in Disguise."

"What about after the fire? Could the killer have followed you and the Reverend down to Doc Pinkerton's?"

"I thought he might try," I said, "so I followed the Reverend back to his house. I made sure nobody else was shadowing him. And then I got another person to take Martha from Doc Pinkerton's to a Safe Haven. Just in case it was the Reverend and not Ludwig Hamm who killed her."

"Good thinking," said Jace. "Where will you go from here? With the Investigation, I mean?"

"As soon as Martha is better," I said, "I am going to ask her what accent the Killer spoke with. If he spoke with a German accent, then the Killer is probably Ludwig Hamm."

"Unless it's someone not on your list," said Jace.

Jace had just planted another Seed of Doubt in my mind.

Stonewall pushed his chair back & stood up & went into his bedchamber. He had not spoken a word & his coffee sat cold & untouched. I heard him peeing into the chamber pot.

"What is wrong with Stonewall?" I said in a low voice.

"He is in a brown study," said Jace.

I said, "You have a study in there? I thought it was another bedchamber."

"It is a figure of speech," said Jace. "It means he is low in his spirits."

"Why is Stonewall low in his spirits?" I asked.

"The news from Maryland," said Jace. "That terrible battle at Sharpsburg, which the newspapers call Antietam."

"That was last week."

"There are reports coming in of terrible losses. Every day the number goes higher. The latest estimate is twenty thousand."

"Twenty thousand men killed?" I said.

Jace nodded. "They say the bodies are all piled up in bloated heaps and not even buried. There are photographs in New York showing corpses with blackened faces, distorted features, and expressions most agonizing. Some people say that battle will end the war."

"Jace?" I said. "Why are they fighting?"

Jace sighed. "There are a lot of reasons," he said. "But the main dispute is about the right to own slaves. The North wants to make the South set their slaves free. The Confederates—that is, the Southerners—reckon they will not survive without slave labor. Plus we don't like being told what to do."

"You're a Reb?" I said.

He sighed again. "I am a Southerner who has seen too much death and killing."

Stonewall's bedchamber door opened & he came back into the room.

"We don't have time for a full lesson this evening," Jace told me in a businesslike tone of voice, "but in light of this recent spate of shootings I am going to give you a useful piece of advice."

Stonewall had pulled a chair up by the fire & was fingering a narrow felt pouch.

"Here is my tip," said Jace. "Just before a person is about to do something big or dangerous, they usually take a deep breath in."

I nodded. That made sense.

"Sometimes," he said, "you will see their whole chest swell up, but that don't always happen. What *does* always happen is that their nostrils get a little wider a split second before they mean to act. This will often tip you off that they are about to throw a punch or draw their piece."

"Nostrils," I said, to show I was paying close attention.

"Correct," said Jace, tapping some ash onto his empty dinner plate. "Of course, you have got to look at the whole picture, but train yourself to notice that flaring of the nostrils."

I remembered how Ludwig Hamm had taken a deep breath right before he hauled out & struck me. I rubbed my sore ear and wished I had known that useful tip before.

"Stonewall taught me that," said Jace. "Didn't you?"

We both looked at Stonewall.

He was still sitting by the fire, staring down at a piece of thread in one hand and a needle in the other.

"I cannot seem to do this," he said in a low voice. I reckoned it was hard for him as his eyes pointed in two different directions.

"Here," I said. "Let me. My eyesight is sharp."

I threaded the needle & handed it back.

Stonewall took the threaded needle and regarded it for a few moments as if it was something he did not recognize.

Then the man who had once pressed a Le Mat revolver to my forehead began to weep.

Ledger Sheet 31

WATCHING STONEWALL CRY made me feel mighty strange. Like the time Ma Evangeline banged her head on the table when she was coming up from cleaning the floor. When someone as brave and fearless as Ma Evangeline or Stonewall starts to cry, you feel your world is collapsing into crumbs.

I looked at Jace.

Jace was blowing smoke out & slowly shaking his head. But he had a soft look in his eyes.

"What's the matter, Brose?" said he. I had never heard him use that name before.

"My pard Tiny used to do the sewing." Stonewall's big head was down & big tears plopped on his mending. "But Tiny got shredded at the Battle of Shiloh."

"Was it bad?" I asked. "Fighting in the war?"

Stonewall lifted his big head. "That is like asking if burning in H-ll is bad," he said. "Everybody told me it would be all trumpets and glory, but it turned out to be mud and blood and minie-balls and bits of flesh and men begging to go home. But Shiloh made the other battles look like paradise."

Stonewall gazed at the wall. His eyes pointed two different directions but he did not seem to be looking at anything. "They say the rout started because of a lieutenant in one of our other companies. They say he was Petrified. Petrified with Terror. I don't know his name but it was his first battle. They say he stood there like a statue while men dropped on his right and on his left. Then his men turned and ran. They swept us along with them."

Stonewall hung his head. "We ran past a regiment of Tennessee boys and they called out taunts after us: 'Flicker, flicker! Yellowhammer!'"

"What does that mean?" I asked.

Stonewall shrugged. "Yellowhammer is the State Bird of Alabama," he said. "We call it the flicker. I guess those Tennessee boys was saying we were scared like birds. I guess they were calling us yellow." He looked down at the needle and thread in his lap.

"War can make people animals," said Jace. "Not everybody stays to fight like a bear. Some freeze like possums and some flee like flickers."

"Well, I was a fleeing yellow flicker," said Stonewall. "If I could of flown I would of. But I had to walk. I set my face west and did not stop except to eat and sleep." He looked up at me. "Took me a month and a half to get here. Jace told me I should've come earlier. Wish I had."

I looked at Stonewall's sad & ugly face and wondered how I would behave in a battle with men getting shredded around me. Would I fight like a bear? Or flee like a flicker? Or freeze like a possum? I reckoned I would freeze, too, because when the Shoshone attacked us two years ago, I found myself sitting on the grass by dead bodies and burning wagons and I do not remember anything that happened before that. It was all a blank.

"What happened to the man who froze?" I asked. "The lieutenant of that other company?"

Stonewall shrugged. "I reckon he is dead. Those minie-balls was so thick they sounded like wasps buzzing around us. If those waspy bullets didn't get him," he said, "our firing squad would of."

"Your own people would've shot him?"

Stonewall nodded. "They shoot cowards and deserters as a lesson to the rest. Specially officers."

"Did you ever kill anyone?" I asked Stonewall.

"P.K.," said Jace, "do you always interrogate people like this?"

"What do you mean?"

Jace leant forward. "I mean you can't just ride a Question straight at somebody like that. It is just like a battle. They will either throw up their hands and flee, or freeze, or they will fight back." He drew on his cigar. "That may well be why this Hamm person beat on you."

I did not know what to say, so I said nothing.

"You got to come at them from the side," he said. "A flanking maneuver is what they call it in the army. Weave your way round to the question. If you want to know where somebody was on Friday evening, ask them if they ever go to the Melodeon or the Dog Fights of an evening."

"There are Dog Fights here in Virginia?"

"That ain't the point. Do you understand what I am trying to tell you?"

I nodded. "Yes, sir," I said. "Don't charge straight at them but come around sideways."

Jace sat back and tapped some cigar ash in the ashtray. "I suggest that you continue to interview the suspects on that list of yours, but try out this new method on them. Sideways, not direct."

I looked at Jace. He sat relaxed & calm & smoking his cigar. He had taught me more useful lessons about Human Nature than I had learned in the previous 12 years. He was helping me with my Murder Investigation & even advising me on how to Interview a Suspect.

It was time for me to do something for him in return.

It was time for me to help him play poker.

Ledger Sheet 32

STILL WEARING MY BLANKET Indian disguise, I went out the nondescript C Street exit of the International Hotel and wove my way through crowds to the Virginia City Saloon on B Street. I did not want to arrive before Jace, so I wandered up & down for a few minutes, making sure that nobody was "shadowing" me.

Confident that I would not be recognized in my disguise, I went past the Flora Temple Livery Stable. Torchlight showed that some carpenters were already at work replacing the south wall. I saw Sissy, Sassy and some other horses in the corral, and the skinnier of the two stable hands dozing against a wall, with a scatter gun across his knees. I heard a soft nickering and turned to see the buckskin mustang with his head raised and his ears pricked towards where I loitered. Had he recognized me? Even in my disguise? That was one clever horse.

I resisted the impulse to go over & stroke him. Instead, I made my way back up to the saloon on the west side of North B Street.

When I enter a saloon, I generally enjoy bursting through those swinging doors, if they have them. The Virginia City Saloon has them, but on this occasion I ducked under so as to enter unnoticed. The room was full of cigar smoke, whiskey fumes, men's voices & the entrancing sound of a banjo.

It was not the first time I had been to the Virginia City Saloon. Less than a week before, a couple of desperados had tried to fill me full of lead there. I was certain nobody would try such a thing again. They say lightning rarely strikes in the same place twice and on that other occasion I had been wearing Disguise No. 3—a pink calico dress and bonnet.

Today I was in a different getup.

Wrapped in my Paiute Blanket and rattling my begging cup, I attracted a few glares but nobody complained outright. It was up to the barkeeper whether Blanket Indians and other undesirable types were allowed to frequent the place. I guess Jace had probably already had a quiet word with the barkeeper, because he just gave me a little nod.

I quickly glanced around and saw Jace already seated at a round table covered with green baize. As usual, his back was to the wall and the brim of his hat cast a shadow over his eyes. I sat where I could see him as well as the feet of the four other men at his table.

My Indian ma taught me to always look for the exits in a room in case you need to make a hasty escape. There was the front door with its swinging butterfly doors. There was a normal wooden back door over near the banjo player. There were also stairs leading to an upper walkway, with numbered rooms of the Virginia City Hotel and a door at each end of the walkway. I myself was flanked by a spittoon on my right and the faro table on my left.

The Virginia City Saloon is pretty well lit, with oil lamps on the wall and a big chandelier with glass globes hanging from the ceiling. There were half a dozen tables with men gambling. A few hurdy girls in low-cut dresses were leaning against the wall or lingering near the bar.

I turned my attention to Jace's table. There were four other men playing cards with him. Two of them had big droopy mustaches and one had a waxed one. The fourth man was Absalom Smith. The reason I recognized him was thanks to his pipe tobacco, the same as Pa Emmet's, and his eyebrows, which almost met over his eyes. I was surprised because I thought he would have been performing at the Music Hall. Then I saw the clock said midnight so I guessed the show at Topliffe's had finished.

"What is put on the table and cut, but never eaten?" Absalom Smith was posing conundrums.

"Undercooked potatoes?" suggested someone at the table.

"No," laughed Absalom Smith. "A pack of cards!"

Over the next hour or so his puns got worse as he got "tighter."

About halfway through the fifth hand Absalom Smith said to the man with the pointy waxed mustache, "Ain't you going to see my raise? Or are you yellow?" His Southern accent was more noticeable, probably because he had been drinking.

"I'm sinking," said the man with the waxed mustache. It took me a moment to realize that he was a foreigner and that he meant to say he was "thinking."

"Flicker, flicker. Yellowhammer," drawled Absalom Smith.

Whenever someone tells me a new expression or word, I suddenly hear it everywhere. I remembered Stonewall saying these very words just a few hours before.

I looked over at Stonewall, who was hunched over the bar. But he was lost in his cups & had not heard.

"What zee h-ll is 'flicker yellowhammer'?" said the man with the pointy waxed mustache. I guessed his accent was French.

"I believe he's calling you a poltroon," said Droopy Mustache No. 1.

"What zee h-ll is 'poltroon'?" said the Frenchman.

"It means a 'big coward,'" said Droopy Mustache No. 2.

The Frenchman looked from one man to another, then folded his cards facedown on the table. "I finish with zis game!" he said.

"Flicker, flicker. Yellowhammer," said Absalom Smith again.

"You shut your mouth or I shut her for you!" said the Frenchman, leaping to his feet.

"Now, boys," said Jace in his deep voice. "Let's keep it civil."

The Frenchman stood for a moment, breathing heavy, then spun on his heel & stalked out of the saloon.

Jace watched him go & shook his head & took a suck of his cigar. "You in?" he asked the others.

They all nodded and finished betting.

"Read them and weep, gentlemen," said Absalom Smith as he spread his cards out for all to see.

His hand must have been good because everybody sat back except Absalom Smith. He leaned forward to rake in the pile of coins.

"Mind if I join you?" asked a familiar voice. It belonged to a tall, slender man with a blond goatee. He spoke with an English accent, like Ma Evangeline's. It was not until he sat down in the Frenchman's recently vacated chair that I recognized him by the small circular scar on his cheek.

It was Langford Farner Peel, the new Chief of the Comstock.

Ledger Sheet 33

YOU HAD BETTER NOT call this fellow a coward or a poltroon," said one of the men to Absalom Smith.

"Or tell him any more of your bad puns," said the other. "He is a famous shootist from Salt Lake City, ain't you?"

"I just want to play a little poker," said Farner Peel, puffing his pipe.

"You are welcome to join us as long as you play fair," said Jace. "My name is Jason Montgomery but everyone calls me Jace."

"They call him *Poker Face* Jace," said Absalom Smith in a loud voice. "So you'd better watch out."

Farner Peel turned to Absalom Smith, the smile still on his face. "And what, if I may ask, is your name?"

Absalom Smith gave a little bow and said in his Southern drawl, "I am Absalom Smith: actor and punster extraordinaire. Singer, too, sometimes." And he began to sing, "'Oh, I'm the fool of the family, and people do what they like with me . . .'" They were the words to the song I had heard him whistle once or twice.

Mr. Jasper Leeky, the barkeeper and proprietor, brought a bottle of whiskey and a fresh glass for Peel to the table. "Compliments of the house," he said.

Suddenly I saw Mr. Jasper Leeky's chest swell & his nostrils flare, just like Jace warned me about. But he did not throw down on Peel. He extended his hand & said, "It is an honor to meet you, sir."

Peel shook his hand & Mr. Leeky filled each man's glass.

I guess Mr. Leeky just needed that breath for courage to shake the shootist's hand.

Everyone took a sip of their drink except Jace, who was dealing.

The saloon fell quiet for a few minutes. I think people were waiting to see if Farner Peel intended to pull out his six-shooters and start blazing.

But he played cards quite amicably & soon the buzz of conversation in the saloon was back to its normal level.

I carefully watched the feet of the men at Jace's table to find out who was confident and who was bluffing. If someone had dancing feet or their toes pointed upwards, I gave a light jingle of my tin begging cup and then put it down with the handle turned towards the man with the Happy Feet.

If someone hooked their feet around their chair legs, or drew them back under the chair, that meant they might be bluffing. In that case I gave the cup a jingle & aimed the handle, but kept it in my hand.

Everything was going well at Jace's table. The men were drinking & betting & everybody won a hand or two, though Jace always won more. The cigar smoke and late hour was making me drowsy. Once or twice I nodded off & had to pinch myself hard to stay awake.

Then something happened.

At Jace's table there was about $400 in the pot: a lot of money, even for Jace. The other three men had folded and this game had come down to Farner Peel and Jace.

Absalom Smith was dealing. Peel and Jace both asked for one card. When they got their cards, Jace remained very still, as usual, but Peel frowned & stroked his mustache & sat back in his chair. I was expecting him to fold, but instead his chest swelled a little as he took a deep breath & pushed three gold coins forward & said, "Sixty dollars."

Immediately after this statement, I saw Peel hook his ankles tightly around his chair legs. He was also sitting as still as a statue & holding his breath. From these clews, I reckoned he was bluffing. I let Jace know by giving my cup a soft jingle & keeping it in my hand, with the handle pointed towards Peel.

I know Jace saw my handle pointing accusingly at Peel, but he did not act on this information by matching or even raising Peel's bet. Instead, he said, "I fold," and put his hand face down on the table.

"Flicker! Flicker!" muttered Absalom Smith, taking a drink. "Yellowhammer."

Langford Farner Peel stood up so suddenly that his chair fell back with a crash. He held his arms away from his body and we could all see the flaps of his holsters were open.

Everyone in the saloon fell instantly silent.

"Don't shoot me!" slurred Absalom Smith, holding up both his hands. "I meant it for Jace . . . not for you."

But Farner Peel was not looking at him. Or at Jace.

"You two," said Peel. "Over by the door. Have you come for me?"

All heads turned towards the door, including mine.

Two men stood in the doorway, each held open one of the slatted wooden doors. After a heartbeat, they stepped inside, their spurs jangling, and let the doors swing closed behind them.

"No," said Boz in his whiny voice. "We ain't come for you."

"We come for him!" said Extra Dub in his raspy voice.

Then they both turned towards me, their guns already in their hands.

Ledger Sheet 34

I DID NOT NEED to look for flaring nostrils to know to move quick.

Five shots rang out in quick succession as I flung myself to the right.

Bang! Bang! Bang! Bang! Bang!

I picked up the full spittoon, hurled it at the desperados, then dived left beneath the shelter of the faro table.

The flying spittoon made Boz recoil against Extra Dub & they both went down into a puddle of slimy tobacco-tinted spit.

Bang! Bang!

Their pistols discharged harmlessly into the

ceiling. One ball hit the chandelier & glass sprinkled down. Women were screaming & men were cursing & some more shots rang out from other parts of the saloon.

Bang! Bang!

From my vantage point under the faro table I saw Farner Peel standing there with two smoking Navy Colts. He was not even breathing hard.

Boz, on the other hand, was writhing and whimpering on the floor. The two black eyes I had given him were swollen so much I wondered he could see out of them. He was slick with tobacco juice and blood.

"Dub!" he whimpered. "Dub, where are you? I is shot!"

"Your friend has departed," said Farner Peel in his English accent. "Look behind you and you will see the doors still swinging behind him."

Boz peered up at Farner Peel. "Why did you shoot me?" he whined. "I warn't doing you no harm."

Peel shook his head. "I detest cowards and bullies," he said in his soft voice. "Rise up and get out of this town. If I see you again, I will put a ball between those two black eyes of yours."

Boz started to struggle to his feet & as he did so he caught sight of me crouching under the faro table.

"You damned puppy!" he hissed. "This is all your fault. I'm gonna get you and cut your throat!"

Bang!

Farner Peel had fired another shot up into the ceiling. It brought down a satisfying shower of dust & plaster.

"I will count to ten," said Peel.

He had barely got to six when the saloon doors were swinging and the space Boz had occupied was empty.

I breathed a sigh of relief and crawled out and dusted off the sawdust.

There was a round of applause from some of the patrons, but Mr. Leeky did not seem happy.

"Sir," he said to Langford Farner Peel, "please do not take offence at what I am about to say. But there was a shooting affray here last week and I only just finished having the ceiling replastered."

"You want me to leave and never come back?" said Peel with a half smile & a raised eyebrow.

"If you don't mind, sir." Mr. Jasper Leeky gave Peel a little bow. I noticed his hands were shaking.

"Very well." Peel picked up his slouch hat and put it on his head and slowly walked towards the exit.

As he passed by me, I said, "Thank you, Mr. Peel."

He gave that strange half smile again and touched his finger to his hat.

Then he, too, went out the swinging doors.

"You! Indian boy!" said Mr. Jasper Leeky. I looked up to see that he was addressing me.

His arm pointed towards the door. "You go, too!" he said. "You bring heap bad medicine."

I gave Jace a sidelong look, but he was flicking a piece of lint from his coat.

I knew he would understand my leaving so abruptly.

I gave Mr. Jasper Leeky a curt nod & bent to pick up my begging cup & went out after the three gunmen.

I glanced around to make sure none of them were lying in wait for me. They appeared to be gone.

Nevertheless, I kept to the shadows as I made my way home through the lively streets.

I reckon it was nearly 2:30 a.m. when I climbed back up my ladder & tumbled in through my half-open window.

I took off my hat & put down my begging cup & I knelt beside my camp bed to say my prayers but my mind was spinning like a top with all the things that had happened since the morning:

I had received a ghoulish parcel containing a Stone Baby with the letters R.I.P. on its belly. I had witnessed a shooting affray & helped the Doc perform a delicate medical operation. I had been swung at & knocked down & nearly kissed. I had met the new Preacher & interviewed four ladies in their corsets. I had seen my first Minstrel Singers & some Dancing Firegirls & also some real Firemen in action. I had got my first Genuine Client, then lost her, then found her & then nearly lost her again to flames. I had nearly got set on fire and/or lynched. Jace had taught me some more useful things about people and I had seen Stonewall blub like a baby. And just now I had stopped two desperados from shooting me by flinging a nearly-full spittoon at them.

I thought, "Yes, this is a good place to learn about the ways of men and the wickedness thereof."

Little did I imagine what the next day held in store for me.

Ledger Sheet 35

I WAS WOKEN on the morning of Friday October 3 by an insistent knocking on the front door of my office.

I unrolled myself from my begging blanket & sat up. My left arm was throbbing from my gunshot wound & from where about three people had gripped me hard the day before. My ear ached from where Ludwig Hamm had struck me. My ankle was still sore from jumping from one balcony to another last week. And now my heart was banging from being wrenched from sleep by urgent knocking.

I felt tired & low, but as I stood up, the sight of that 100-mile view of far-off deserts & mountains & the sun gilding Sugar Loaf Mountain revived my spirits a little. Through the soles of my moccasins, I could feel the steady thump of a thousand Quartz Mills pounding ore into silver-filled dust. That thudding came right up through the stilts on which my back room was propped. It was like the mountain's heartbeat.

I had fallen asleep still dressed in my moccasins & buckskin trowsers & faded red flannel shirt & wrapped in my Paiute begging blanket. My hair is still real short from where Ma Evangeline shaved it against nits, so I did not have to comb it or do anything else to get ready except put on my dark blue coat with the brass buttons.

When I came out of my bedroom I could see the shape of a figure in my door window. As I got closer, I saw it was Mr. Sam Clemens. He was looking back across the street towards the Shamrock Saloon. When he heard the key in my lock he turned & smiled down at me & took the pipe from his mouth.

"No flowers grow here, and no green thing gladdens the eye," he drawled, pointing with his pipe, "but saloons spring up like weeds. That one seems to have appeared overnight. Did you hear about Murphy who was shot yesterday? They say he might live! I reckon this rarified atmosphere carries healing to gunshot wounds."

I said, "What do you want?"

"You know, P.K.," he said, strolling into my office, "now that you have set up as a Private Eye, you might consider adopting a more formal way of greeting your clients. 'How may I help you?' or 'What is troubling you?' are both preferable to a blunt 'What do you want?'"

"How may I help you?" I asked, stifling a yawn with my hand.

"Oh, I am sorry," he said, puffing on his evil-smelling pipe. "Did I wake you? Were you up till all hours at some saloon last night?" He chuckled & then stopped when I nodded.

"Yes," I replied. "I was over at the Virginia City Saloon until about two a.m. Two desperados came gunning for me but I distracted them with a spittoon long enough for Farner Peel to draw his piece & scare them out of town."

"Dang it, Pinky," he drawled. "You have the Devil's Luck. You always seem to be in the right place at the right time." He clasped his hands behind him & rocked back on his heels & gazed up at the sky-window & puffed. "What I would have given to live by myself and frequent saloons until two a.m. when I was your age," he said. "What a life."

"It is no Feather Bed," said I. "Being a Detective is harder than I thought it would be."

Sam Clemens removed the pipe from his mouth and scowled at it. "Dan De Quille got wind of that Shooting last night. He has already conducted interviews and written it up," he said. "Dan found Boz nearly bleeding to death and turned him in and got the two hundred dollar reward."

"He turned Boz in?" I said. "So I don't have to worry about him?"

"I reckon not."

"What about Extra Dub?"

Sam Clemens shrugged. "Some witnesses saw him tearing away towards Carson City at a prodigious rate," he said. "His horse was shedding foam-flakes like a ship in a typhoon."

"That is good news," I said.

I sat behind my desk and he sat in my Client's chair before me.

I poured myself a cup of cold coffee.

"You going to share that with me?" he drawled.

"I only have one cup," I said, taking a sip. "Besides, it is cold and black."

"Like your heart," he muttered. Then he sat forward and said, "P.K., I have a problem. I got my job at the Territorial Enterprise by writing the occasional witty Letter to the Editor. But now they want me to fill two columns every single day. And by God, that ain't easy, especially as Dan gets first choice on all the Shootings and really exciting things. At the moment, my notebook is barren. Bereft of ideas. Blank as a desert."

I nodded, to show I was listening.

He tipped his chair back and continued, "After the gun duel between Patrick Murphy and Farner Peel that was snatched from me, I happened upon a beautiful fistfight down on C Street. But as nobody was killed or mortally wounded, my paper will not publish the details. Then my hopes soared when I heard the fire bell yesterday evening. I rushed across the street to the Flora Temple Livery Stable but by the time I got there the fire was almost out. Those Firemen are so doggone rapid that they prevented any loss of man or beast. It seems fistfights and fires without deaths are of no consequence to anybody." He puffed his pipe & said, "I do pine for murder."

I said, "I am trying to solve the murder of Short Sally."

He waved his pipe. "Last month's news."

I kept quiet. I did not want him muddying my waters anyway. He seemed to twist every fact he got hold of.

Then he leaned forward. "Yesterday Dan suggested I go down to the Coroner and get some stories from him. You know, children run over by Quartz Wagons or puppies fallen down Mine Shafts. Now that was a good idea, the reader loves that sort of Tragedy. The only problem is that the Coroner and I are feuding."

"Do you mean Mr. G.T. Sewall?" I said. "A big red-faced man with a silver-tipped walking stick?"

"That is the varmint!" cried Sam Clemens & pointed at me with his pipe stem. "See? You arrived the same afternoon I did and already you know more about this town and its denizens than I do."

"I do not like G.T. Sewall," I said.

"Nor do I," said Sam Clemens. "So here is my proposition to you. I will pay you a dollar to go down to the Coroner and find out if there have been any grisly or gruesome deaths recently."

"No," I said.

"What do you mean: no?"

"I mean I went down there yesterday to ask about my Case. He thought you had put me up to it and he almost brained me with his silver-tipped walking stick. He already thinks I am in cahoots with you."

"That could be a problem." Sam Clemens sat back & puffed on his pipe.

I sat back, too, and took a sip of yesterday's cold black coffee.

I had an idea. "Would your readers like to hear about a man cut in half by a Quartz Wagon?"

He shook his head. "Too commonplace. We had one of those last week. I need something new. Something fresh."

I thought, "I'll bet you would like the story of a little girl who witnessed a crime and now the killer is after her." But I did not say it.

After a moment Sam Clemens sat forward. "You could go down in *disguise*," he said.

"My disguises are for shadowing people," I said. "Not for interviewing them. They only work because they help you blend in to the background. They don't bear close examination."

"There is one disguise you have that might work," said he.

"Which one is that?" I asked. But already I thought I knew what he had in mind.

"That one where you dress up as a little girl," he said. "It quite transforms you."

"That is a time-consuming disguise," I said. "I am in the middle of an important investigation. I have to check the whereabouts of various suspects on the evening of Friday last."

"Give me their names," said he. "I will question them with

tact and discretion, under the pretence of writing an article. I will find out if any of them are unaccounted for."

I took another sip of cold black coffee & pondered his proposal.

It was a good one. I had not had much luck interviewing suspects. They always seemed to get mad at me, probably because I came straight at them as Jace had said. It might be that Sam Clemens was better at flanking maneuvers.

"All right," I said. "I will question my next-door neighbor, Mr. Isaiah Coffin. If you question a barber named Pierre Forote, a policeman named Isaac Brokaw and a telegraph operator named Yuri Ivanovich, then I will visit the Coroner for you."

I did not say it out loud, but I thought, "If my disguise is convincing enough, I might even get some more clews about Short Sally's Killer."

Ledger Sheet 36

BEFORE I WENT DOWN to the Coroner's Office to get news of grisly murders and/or gruesome deaths for Mr. Sam Clemens, I fortified myself with a hearty Detective Breakfast of two mutton chops, eggs & buttered toast with marmalade.

Then I went next door to interview Suspect No. 6 on my list. I was still pretty sure No. 1 had done it—Ludwig Hamm—but this would give me a chance to practice my interview skills.

I knocked at the door of Isaiah Coffin's Ambrotype & Photographic Gallery.

His Chinese assistant, Ping, opened the door with a scowl.

"How are you, Ping?" I asked carefully. "How is everything at home?"

He shrugged. "All right. Everyone still asleep," he said.

I nodded to show I understood. "May I come in?"

"Why?" he asked.

"I need to borrow a costume," I said. "And also to question your boss."

"He busy," said Ping. "He is teaching me to mix chemicals. Also, he is vexed because you keep borrowing clothings. He say you wear and tear."

"I will pay him for any damaged goods," I said. "Please let me by?"

Ping stood back to let me by. He was wearing an apron over a smart gray worsted suit. The suit looked store-bought. I reckon he had bought it with some of the $500 I gave him for helping me the previous week.

Ping followed me into the clothes cupboard.

The door to the small Dark Room was open. I saw & smelled Mr. Isaiah Coffin mixing chemicals. Isaiah Coffin is tall & slim with a wispy billy goat beard & one eyebrow almost permanently raised.

"Good morning, P.K.," he said in his English accent. "How are you today?"

"I am well, thank you. Ping says you are vexed at me."

"Ping is quite correct," said Isaiah Coffin, raising his raised eyebrow even higher. "You have been using up my costumes. Wear and tear, my boy, wear and tear. My problem, you see, is that they belong to my friend Maguire. I'm only storing them until he opens his theater."

"May I borrow the Prim Little Girl costume one last time if I buy a replacement?"

"I suppose so," he said. "As long as your replacement is of the same quality."

"Thank you," I said. I went behind a rack of clothes and began to change. I could have taken my costume to my own place next door but I wanted an excuse to stay & question him.

I remembered Jace's advice so I tried coming at Mr. Isaiah Coffin from the side: a "flanking maneuver."

I cleared my throat and said, "Mr. Coffin, do you ever go to the Melodeon or the Dog Fights of an evening?"

He stuck his head out of the small room and frowned at me. "What?"

"Topliffe's Theatre, for example. Do you ever go there?"

"B'yen syoor," said Isaiah Coffin. "I love the theater in all its forms."

I unbuttoned my faded red (not pink) flannel shirt. "Were you there last Friday by any chance?" I asked. "Only I noticed the poster said a woman was doing a 'Fancy Dance' and I was wondering what that was."

"I was not there," replied Mr. Isaiah Coffin. "I had a Secret Meeting. But I imagine a 'Fancy Dance' is some sort of energetic jig."

"Secret Meeting?" I said, turning to face his open door. "What Secret Meeting?"

"It is a secret," he said, his voice was muffled as he bent over a tray.

I tried coming at him from another side.

"Where do you live, Mr. Coffin?" I asked, as I slipped on the calico dress.

"I live in a boardinghouse south of here, near the Divide."

"Were you up late last Friday night?" I asked, as I pulled on the bloomers. "At your 'Secret Meeting'?"

His head appeared over the clothes rack & almost made me jump out of my dress.

"Why all these questions?" he asked.

"Just curious," I said.

"Cease and desist," he said. "I am teaching Ping how to develop tintypes and we are using dangerous chemicals. You are distracting me."

"I apologize," I said. "I will not bother you anymore."

They closed the door of the small dark room behind them & I sighed.

My flanking maneuver had failed. I hoped Sam Clemens was having more luck with the French barber, the American policeman and the Russian telegraph operator.

I finished changing into my Prim Little Girl Disguise. It takes about five minutes to do up all the little buttons on each boot. I was glad I did not have to wear such an outfit every day.

The strange thing about wearing a disguise is that it makes you feel different. It is a little like adopting a person's posture. Wearing a calico dress & boots & bonnet, you can almost imagine what it would be like to be a Prim Little Girl. It changes the way you walk and the way you see the world. Your dress prickles your neck & your bonnet blinkers your vision & your too-tight white button-up boots make you take wincing, mincing steps. Bloomers feel strange, too, because a breeze comes up under your skirt & whistles around your nether parts & this can be unsettling. The temperature had dropped so I also took a knitted, woolen woman's shawl. It was a shade of purple and did not match my pink calico dress but that could not be helped.

When I took my own clothes back next door, I observed there were still no clients waiting outside to hire me.

I thought, "I had better solve this case or my career as a Detective will soon be over and I will never get to Chicago."

When I finally got down to the Coroner's office it was about 11 o'clock a.m. The door was closed.

I knocked politely.

"Come in!" said a voice from within.

I opened the door. Sure enough it was that red-faced bully G.T. Sewall.

"Good morning, sir," I said in a little girl's voice. I kept my head down as if I was shy so he would not get a good look at my face. Under my pink bonnet I was wearing a wig with black ringlets. "Are you the Coroner?" I asked. I perched on the edge of a wooden chair facing his desk.

"I am," he said. "What brings you here?"

"My brother has gone missing," I said. "My ma sent me to see if you've had any deaths recently. She is too upset to come herself."

This was the story Sam Clemens had coached me to say. He said to be as vague as possible about "my brother."

"You look familiar," he said. "Have we met before?"

"No, sir," I lied. I caught myself pulling the prickly lace

collar away from my neck & forced myself to sit still with my hands in my lap.

"You Mexican?" he said, squinting at me. "You got a kind of tinge to your complexion."

I lowered my head even more. "Only on my pa's side."

He said, "Well, some prospectors did find the body of a young man yesterday evening, but he ain't Mexican."

"My brother had a different pa," I said, still keeping my head down. "So it could have been him. How did he die?"

"Appears to have been kicked by a mule or horse. They found him down in Six Mile Canyon with a hoof-shaped dent in his skull."

This sounded interesting. I sat up a little straighter. "May I see his body?" I asked, glancing towards the morgue.

(Sam Clemens had told me to ask this so I could examine the body & make note of any grisly wounds.)

"Trust me, little Missy, you do not want to do that. The coyotes have been at him. Besides, his body is not here. It is at the undertakers."

"Oh," I said. "Have you heard of any other grisly accidents?"

"Well, there were two shootings yesterday but both men are still clinging to life. One of them was Irish. Name of Murphy. You ain't part Irish by any chance?"

I shook my head.

He said, "Then there was that killing down on D Street. Two drunks arguing about the war and that new proclamation. The Reb forked the Yank."

"Forked?"

"Yes, sir. Stabbed him in the neck with a fork. The Yank

received a mortal puncture to the carotid artery. He bled out in about five minutes."

"Mortal? Does that mean he is dead?"

"It does indeed," said G.T. Sewall.

I pondered that for a moment. I had seen two men survive being riddled with bullets at close range and yet here was a man who died in less than five minutes from a fork-inflicted wound. I reckoned Mr. Sam Clemens would like this story.

"May I see the body?" I asked. "He might be my brother."

"I doubt he is your brother. That one's forty if he's a day."

"It might be him," I said. "May I look at him?"

"You have a forty-year-old brother? What is your name, anyway?" he said, narrowing his eyes at me. That was Expression No. 5: Anger or Suspicion. Or both.

Sam Clemens and I had not decided what my name was to be.

I needed to think of one quick.

"Maisie," I said, using the name Dan De Quille had given me the week before.

"And your last name?"

"De Quille," I said. "Maisie De Quille."

"What? You're Dan De Quille's little girl?"

"Yes. I am Dan De Quille's little girl."

"Why you are telling a big story! Dan ain't Mexican!"

Too late I remembered I had told him my pa was Mexican.

"Also," said G.T. Sewall, rising up from his chair, "I happen to know that Dan's family ain't here in Virginia. He left them all back east. Also, his real name ain't even Dan De Quille."

This was news to me. I looked up. "It ain't?"

"No. It ain't. Now, who are you?"

I quickly looked down & tried to think of a convincing reply.

"Why, you're that danged Injun boy who came round yesterday, ain't you? Only today they dressed you up as a girl! That varmint Sam Clemens sent you, I'll bet. You tell that conniving skunk that he will get no information out of me. As for you ..." G.T. Sewall lunged for his silver-tipped walking stick.

I did not hear the rest of his threat for I was out the door faster than a cricket from hot embers.

Ledger Sheet 37

I ESCAPED THE CORONER by dashing in the trades-man's entrance of the International Hotel & up the wooden stairs & out its B Street entrance. Nobody took any notice of a breathless little girl in shawl and bonnet.

As I emerged onto B Street I was almost knocked off my feet by a tide of off-duty miners & shop-keepers & even some women hurrying south along both sides of the street.

"Gonna be another duel!" I heard someone say.

I offered up a prayer of thanks and let myself be carried away by the swirling tide of people.

Presently I found myself outside the Niagara Hall & Billiard Saloon.

I squeezed through the crowd so I could hear what the people at the front were saying.

"He is crazy," said a man.

"Do you think he will do it?" said another.

I emerged into open space at the front of the crowd. My bonnet had got shmooshed down over my eyes. When I adjusted it, I saw nothing but the doors of a saloon.

I tugged the frock coat of the man to my right. "What is it?" I asked him. "What is happening?"

"You run along home, now, li'l gal," said the man. "They is going to be trouble here in not too long."

"What trouble?" said a man's voice behind me.

"Some crazy Irishman," replied another. "Pat Lynch was sweeping the front when this fellow comes up and says, 'Pat, what sort of a corpse do you think I'd make? Do you think I'd make a good-looking corpse?'"

"He calls himself El Dorado Johnny," said another man. "He's packing a pair of Colt's Navy revolvers."

"Pat tried to stop him from going inside but he would not listen," said the first man.

"Who is he looking for?" asked a woman.

"That Farmer Peel!" said the first man. "The one who has been calling himself Chief of Virginia City."

The crowd gasped & took a communal step back as a man swung out through the saloon doors.

But it was only a red-bearded, flannel-shirted miner.

"Trouble's afoot," he said. "I'm skedaddling."

Instead of dispersing, the crowd shuffled forward. I was right at the front with a good view.

Nobody told me to go home now. Everyone was too intent on trying to hear what was happening inside. It had gone so quiet that we could all hear a young man's voice.

"I said are there any Chiefs around here?" came the too-loud voice of a drunk. "My name is John Dennis. They call me El Dorado Johnny."

There was a pause. Then another voice replied, too soft for us to hear.

"Anyone can take it as likes!" said the loud first voice.

For a moment there was utter silence apart from the rhythmic thudding of the mountain & the distant tinkle of piano music coming from another saloon. Then the doors of the saloon swung open and a hatless young man with slicked-back hair & silver spurs backed onto the boardwalk, fumbling with his holster. Sure enough, it was the young man who had come into the Fashion Saloon the day before: El Dorado Johnny. Everybody scattered like quail when the hawk lands, but I stuck to my spot.

Bang! Bang! Bang!

Farner Peel burst through the swinging doors with his guns blazing.

The young man fell at my feet, his guns only half out of the holsters.

A woman screamed and three men uttered profanities not fit for publication.

Two of Farner Peel's shots had struck El Dorado Johnny in the chest. One ball still had a piece of burning wad attached & a little flame burned on his lapel. But it was the third bullet smack dab in the middle of his forehead that had killed him. He had fallen off the boardwalk and landed in the thoroughfare right at my feet. For a moment I saw the look of puzzlement in his long-lashed blue eyes. Then the spark of life faded. I guess my upside-down, bonnet-framed face was the last thing that met his dying gaze.

"Dang!" A man knelt over Johnny's body & patted out the fire on his coat. He turned & glared up at Peel, who was still up on the boardwalk. "That ain't fair! You did not fight by the rules of duello. You were supposed to wait till you were both outside and facing each other."

"Are you making an official complaint?" said Farner Peel, his smoking pistols still in his hands.

"No," said the man, lowering his gaze. "No, I guess I ain't."

Farner Peel looked around. I could tell by the way he was swaying slightly that he was "tight."

"Anybody else?" he said in his English accent. "Anybody else want to come at me with guns or knives or forks, or anything else?"

Nobody uttered a peep, so he holstered his guns & turned & went back into the saloon.

People were just starting to talk again when he came back out through the swinging doors of the saloon.

Everybody fell silent.

"I do not believe I will frequent this saloon in future," he said, and started off north towards Union Street.

A man in an apron followed Farner Peel out and watched him go. Then he looked down at the corpse & shook his head.

"Bring poor Johnny in here, boys," he said in an Irish accent. "Put him on the billiards table. He wanted to be a good-looking corpse and he will get his desire. Free drinks for the first four men to carry him in," he added.

Instantly, four men lifted El Dorado Johnny's corpse & carried it into the saloon.

I went in after them & watched them lay him out. The barkeep gently closed the eyes of the corpse & after that he looked better. More peaceful. Less surprised. Good-looking, even.

I thought, "I'll bet Mr. Sam Clemens will be happy to hear about a shooting duel between Farner Peel and El Dorado Johnny, who is now a good-looking corpse."

Then I thought, "This is even better than a Yank forked by a Reb."

And finally, "I wonder if he has any information for me."

I hated running in those too-tight white boots & breezy bloomers while holding down my bonnet with my left hand & clutching my purple shawl with my right.

But news like this could not wait.

Ledger Sheet 38

WHY, HELLO, MAISIE," said Dan De Quille as I flung open the door of the Enterprise. He gave me a wink. "How are you today?"

Most of the desks were unoccupied, but Dan sat at a rolltop desk near the window.

"Is Sam Clemens here?" I was somewhat breathless from running in the thin Virginia City air.

"Why, no, he has gone down to Silver City to do some research. He won't be back until this evening."

That surprised me. I thought Sam Clemens was interviewing witnesses for me. Dan's statement should have given me pause for thought, but I thought he was wearing Expression No. 1—a Genuine Smile—so I did not question it at the time. Also, I was distracted by the intense stares of some of the reporters and especially by Horace, the Printer's Devil. He was coming towards me with a strange look on his face. He must have been setting print, for his apron & fingers were covered with ink & he had a smudge of it across his freckled nose.

"Hello, Maisie," said Horace. "How are you today?"

"Not now, Horace," said Dan De Quille, and turned back to me. "What do you want with Sam?"

"Nothing," I lied.

"You must want something," he said. "You came running in here as if pursued by desperados." His smile vanished & he half rose from his chair. "You ain't being pursued by desperados again? Will I be obliged to flee to Carson City and live there under an assumed name?"

That reminded me of something.

I said, "Is your real name Dan De Quille?"

"Why, no," he said, settling back into his chair. "That's my Nom de Plume."

"Your what?"

"Nom de Plume." He wrote it out on a slip of paper & held it up for me to see. "It is French for 'pen name'. Lots of writers and reporters have them. It is the done thing. Mine is 'Dan De Quille'. It is not only a false name, but it's also a pun. Do you get it?"

I shook my head.

He held up a quill pen and said, "It sounds like 'dandy quill.'"

"Oh," I said. And then, "What is your real name?"

"William Wright," said he.

I thought about this for a moment.

"Is Charles Dickens his real name?"

"Yes, but he sometimes writes under the name 'Boz.'"

"What about Mr. Sam Clemens?" I said.

Dan laughed. "That's Sam's real name. But he has got a quiver full of pen names. Can't seem to settle on one yet. My favorite is 'W. Epaminondas Adrastus Blab.' But around here he usually signs off as 'Josh.'"

"I did not know that writers and reporters could have other names," I said.

"Not just writers and reporters," said Dan De Quille. "Desperados often adopt an Alias, while actors and actresses call it a Stage Name. Soiled Doves and other such sporting ladies are liable to put on a colorful name, too. You don't suppose Belle Donne is her real name, do you?"

I stared at him.

"Pseudonym," he said. "Some people call a false name a 'Pseudonym.'"

"Sioux what?" I said.

"Pseudonym," said Dan. He wrote that out for me, too. (I never would have guessed a word that sounded like soo-doe-nim had a P at the front.)

"Yes," said Dan, "anybody can rename themselves if they so desire. Especially if they have a past or a secret life."

I said, "I guess P.K. Pinkerton is a sort of Pseudonym."

"Oh?" he said, lighting his pipe. "What is your real name?"

"The name my Indian ma gave me when I was born," I said. "Glares from a Bush."

"Ha-ha," said Dan De Quille. "That is amusing. Now, tell me why you really came here."

I said, "I came to help Sam Clemens as part of a deal we struck, but I reckon he was pranking me."

Dan nodded. "Sam does love a prank." He puffed his pipe a little and then said, "Why don't you tell me your news?"

For a moment I hesitated.

Then I thought, "Why not?" Sam Clemens had let me down. Dan De Quille got first crack at Shootings anyway.

I reckoned I might as well tell him.

I took a deep breath & spilled it out. "Farner Peel and El Dorado Johnny just had a duel at the Niagara Music Hall & Billiard Saloon up on B Street," I said. "Johnny went along to the barber yesterday. He said he wanted to be either the 'Chief of the Comstock' or a 'Good-Looking Corpse.' Peel put a Navy ball in Johnny's forehead & killed him outright. Another ball set his vest on fire. Johnny is now laid out in state on the billiard table in the saloon."

"By God, Pinky!" cried Dan, leaping to his feet. "A good-looking corpse with a smoking vest. That is pure gold!" He flipped me a silver half-dollar, grabbed his hat from the rack & cried, "Bless you, my child!"

And he was out the door.

Horace had not gone away. He was still standing & gazing

at me. Now he stepped closer. "Are you all right, Maisie?" he said. "You ain't hurt?"

"No," I said, backing towards the door. "No, I am right as rain."

"Why did he call you 'Pinky'?" said Horace. "Is that your nickname? It is real purty. Almost as purty as you are."

He was advancing as he said this & I was retreating. I clutched my shawl around me for protection.

He swallowed hard. "Miss Pinky? Do you suppose I could have a kiss?"

"No," I said, groping behind me for the doorknob. "I do not like to be touched. Good-bye."

I found the handle & turned it & flung open the door & fled into the chilly October morning.

As I hurried along the clattering C Street boardwalk, I thought, "What is it about Virginia City? Folk either want to kill you or kiss you."

When I was certain I was not being pursued, I slowed to a walk, which in those tight boots was more like a limp.

I limped back to my office & went into my back room & changed back into my buckskin trowsers & flannel shirt.

I felt grumpy and low.

My shot arm ached & my ear was still sore.

That varmint Sam Clemens had let me down.

Now I would have to interview the French barber Pierre Forote, the American policeman Isaac Brokaw & the Russian telegraph operator Yuri Ivanovich, to strike them from my list of suspects.

Unless Martha was awake.

If she could tell me what kind of accent the Killer had, it would be a simple way of eliminating suspects.

I sent up a prayer that Martha would be conscious & I made my way down to the Extra-Safe Haven.

My client's surroundings were unusual, but she was awake & conscious.

"Martha!" I said. "You are awake!"

Martha nodded weakly. She was propped up in a makeshift bed in the corner of a room. She was clean and there was no straw in her hair.

I said, "How do you feel? Do you still have a fever?"

She shook her head.

"Are they looking after you?"

She gave a small nod, then said in a faint voice, "Only the food they's giving me is mighty peculiar."

"Martha," I said, "I need more help figuring out who killed Miss Sally. I have a list of suspects and each of them would have spoken with a different accent. Yuri Ivanovich would have used a Russian accent, Pierre Forote is French, Isaiah Coffin is English and Ludwig Hamm is German. Or the killer might have been an American."

Martha closed her eyes. "Why you telling me all them names? I done told you his name already."

"You what?" I came closer to hear her better.

She opened her eyes. "I done told you his name yesterday, before you run out on me. I remembered Miss Sally call him Dee Forest. Lieutenant Dee Forest Robards."

I stared at her in disbelief & dismay.

Martha hadn't told me that she would be hiding in a

forest. She hadn't mentioned a "bear" or a "bar." She had told me the Killer's name: Dee Forest Robards.

For a whole day and a half I had been trying to find a man whose name I should have known all along.

I thought, "Of all the Detectives in the world, I must be the worst."

Ledger Sheet 39

DEE FOREST ROBARDS?" said the Rev. C.V. Anthony, whom I had unfairly suspected. "No, that name does not ring a bell."

I heaved a deep sigh. I had been asking everyone I knew if they had heard of Dee Forest Robards. They hadn't. The Methodist pastor was my last chance.

"I am sorry," said the Rev. C.V. Anthony, "I have only been here in Virginia a few weeks. That is why I am not familiar with all my parishioners yet. However, I do have some records left by my predecessor. Let me look. By the way," he added, "it's probably spelled D-e-f-o-r-e-s-t. One word.

Southern folk often give their children family names as Christian names."

I nodded & offered up a silent prayer as he went over to a big leather book. He was puffing a cherrywood pipe.

They had told me about the possible alternate spelling of the name over at the Territorial Enterprise, but none of them had ever heard of him. The Virginia Directory had no record of a Dee Forest or D. Forest Robards or Deforest or any combination of those names. Doc Pinkerton and his wife had never heard the name. Nor had Isaiah Coffin nor Titus Jepson nor any of the girls down at Big Gussie's Boardinghouse nor any of the barkeepers at the saloons near my office.

Worst of all, the two people I relied on the most had left town. The man at the International Hotel told me that Jace and Stonewall had gone to Carson City and he did not know when they would return.

So the Rev. was my last hope.

"People come and go in a mining camp like this," said the Rev. C.V. Anthony as he leafed through the crinkly pages of the fat leather volume. "These records are already out of date." By and by he turned to me and shook his head. "I'm sorry but I can't find anybody with the name Robards or Deforest, or even Forest. Do you suspect this man in your murder investigation?"

I nodded dejectedly. "Martha remembered his name."

He frowned and said, "P.K., you should leave this investigation to the Law. I don't think a child your age should be interviewing Soiled Doves and frequenting saloons in search of a murderer. How is Martha, anyway?"

"She is better. She is in a Safe Haven." I sighed again. Would I ever understand people? "Reverend Anthony, sir," I said, "why do people kill each other?"

"You mean 'murder' as opposed to 'kill' in self-defense or wartime?"

"Yes, sir," I said.

"Because we are sinful, P.K.," he said. "Men kill because they covet their neighbor's possessions or because they are thwarted in love. They kill to defend their wounded pride and sometimes even their vanity. In this town, men often kill each other merely because they are inebriated."

I nodded even though I did not understand most of what he had said.

"Hello, Charles!" boomed a voice behind me. The Reverend and I both turned to see a tall, big-bearded, well-dressed man come into the church.

"Hello, Bill," said the Reverend. "How are you today?"

"Capital!" cried the man. "Capital! And you?"

"Very well, thank you. We were just discussing the nature of evil and why men kill other men."

"Why, I can tell you that," said the big-bearded man called Bill. "Man kills for three reasons: love, anger and greed."

I liked his answer & I liked him. He was about 6 & ½ feet tall & skinny with a beard the size of a small sagebrush. I was pretty sure I would not confuse him for anybody else. I took out my Detective Notebook and wrote down: *love, anger & greed.*

"You don't really mean 'Love,' do you?" said the Rev. C.V. Anthony.

"All right," said Bill. "Lust then. Or Jealousy as a result of love or lust."

I crossed out *love* and wrote down *jealousy* in its place.

So now my Detective Notebook said: *jealousy, anger & greed.* That would be easy to remember because the first letters spelled out *JAG*.

The sagebrush-bearded man said, "Who is the miniature philosopher with whom you are discussing such important topics, Charles?"

"This is P.K. Pinkerton," said the Rev. C.V. Anthony. "He is Virginia's newest private detective."

"Great Caesar's ghost!" exclaimed the tall man. "I saw your shingle go up across the road but I had no idea you were so young. I do not believe I have ever encountered a Child Detective before."

"Now you have," said I.

"P.K.," said the Rev. C.V. Anthony, "please allow me to introduce Mr. William Morris Stewart, the 'great lawyer' of the region."

I stared at him. According to my dead pa, Lawyers were worse than gunmen or desperados. He called them the "Devil's Own" & said they were smooth-talking crooks bent on making you give them all you had.

I said, "According to my dead pa, Lawyers are worse than gunmen or desperados. He called them 'the Devil's Own.'"

Mr. William Morris Stewart stared at me openmouthed for a moment. Then he tipped back his head and roared with laughter.

The Rev. C.V. Anthony raised one eyebrow at me. "P.K.," he

chided. "That is a rather hurtful thing to say right to a man's face. Even a Lawyer's."

"Not at all!" cried Mr. William Morris Stewart, wiping tears of laughter from his eyes. "Not at all! That is about the first honest thing anybody has said to me in this town. Son," he said, "if you are ever in need of a Lawyer, please come to me. I enjoy your refreshing approach to life. One day I might even have use for a Private Eye such as yourself. And if you ever have need of my help"—here he handed me a business card— "my Virginia City office is right across the street from you."

As I pocketed his card, I wondered if despite all Pa Emmet's warnings the Lord might possibly be inclined to use a Lawyer for good and not evil.

"There is something," I said.

"Name it!" he cried.

"Have you ever heard of a man called Deforest Robards?"

Mr. William Morris Stewart tipped his big head on one side & pursed his lips. "Why, no," he said presently. "No, cannot say as I have. But I have contacts in Washington and Richmond. I will telegraph them at once. However," he added, "I would not get my hopes up if I were you."

It appeared the trail had gone cold. My quarry had eluded me. I miserably nodded my thanks & trudged back up to my office.

Ledger Sheet 40

BACK AT MY OFFICE, I sat at my desk and rocked back and forth, humming quietly. I was hungry but there was no food in my office and I did not feel disposed to go shopping.

I was too low.

I thought I had solved my first big case but it appeared I was dead wrong. I had not even come close to identifying the man who killed Sally Sampson.

I had gone to the Scene of the Crime.

I had looked for Clews.

I had interviewed witnesses and listed the suspects, first narrowing it down to six & then adding a few to make nine.

But now it appeared that the Killer was none of these. It was someone so clever that nobody had even heard of him. It was as if he had disappeared, and yet he must still be in town for he had tried to burn down Martha's hiding place.

I was in a "brown study."

To take my mind off my troubles, I took out my Big Tobacco Collection & started to arrange it across my desktop. As I worked, I observed interesting details, viz: "Banana" brand Cuban cigars have slightly yellow tobacco, like a banana. Connecticut "Cinnamon Blotch" cigars are reddish-brown with white specks. "Maple Leaf" snuff has a faint whiff of maple syrup.

The varying shapes & colors of the cigars consoled me. The different smells of the plug tobacco comforted me.

I had over 100 different samples and I could match the shreds to their boxes and/or tags real quick now. For those tobaccos with no store-bought label—like Sam Clemens's Killickinick—I made my own from carefully folded & torn pieces of loose ledger pages.

I was just making a label for the Reverend's "Cavendish Gold" pipe tobacco when the door flew open with a bang.

In came Isaiah Coffin, my next-door neighbor.

"You have wounded me!" he said. "And I am hurt."

"Where?" I said. "Where did I hurt you?"

"Here!" he said, pressing his hand to his heart. "I have been a good neighbor and supplier of disguises. And how do you repay me? By putting me on a list of murder suspects."

I opened my mouth to reply but I did not get a chance to speak.

"Furthermore," he said, "you told Belle that I frequented Miss Sally Sampson and that I am a suspect in her murder. That is a lie, sir. A dam lie!"

"Then why did you visit her?" I said.

He slapped down a passel of little photographs onto the Tobacco Collection spread on my desk.

"I was taking Cartes de Visite of her. Fully clothed, as you see. She did not want to soil her frocks and gowns by trudging them up to B Street."

I stared at the photos. They showed a pretty blond woman in a variety of dresses. At the bottom of one, someone had printed SALLY SAMPSON SEAMSTRESS.

"What about Mrs. Zoe Brown?" I said. "You called on her. I saw you."

"I was buying Belle a hat."

"From a Nymph of the Night?"

"Mrs. Zoe Brown is not a Nymph!" said Isaiah Coffin. "She is the best milliner in Virginia City."

"Millionaire?" I repeated, stupidly.

"Milliner! It means 'hat-maker.'"

"What about your 'Secret Meeting' that Friday night?"

At this he took a step back & stood up extra straight & looked down his nose at me. I saw his nostrils flare as he puffed out his chest.

At that, I crouched down behind my desk but he did not hit me or shoot me.

He only said, "That was a secret meeting to discuss the formation of a new chapter of Yoof."

"Yoof?" I said, resuming my seat.

"Yoof, sir. Yoof!"

Seeing my blank look, he sighed & rolled his eyes heaven-ward & spelled it out. "I-O-O-F!" he said. "The Independent Order of Odd Fellows. It is a venerable order not unlike that of the Masonic Temple."

Now I did feel bad. Foolish & bad.

He turned & stalked to the door & went out.

Before the door had closed completely, someone else shoved it open.

It was Sam Clemens.

His eyes were narrowed and he was clamping his pipe stem with his teeth.

"Dang you, P.K.," he said, pulling the pipe from his mouth. "This time I am really mad at you. Spitting mad! You gave that story to Dan after I struck a bargain with you. I went and interviewed the Russian, American and Frenchman and eliminated them as suspects and have been patiently sitting at my desk waiting for your Scoop!"

"You have?" I said. "You did? But I've been to the Enterprise twice today and I did not see you."

"Well, I was probably still interviewing your suspects. Anybody would have told you that if you had asked."

"They told me you were down in Silver City."

"Why would I be down in Silver City when I have been laboring for you?" Sam Clemens spoke so forcefully that some drops from his mouth sprayed out. I guess that is what they mean when they say "spitting mad."

"You know those boys love pranking me," he continued. "You should have persisted. And what about the Coroner? What happened when you went down there?"

I hung my head. "He saw through my disguise," I said. "He drove me out with his walking stick."

"Doggone it, P.K.! How do you expect to be a Detective if you cannot even fool a fool like Sewall? You are a miserable detective. Worst I ever seen."

Then he caught sight of my cigar butts and tobacco crumbs spread out in alphabetical order on the desk. "You and your foibles and eccentricities!" he cried. "This is all flapdoodle!" He drew back his arm and with one motion he swept the Big Tobacco Collection off my desk and onto the floor.

As a final insult, he kicked the ghoulish Stone Baby in its cigar box.

"Ow!" he yelled. He hopped on one foot and let loose a stream of profanities such as I have never heard before nor hope to hear again. Needless to say, they are unfit for publication.

Abruptly he halted in mid-profanity.

He looked down at the Stone Baby & a strange expression transformed his face.

I could not read it.

Without another word, he turned on his heel & limped quickly out of my office.

Scarcely had the door closed behind him when it flew open for the third time in as many minutes.

There stood Deputy Marshal Jack Williams and another man, whom I found out later was a police officer.

"P.K. Pinkerton?" The Deputy fixed me with his cold & unblinking gaze.

"That is me," I said.

"There is something not quite right about you," he growled, "and I am gonna find out what. In the meantime," he said, "I have a warrant for your arrest. Come with me."

"What?" I said. "Why? What for?"

For the first time I saw him smile.

His mouth stretched sideways but his eyes remained cold & narrow. It was definitely Expression No. 2—a Fake Smile.

"I am arresting you for the brutal murder of a woman named Sally Sampson," said he. "You do not have to come along peaceably," he added, "I will enjoy taking you there by force."

Ledger Sheet 41

I WAS ON A HIGH MOUNTAIN PEAK—happy & calm—but someone was trying to topple me off it.

"P.K.?" said a voice from a long ways off. "P.K. what is wrong?"

I ignored the voice. My gray stone mountain was as narrow and jagged as a pine tree and it stood among many other such peaks, but it was the tallest. At the top of my peak was a small flat place. I sat on a soft & shaggy buffalo skin. I could see for a thousand miles in every direction. I was higher than the Thunderbird. I was so high that I could almost touch God. There came only the sound of the wind & of chanting.

And the irksome voice.

"P.K.?" said the irksome, faraway voice.

"I'll rouse him, by God!" said another distant voice.

"No," said the first. "Let me try one more thing."

Then I heard a man's voice softly praying.

He was praying like Pa Emmet used to do, so I came back down to earth. The chanting ceased inside my head and I opened my eyes.

Everything seemed strange. I seemed to be inside the mountain, not atop it. I blinked. Everything around me was gray stone. Then I remembered: I was in Jail. Two men were in the cell with me.

"P.K.?" A face loomed into view. A man's face with blue eyes & a fair mustache & beard. He looked vaguely familiar.

"Who are you?" I said. My tongue was sluggish and my voice sounded strange.

"It is me, the Reverend Charles Volney Anthony. Do you realize you were rocking back and forth, chanting? The jailer says you've been doing that for a couple of hours."

"Course he knows!" said the angry voice. "He's been doing it to vex me."

"P.K.," said the Rev. C.V. Anthony, "I've brought someone who might be able to help you."

"Hello, P.K.," said another voice. Not the angry voice. With great effort I turned my head. Another blue-eyed man with a huge beard loomed into view. My Indian mother called white men "owl-people" because they look like owls with their staring white eyes and feathery faces. I nodded to myself. These two certainly looked like owls.

"It is me," said the bearded man. "Bill Stewart. I found

something about that man you were looking for. Deforrest Robards. He spells his name with two Rs."

I blinked again and he began to look less like an owl.

"He is a deserter," said Bill Stewart. "A Lieutenant in the Twenty-Second Alabama Infantry Regiment."

I blinked. I was trying to remember who "Bill Stewart" was.

The man spoke again. "Do you hear me? Deforrest Robards is a Confederate Lieutenant who gathered together a band of volunteers, mainly upon his father's insistence. But when he led them into a battle at Shiloh, he froze with terror and then ran, causing a rout of his men and great loss of life. They want to bring him back to stand trial and face a firing squad if necessary."

Then it came to me. "You are a lawyer," I said. "Mr. William Morris Stewart. My foster pa said Lawyers were the Devil's Own."

"We covered that ground already," said Mr. William Morris Stewart. "You can drop that line."

"P.K.," said the Reverend Anthony. "You seemed to be in some kind of trance. Have you been drinking?"

With great effort I turned back to the first owl. "No," I said. "I promised Ma Evangeline never to kill a man, nor drink nor gamble."

"Smoking opium?" asked Mr. William Morris Stewart.

"No," I said. "I am not a dope fiend."

"Then what is it?"

I said, "Ma Evangeline called it 'the Mulligrubs.' It happens when I am scared or low."

Mr. William Morris Stewart put his big arm around my

shoulder and leaned forward. "Do not be scared," he said, "and do not be low. I will be your Champion."

"Why would you bother?" I said, staring at the floor of my cell. "I called you 'the Devil's Own.'"

"I will be your champion," he said, "because you remind me of my mother."

I looked up, startled out of my fog.

"My mother never told a falsehood," said Mr. William Morris Stewart. "She often came across as blunt. You are about as honest as she, and a sight more honest than some Methodist reverends I have met, present company excepted. For this reason I am happy to represent you. Now, can you tell me what happened?"

I thought for a moment & tried to order my thoughts. Then I shook my head. "Too jumbled," I said. "Everything is too jumbled and tangled in my head."

Then I had an idea.

"In my office," I said, "are some blank ledger books on one of the shelves. Bring me one and I will write things down."

"Ledger books?" said Mr. William Morris Stewart. "Why ledger books?"

"Because I wrote up my first case on ledger sheets," I said, "and so I bought a dozen more for future cases, along with half a dozen small notebooks like this one." I showed them the Detective Notebook in my pocket.

"But why ledger books?" said the Rev.

"So they would look even on the shelf," I said.

Mr. William Morris Stewart shook his head and gave a half smile. "Do you need anything else?"

I nodded. "Coffee," I said. "Black, please. Also I am hungry."

And that was how I came to be here in prison, accused of committing the very crime I have been diligently trying to solve. Now it is late & my coffee is finished & both pieces of layer cake that my Lawyer brought me for dessert. Even the night jailer is asleep so I am going to sleep as well.

I have written this account as fairly & accurately as I could.

I will swear on the Bible to that.

You can see that Deputy Marshal Jack Williams has got it in for me because he blames me for the recent spate of shooting affrays here in Virginia City & because I am a Misfit & half Indian.

Yes, I confess I am half Indian.

Yes, I confess I vanquished the previous Chief of the Comstock last week and maybe that caused some competition for the position.

Yes, I confess that Trouble seems to follow me wherever I go.

But, no, I did not murder the Soiled Dove who went by the name of Short Sally Sampson. It is true that I do not have an alibi for most of that night apart from the few hours I was in an Opium Den, but if you read my account of that case and also of this one, you will know that I am guilty of nothing more than trying to help a poor frightened girl & of searching out the Truth behind a dastardly deed that the Law had forgotten.

Dear Mr. Judge and/or Gentlemen of the Jury: please judge me NOT GUILTY and set me free to solve this crime.

Ledger Sheet 42

AS YOU CAN PROBABLY TELL from the fact that I am now writing in ink, not pencil, I am not in Jail anymore.

Here is how it happened.

After I wrote the account you have just read, I put down my pencil, climbed onto the hard & narrow shelf of my cell & fell asleep upon the instant.

The next morning I was woken by a cheerful argument.

It was the night jailer and a new jailer I had not seen before. I guessed he was the Saturday Jailer as it was Saturday. They were debating something in the newspaper.

One of them kept saying, "It's true, I tell you."

"No, it ain't," said the Night Jailer. "I am telling you. It's a big Hoax."

"No! They really found a Petrified Man out there in the desert. Place called Gravelly Ford."

"I ain't never heard of no Gravelly Ford," said the Night Jailer.

"But they wouldn't of printed it if it warn't true." He picked up the paper and read. "Listen to this. This is how they describe the posture of the man."

When he said the word *posture* I remembered what Jace told me & I adopted the pose as he read the description.

"'The body was in a sitting posture,'" began the Night Jailer, "'leaning against a huge mass of croppings; the attitude was pensive, the right thumb resting against the side of the nose; the left thumb partially supported the chin, the forefinger pressing the inner corner of the left eye and drawing it partly open; the right eye was closed, and the fingers of the right hand spread apart.'"

I found when I adopted this posture that I was thumbing my nose with my right hand like Belle Donne, and pulling down the lower lid of my left eye, just like Mr. Absalom Smith at Topliffe's Theatre when he was telling a joke.

"Thar!" cried the Night Jailer. "Look at the boy! He's doing what the paper describes. See? That reporter is cocking a snook at us."

The other prisoners were laughing and nodding.

"But they wouldn't of printed it if it warn't true," repeated the Saturday Jailer.

"Course they would. Look at the name of the fellow who wrote it."

"Josh?" said the other one. "What does that prove?"

"Well, 'josh' means 'joke', don't it?"

"It could be his real name."

"Don't be a numbskull," said the Night Jailer. "Those fellows hardly ever use their real names."

At that moment I had a Revelation.

It was as if the Clouds of Heaven had parted and God had sent a great Sunbeam of Illumination into my brain.

Martha had heard Sally call the Killer "Deforrest" & "Lieutenant Robards."

My Lawyer had told me that a "Lieutenant Deforrest Robards" was a deserter from the Reb Army.

But why would a deserter who had escaped to a new town keep his real name?

He would adopt a false name, like Sam Clemens who called himself "Josh" & a whole passel of other Pen Names to boot. I suddenly realized I knew lots of people with false names: Dan De Quille, Poker Face Jace, Stonewall, El Dorado Johnny, Whittlin Walt, Boz & Extra Dub. Then there was Big Gussie & her four girls: not one of them going by her real name. Even I have used different names from my Indian one, and sometimes I go by the name "Maisie."

In fact, I knew more people with fake names than I knew with real names.

Lieutenant Deforrest Robards might be known to

hundreds of people here in Virginia City, but not by his *real name.* Only Short Sally Sampson, an "old friend" of his, had recognized him & called him by his true name, in Martha's hearing.

Like dominoes, that revelation gave me another: that had been the motive for the murder! Short Sally had recognized the coward Deforrest Robards. Maybe she had taunted him. Maybe she had threatened to expose him. Maybe both. If he was found out he would be sent home to be tried, and then hanged or shot, because he had been an officer with men under his command.

My heart was beating fast with excitement. Everything made sense now. It was the "dam domino effect."

That meant I could go back to my list of suspects.

I pulled out my Detective Notebook and opened it with trembling hands.

Here was the list I had compiled:

SUSPECTS IN THE MURDER OF
SALLY SAMPSON
(Tall, Slim Men with Fair Hair & Smallish Beards Known to Have Frequented Sally)

1. Ludwig Hamm, barkeeper, German
2. Pierre Forote, barber, French
3. John Dennis, miner, American
4. Yuri Ivanovich, telegraph operator, Russian
5. Isaac E. Brokaw, policeman, American
6. Isaiah Coffin, photographer, English

Others who fit the description but were not
known to have visited her

7. Farner Peel, shootist, English
8. Absalom Smith, actor and punster, American
9. C.V. Anthony, reverend, American

I now knew the Killer—Lt. Deforrest Robards—was a Confederate, so that meant I was looking for a man with a Southern accent. I started to strike through the names of those who were not American, but then I stopped.

What if he had changed his accent as well as his name?

Then another even more terrible thought occurred: what if he had changed his appearance, too?

After all, did I not disguise myself and use other names & accents from time to time?

What if he had shaved off his mustache & beard & dyed his hair black?

What if he now put on an Italian accent? Or French?

What if he was not even on my list?

Those thoughts made me dizzy.

I needed to find something else that would identify the Killer. Something not connected to his name or appearance or accent. But what?

I went to the bars of my cell & gripped them hard & thumped my head softly against the cold iron: What? What? What?

"Stop that banging," said the Saturday Jailer. He was sitting at the desk, reading the paper & drinking coffee & smoking a pipe.

I could tell from the odor of his pipe that he was smoking No. 81 on my list: "Taylor Made," which comes in a muslin pouch with a blue seal and white letters.

Then the Lord above sent down another ray of Illumination: whiz! Right into my brain.

This idea was so brilliant that I whooped & did a Victory Dance around my cell.

The jailer jumped out of his chair so fast that he dropped his pipe in his coffee & got riled & told me to "Stop that god-awful noise."

But I did not care.

I knew how to identify the Killer.

Ledger Sheet 43

MR. WILLIAM MORRIS STEWART arrived as I was eating some slimy porridge cooked up by the jailer. I almost dropped the tin plate in my eagerness to address him. I went to the bars of the cell and gripped them.

"Mr. Stewart," I said. "Is there some way you can get me out of here? Even for just a few hours? I know how to find the Killer of Miss Sally Sampson but I cannot do it trapped in here."

"I suppose so," said Mr. William Morris Stewart, "but someone will have to post bail." He looked at the Jailer. "How much to bail out this little Indian?"

"Two thousand dollars," said the Jailer without even looking up.

"Two *thousand*?" said Mr. William Morris Stewart.

"He's wanted for murder, ain't he?" said the Jailer, puffing his pipe & turning a page of the paper. "Anyways, that's what the Deputy Marshal said."

"I have nearly fifteen hundred dollars in my account at Wells, Fargo & Co.," I said.

Mr. William Morris Stewart shook his big head. "We'll still have to raise over five hundred. Do you know anybody who could lay their hands on five or six hundred dollars?"

My first thought was Jace. He certainly had thousands & he would bail me out in a flash. But he had vamoosed to Carson City & I did not know when he would be back.

Then I had another idea.

It was a long shot but worth a try.

"Do you know a Boarding House owner called Big Gussie in a brick house down on D Street?" I asked.

Mr. William Morris Stewart gave me Expression No. 4: Surprise. Then he said, "Course I know Gussie. Everybody knows Gussie."

I said, "She told me to call on her if I ever needed anything."

He said, "I will go down there as soon as you write me a note of release to Wells, Fargo & Co."

He was as good as his word and within an hour he was back with a heavy pouch full of gold.

"I withdrew fourteen hundred from your account," he told me as he made the Saturday Jailer sign a Receipt. "Big Gussie and her girls raised the remaining six hundred. They are mighty fond of you down at the Brick House."

"That is good," I said. "For that is where I am bound right now."

"I am a student of crime and punishment," said Mr. William Morris Stewart, as the Jailer unlocked the door of my cell. "Mind if I accompany you?"

I came out of the cell and looked up at him. "I like to work alone," I said, "but you have been a Friend to me this day so, yes, you may come."

As we walked out into the crisp and clear October morning, I told Mr. William Morris Stewart my reasoning.

I told him how Martha had hid out for days at the only place she knew apart from Sally's: The Flora Temple Livery Stable. She had lived on oats and water from the trough and hid in a pile of hay. But she got more and more desperate. Early one morning, she heard the men at the Flora Temple Livery Stable read my Advertisement in the *Enterprise*.

Hunger & desperation outweighed fear and she made her way up to my office.

"But there are not many dark-skinned girls here in Virginia City," I said. "She had the bad luck to be spotted by Robards, the very man she had been avoiding. He must have followed her to my office," I said. "When I went out to get her some food, he came and peered into the window. Maybe rattled the door. I had locked it, but Martha panicked and went out my back window and down a rickety ladder and then doubled back up to the stables. Robards lost her trail but he loitered near my office and followed me instead. I believe he hoped I would lead him to Martha so he could kill her, she being the only witness to his terrible deed. I thought I lost him but I must have been wrong, because when I finally figured out where she was hiding and went there, I led him straight to her. He tried to burn the place down."

"Yesterday's fire at the Flora Temple Livery Stable!" cried Mr. William Morris Stewart. He thrust his arm out to stop me jumping down onto C Street in front of a Stagecoach.

"That's right," I said, as we waited on the boardwalk for the stagecoach to drive past. "But Virginia City's finest were quick to quench the blaze and no one died."

"That poltroon!" exclaimed Mr. William Morris Stewart, as we crossed over. "He was willing to burn down a whole stable—nay, an entire town!—just to keep his secret safe. And you say she did not even get a good look at him?"

"That's right. But he does not know that."

"Where is Martha now?"

"In a Safe Haven," I said. As we turned down D Street I continued explaining. "This morning, when the Jailers were reading that article about a Petrified Man found over by Gravelly Ford, one of them said reporters hardly ever use their real names. That is when I realized that Robards might be using a fake name, too."

"Great Caesar's ghost, you're right!" cried Mr. William Morris Stewart. "Plenty of people here in Virginia have fled the war, but Robards is a special case. Not only is he a Confederate officer, he is a coward who froze under the pressure of battle and caused the deaths of many men."

"But Short Sally did not know he was a deserter when she caught sight of him up at Topliffe's last Friday night," I said. "And he was not going to risk her finding out and betraying his secret. Or telling people his real name."

"So that's why she was murdered," said Mr. William Morris Stewart.

I nodded. "It might be that he disguised himself, too," I said, "and if he changed his appearance once, then maybe he did it again after he killed Short Sally."

"So how will you find him?" said Mr. William Morris Stewart. "Sally Sampson was the only one who knew him in the South and now she is dead."

I looked up at him. His head appeared to me as a beard topped by a slouch hat with a big Cuban cigar sticking out between the two.

"A friend of mine claims that a man's tobacco is his first love," I said.

"So?"

"So a man might think to change his name & even his appearance but it might not occur to him to change his brand of tobacco as well."

"Quite right," said Mr. William Morris Stewart, nodding. "It might even be a comfort to him. A familiar comfort in a strange new world."

"Yes," I said. "That is why we are here at Short Sally's crib. She had not had any Gentlemen Callers in nearly a month. Plus, Martha swept the crib every morning until it was speckless. The Killer, Lieutenant Deforrest Robards, must have been the last person to visit her. My idea is this: all the furniture might be gone, but the Killer might have left a cigar stump or a shred of tobacco."

"But what good would a shred of tobacco be?" said he.

I smiled. "I can identify over one hundred different types of smoking, chewing and leaf tobacco. And I can do it with no more than a shred or two."

"Great Scott! But how?"

"Partly my Indian tracking skills," I said, "and partly that I like collecting things. Ma Evangeline called it one of my Eccentricities. I have an extensive tobacco collection back at my office. You are smoking a cigar called 'La Honradez.'"

"Great Caesar's ghost! You are absolutely correct!"

"I can tell by the color and shape and the smell of it, too," I said.

We had reached Sally's Crib with its yellow door. Outside stood a horse and a wagon loaded with furniture.

The door of the Crib was open.

It was clear what was happening: a new Nymph of the Night was moving in.

I ran inside.

A pretty Lady in a dark green velvet dress & matching hat stood with her hands on her hips, looking around. "Great Mary Mother of God," she said in an Irish accent. "They have not even swept the place."

"Hallelujah!" I said. Then I got down on my hands & knees and I began to sniff around at the dust & fluff still lying at the edges of the floor where it met the wall.

"What in the bejeezus are you doing?" asked the pretty lady in the green velvet dress.

"That there is P.K. Pinkerton, Private Eye," came the deep voice of Mr. William Morris Stewart. "He is just nosing around for clews. Found anything, P.K.?"

"Just a moment," I said, holding up one hand. Then I resumed my sniffing.

A moment later a scent in the southeast corner of the room stopped me short. Could it be?

Yes, it was.

All the little hairs on the back of my neck stood up.

I carefully picked up two small shreds of tobacco and placed them in the palm of my hand. They were the right color and texture.

I stood up & turned & faced the front of the room.

Mr. William Morris Stewart stood there, flanked by the Lady in Green. Big Gussie had appeared, along with her four girls: Irish Rose, Honey Pie, Spring Chicken and Big Mouth Annie.

"Do you know who done it?" rasped Gussie; she had a broom and dustpan in her hand.

I looked down at the two little shreds of tobacco in the palm of my hand.

"Yes," I said happily. "I know who done it."

"You know from *that*?" said Mr. William Morris Stewart, stepping forward and peering into my hand.

"Yes, sir," I replied.

All the Boarding House Girls crowded around, saying "Ooh!" and "Ah!"

Only the recently arrived Irish Lady kept repeating, "Who done what?"

"P.K.," said Mr. William Morris Stewart. "I am mighty impressed with your deductive skills. But even a great lawyer such as myself might need more than two shreds of tobacco to convict a man of desertion and murder. Do you have anything else up your sleeve?"

I thought for a moment & then nodded. "Yes," I said. "I believe I do."

Ledger Sheet 44

I WENT BACK TO MY OFFICE & got in a disguise so I would not be followed by Deforrest Robards who was still at large. Then I let myself down the rickety ladder at the back of my office & went by a round-about route to see Martha in her Safe Haven.

She was with Ping's family down in Chinatown.

Two nights before, I had gone to Ping's uncle's Laundry & found Ping there. For a fee of $20 a day, he had agreed to protect & care for her.

When I now showed up at Hong Wo Washer's in my Prim Little Girl disguise & asked for Ping, a pretty Chinese girl shook her head. I was pretty sure I had seen her the day before but I could not be sure, as I am not so good with faces.

"I am P.K. Pinkerton," I said. "I was here yesterday. I need to see Martha."

The Pretty Celestial smiled & shook her head once again.

"Me seek little girl," I said. "Dark skin. You protect." I pointed to myself. "Me want see her."

Another smiling shrug.

"Look," I said, lifting my bonnet and part of my wig, too. "It is me!"

"Ah!" cried the girl. She laughed & clapped her hands & looked over her shoulder & called out something. Four other Celestials appeared out of nowhere & came up to me & circled around me, looking me up & down, and discussing me in rapid Chinese. When one of them came closer & tried to lift my wig to look under it, I thought, "Enough is enough."

"Stop!" I cried. "I want to see Martha."

Ping's sister or cousin or whoever she was led me through a maze of rooms & corridors. I had been here the day before but I was just as confused by the twists & turns as I had been then.

I felt confident that nobody from outside would ever find Martha in this rabbit warren. This was certainly a Safe Haven.

Finally the Pretty Chinese Girl stood to one side & gave me a little bow. Here was the small wooden shed I had seen yesterday. It was still filled with sheets & tables & steam & the smell of starch. Martha was nestled in her large pile of crumpled sheets in one corner of the laundry. She was wearing pale blue Chinese pajamas & playing with some kind of

Chinese puzzle. Her head was uncovered and I could see that her hair had been washed & plaited. They must have used a different pomade, because she smelt like Chinese incense.

"Who's that?" She looked up from her puzzle as I came forward.

"It is me," I said. "P.K. Pinkerton. I am disguised as a Prim and Proper Girl."

She sat up in her nest & clapped her hands & gave Expression No. 1: a Genuine Smile. "Why, P.K., you look just like a gal! What a pretty dress and bonnet."

"You seem much recovered," I observed.

"Yes, sir!" Martha gave me Expression No 1 again: a Genuine Smile. "An old Chinee lady give me some foul-tasting tea but I slept and slept and Doc Pinkerton just left and he says I'm all better now. He says he could not have cured me no better himself. He says I just need to rest."

I nodded and came a little closer. "Martha," I said in a low voice. "I think I have found Lieutenant Deforrest Robards."

"Oh!" she cried, and covered her mouth with both her hands. "You found him?"

"I think so," I said. "But I want to be sure. Miss Sally called him by his real name, but he is using another one here in Virginia. He may have changed his appearance, too, but my lawyer says that in the heat of passion people usually use their normal voices. So what I am going to ask you now is very important. Can you tell me what kind of accent the Killer had?"

"What do you mean?"

"Was it German? Or Irish? Or English? Or French?" I paused and then said carefully, "Or Southern?"

She frowned. "Why, none of those," she said. "He didn't have no accent at all."

My spirits sank. I had been certain of another reply. "No accent at all?" I said. "Are you sure?"

She nodded. "You bet. He sounded just like me and Miss Sally."

My spirits revived a little. "So he had an accent like yours?"

She laughed. "I don't have no accent, silly! You are the one with an accent."

I said, "I have an accent?"

"Course!" she said. "You sound like a Mississippi Yankee!"

"But you do not have an accent?"

She put her hands on her hips and tipped her head to one side. "Course not. I talk normal."

I nodded, happy again.

"Martha, when Lieutenant Deforrest Robards killed Miss Sally you were in the back room peeking through the latch hole. I know you can't see faraway things very well, but you heard him clearly, didn't you?"

She nodded, wide-eyed, and said, "The two of them woke me up with they yelling."

"When he was yelling," I said, "did he ever say anything like this?" I leaned in & whispered something in her ear.

"No," she said. "He never."

My spirits sank again.

Then Martha said, "It was Miss Sally that said that. Right before he strangulated her."

Now I knew for sure who the Killer was.

Ledger Sheet 45

MARTHA, I SAID, "if I can find Lieutenant Deforrest Robards, would you testify against him in a court of law?"

Martha looked at me & then slumped down in her nest of sheets & dropped her head in her hands. She said something but her reply was muffled. That and her heavy Southern accent made it hard for me to understand.

"What did you say?" I asked, scrouching down beside her.

"I fear he will get me," she said. "I ain't even sure what he looks like. But he knows me."

"He would not dare to hurt you in a public

place," I said. Then I added, "You have been very brave so far. Fortune favors the brave. All you have to do is face him and point at him and say 'you done it.'"

She was quiet for a moment, her head still down. Then she shook it. "I just can't. I ain't as brave as you."

I nodded & stood up & looked around the starch-smelling shack full of crumpled snow-white sheets all waiting to be ironed.

I had solved the biggest Mystery in Virginia City but it seemed there was no way to convict the Killer.

"P.K.?" said Martha. She was looking up at me.

"Yes?"

"You are mighty brave. Why don't you be me?"

"Beg pardon?"

"You look just like a gal in that getup. Why don't you make your skin a tad darker and pretend to be me? Then *you* point the finger."

I shook my head. "I have tried lots of disguises," I said. "But that would be the hardest. The men who dress like that don't even look real."

Martha stood up. "Not like one of them minstrels that uses boot polish," she said. "But if you get some burnt cork and cream you could mix up a natural-looking dark. But it ain't just skin color. You got to walk and talk like me." She pointed to her nightdress and sleeping bonnet, lying folded & clean on a tabletop nearby. "Put those things on and I will show you."

And so began one of the strangest hours of my life. Martha showed me how to walk like her and coached me in saying a phrase we had devised: "There is Short Sally's killer. His real name be Deforrest Robards. He is a Reb that froze in a battle and then run off. They are after him."

I had thought up the accusation, then Martha had put it in her own words. She told me Miss Sal had taken her to the Melodeon once or twice and that she wanted to be an actress or singer when she grew up.

As we worked together in that small room, Martha became more and more lively. She seemed a different person from the terrified girl I had met two days before.

I said, "You seem very different from the terrified girl I met two days before."

She said, "That is because I now have friends like you and these nice Chinee people to protect me. And nobody beating on me now."

"Did Miss Sal used to beat on you?"

"Only a little. But she didn't mean nothing by it. It was for my own good. She risked her life to save me. She told me that every day."

I said, "Would you like this here pink calico dress and bonnet? You can have these button-up boots, too. They are too tight for me but I reckon they will fit you."

Martha looked up at me, her eyes wide in Expression No. 4. Then her mouth spread into a Genuine Smile.

"For keeps?" she breathed. "You ain't joshing me?"

"For keeps," I said. "I am not joshing you. I must now climb into another disguise."

I paid Ping's pretty cousin $2 to get me my own Chinese boy getup. Ping's cousin also showed me how to tie up

Martha's clean nightdress and bonnet—with my curly dark wig hidden inside—so that it looked like clean laundry to be delivered. Wearing my straw plate hat and carrying the parcel, I looked like a Chinese boy delivering laundry.

"Oh, P.K.!" said Martha, when I appeared. "You look just like a Chinee boy. You could be an actor, too."

She had my pink calico dress on and the second white boot half buttoned.

"You look fine, too," I said. "Do the boots fit?"

"Yes, sir, they fit like they was made for me."

I said, "I must go now."

Before I could stop her, she jumped up and kissed me on the cheek.

I usually do not like to be touched but she did it real quick so I did not mind too much.

"Wish me luck," I said, straightening my straw plate hat.

"Fortune favors the brave," she said.

I left her sitting on her pile of clean sheets, doing up the buttons on her left boot.

In my Chinese-laundry-boy disguise I made my way up from F to B, being careful that nobody was shadowing me. It was a fine sunny morning, and almost warm. When I got up to B Street I did not go into my office.

Instead I went across the thoroughfare to the Law Offices of Mr. William Morris Stewart, Attorney at Law. It was 11:20 a.m. on a Saturday morning, but I could see my sagebrush-bearded lawyer through the door window. He was sitting at a desk, going through papers & smoking a cigar.

I tapped on the door, then tried the handle. It was open.

Although he had taken his leave of me just an hour and a half before, he did not recognize me.

"It is me," I said. "P.K. Pinkerton. I am in disguise."

He was so astonished that his La Honradez cigar fell out of his mouth onto the desk.

"By Jove!" he said, quickly retrieving the cigar before it set his papers alight. "P.K. the Celestial! You are a veritable Pandora's Box of surprises. Come in to my private room."

He led the way into an inner room with a big walnut desk & leather armchair & oil painting & some high-up windows. I guess this was where he received his most important clients.

I quickly explained to him why I was in disguise & I told him I had asked Martha to testify against the man who killed Short Sally. Before I could finish, he interrupted me.

"Even if that little gal had eagle eyes and a memory like a dictionary," he said, "it wouldn't wash. Last year they passed a law that no Negro, Mulatto, Chinaman, Indian—or even half Indian like you—can testify against a white man in a court of law."

"Well then, what if Martha could point out the Killer in a crowded public place?"

He pursed his lips, then nodded slowly. "That might make people sit up and take notice. Maybe force the Law to do something." He took a long suck of his cigar and slowly blew out the smoke as he shook his head. "But from what you've told me about her, that ain't going to happen. She is too scared."

"You are a good judge of people," I said. "You are right. But

Martha and I have come up with a clever plan of making that happen."

He leaned forward. "Tell me," he said.

"I am going to bait a trap for him," I said, "just like you would bait a trap for any sneaking varmint."

"What will you use as bait?" said Mr. William Morris Stewart.

"Me," I said. "I will use me as bait."

Ledger Sheet 46

A QUARTER OF AN HOUR LATER, at 11:45 a.m., I was knocking on the stage door of Topliffe's Theatre. When it opened, who should look out but Miss Belle Donne! She was yawning and her light brown hair was coming unpinned here and there.

Seeing what she thought was a Chinese boy in blue pajamas and a straw plate hat, she spoke in Pidgin English. "What you want?" she said. "You deliver laundry?"

"Let me in, Belle," I said. "It is me, P.K. Pinkerton. I am in disguise."

Her eyes went wide, then narrowed into Expression No. 5. "Go away, P.K.," she said.

"Did you sleep here last night?" I asked, using my Detective Skills.

"Yes," she said. "Isaiah and I had a bad fight and it is all your fault. Now go *away!*"

"Belle!" I put my Chinese clog between the door & the doorjamb. Then I leaned my weight against the door, to push it open. "You have got to help me."

"I don't *got* to do anything," she said, pushing the door from her side.

"He only visited Sally because he was making little photographs of her," I said.

She continued to resist.

"And he only visited Miss Zoe Brown to buy you a new bonnet."

She suddenly stopped pushing, so that the door flew open & I tumbled into the room.

"Oh, Pinky!" she cried, wringing her hands together. "I have been so miserable without him. I almost went and smoked a pipe. But I resisted Temptation and only had a few glasses of whiskey instead."

I got to my feet & picked up my laundry parcel & dusted myself off. "I am glad you did not give into Temptation," I said. "Now tell me, did you ever watch those Minstrel Singers putting on their black faces?"

She nodded. "I watched them do it last night."

"Can you help me do it to myself? Only I want to look real."

"You want to look like a Negro boy?"

I shook my head; held up Martha's clean and folded nightdress. "I want to look like a particular Negro girl; one who has been frightened out of her bed in the dead of night."

Belle's eyes grew even wider. "You want to dress up as a Negro *girl*?"

"Yes," I said. "Remember I told you how a Detective must wear Disguises sometimes?"

She nodded.

"Well, I hope to entrap the man who killed Short Sally in so doing. Will you help me?"

"You bet!" she said. "I will enjoy helping you get yourself up as a poor little black girl. Follow me."

Ledger Sheet 47

I TOLD BELLE ABOUT MARTHAS IDEA of mixing burnt cork with some sort of cream those theater people use. This made the color look less like boot polish. As she helped me stain my face and hands, I told her about my investigation & my plan. She thought it very bold & clever.

At one point she asked me where Martha was hiding but I had learned not to trust Belle farther than I could throw her, so I replied, "She is in a Safe Haven."

Belle found me some big old shoes which just about fit. The sole-leather of one of them flapped like a dog's tongue in hot weather, but I thought they suited the disguise. Those shoes also meant I did not have to black my bare feet.

Finally, Belle put Martha's night bonnet on me and stood back to look me up and down.

"Well?" I said. "How do I look?"

"Try it without the wig," she said. "Negro girls don't have hair like that."

I took off the wig with its swinging black ringlets & put Martha's cotton night bonnet back on.

"Dang!" she said. "If I did not know it was you, I would not have known it was you." She took my shoulders and turned me to face a full-length mirror. "See for yourself."

There in the mirror stood a poor little Negro girl in a white nightdress & bonnet & clumping old shoes.

The girl in the mirror was standing upright, with square shoulders & arms hanging down. Martha had spent an hour coaching me on how to stand. I clasped my hands together in front of my chest & hunched my shoulders & pulled my head in like Martha told me she did when she was afraid.

"P.K., that is bully!" cried Belle, clapping her hands. "That is even better than perfect. Where are you going now? I want to see this."

I said, "I am going up to Currie's Auction House up on Thirteen North B Street. Mr. William Morris Stewart should have got the word out by now."

"What word?"

"That someone witnessed Short Sally's brutal murder and that they will publicly name the Killer immediately following the auction of Sally's goods."

"Well, come on then!" Belle quickly pinned up her hair & put on the same feathered hat she had been wearing the first time I saw her.

"Wait," I said. "I need another disguise."

"What do you mean?" She had her hands on her hips. "We just spent half an hour getting you to look like Martha."

"And the Killer will be on the lookout for her," I said. "If he kills me on the way to the auction house I will not have a chance to publicly denounce him."

"Plus you will be dead," she pointed out.

I nodded. "I need way of getting inside Currie's without him spotting me," I said. "I need a Trojan Horse."

She said, "You want to ride up there on a horse? It is only a block away."

I pointed at a medium-sized wardrobe with costumes hung in it. "No. I want to ride up there in that wardrobe."

"What?"

"I will hide in there and you hire a couple of men to haul it up to Currie's. Pretend you are bringing it to auction." I pulled a coin out of my medicine bag. "You can use this to pay them."

"Oh!" she cried. "What a bully idea! We can take it right up to the auction room and nobody will suspect."

So it was that a short time later I found myself being transported in the camphor-scented darkness of a pinewood wardrobe up to Currie's auction house.

I was jostled as the two men deposited my conveyance on the ground and I heard the deep voice of a man saying, "Sorry, miss, but they is having an auction at the moment and it is busier than a beehive with a bear outside."

"Will you bend down?" came Belle's voice, "so that I may whisper in your ear?"

A moment later I heard the deep-voiced man say, "Follow me, miss!"

Once again I was heaved up and jounced and jostled. I could hear footsteps on wooden stairs and I heard Belle's voice say, "Easy there!" and then, "Bring it in here," and finally, "That will do fine, right there."

The footsteps of my porters receded and I heard the voice of an auctioneer, loud but muffled through the doors of the wardrobe.

A moment later one of the doors squeaked open and Belle's whispered voice said, "Come on out. It is safe."

I emerged into a dim area cluttered with furniture, boxes and other such things. I could hear the auctioneer's voice clearly now. He was just up ahead. We were right on stage!

Belle was crouched down behind a black walnut rolltop desk with her finger in front of her lips.

Then she beckoned me and I followed her through a forest of furniture towards the auctioneer's rapid voice.

"Eight-fifty, eight-fifty, eight-fifty, NINE!" cried the auctioneer.

He was a man in a top hat and blue-velvet frock coat standing behind a podium. He had a wooden mallet & he looked very high-tone.

"Nine, going once," he said. And then, "I have nine-fifty!"

We both moved forward at a crouch. Belle's hoop skirt kept getting shmooshed so I led the way to a heavy walnut dresser with a mirror on top. There was about a one-inch crack between the top of the dresser and the mirror. We both brought our faces closer to that long & narrow spy hole.

"Nine-fifty, nine-fifty, nine-fifty, TEN!" The auctioneer's voice was very loud.

Peeking through the crack, I saw a big bright room with two big west-facing windows showing buildings across the street and the steep side of Mount Davidson. The auction room was three quarters full, with about equal parts men & women. Belle and I were up on a stage near the auctioneer so the audience's faces were gazing up at us, or rather the furniture we were hiding behind. That meant I could identify lots of people I knew.

"Ten! Ten! Ten!" said the auctioneer. "Ten-fifty! 'Leven! 'Leven-fifty!"

I saw Big Gussie & her four Girls. Mrs. Zoe Brown was standing with them, dressed in black with a black-feathered hat to match.

I saw my Lawyer, Mr. William Morris Stewart. He was hard to miss as he stood about a head taller than anyone else.

"'Leven-fifty, 'leven-fifty, 'leven-fifty, TWELVE!"

I saw four of the men from my List of Suspects:

Mr. Isaiah Coffin, photographer.

The Rev. C.V. Anthony, Methodist pastor.

Mr. Absalom Smith, actor & punster.

And Langford Farner Peel, shootist.

One of them looked different than he usually did because he was *in disguise*, but I knew him by his pipe & tobacco, and by his eyebrows.

He was the Killer.

Ledger Sheet 48

THE AUCTIONEER WAS SAYING something but I was not listening to him.

I was watching the Killer. He was disguised as a miner, with a long linen duster coat over a red flannel shirt, pantaloons tucked into boots, a small slouch hat and a big black fake beard. He had his hand in the pocket of his duster coat & he seemed to be looking right in my direction!

I thought, "Surely he cannot see me in the shadows back here."

Then I thought, "He will not dare shoot me in front of a hundred people. He is a coward and a poltroon."

Just to be safe, I started to sink back down behind the dresser.

BANG!

I nearly jumped out of my skin as the auctioneer brought down his gavel. "Sold!" he cried. "To Miss Gertrude Holmes for twelve dollars! One hardwood whatnot."

That bang had made me jump and the auctioneer must have seen the movement out of the corner of his eye. He turned his head & for the first time he noticed me & Belle scrouched down behind the black walnut chest of drawers. His eyes got wider. Belle put a lace-gloved finger to her lips & then pointed to me in my Martha-disguise.

The auctioneer gave us a very slight nod & then turned back to the audience. I reckoned he was Mr. J.C. Currie, the proprietor of the auction house, whom my Lawyer had promised to brief about our plan.

"That completes the sale of the estate of Miss Sally Sampson," said Mr. J.C. Currie in his carrying voice. "Like many of us, she was not perfect, but she was brave and beloved of many."

"What is this," came a man's Southern-accented voice, "an auction or a eulogy?"

There was a smattering of laughter, then some women hushed him.

Mr. Currie bowed his head until people were quiet. "I know you were all saddened to hear of the untimely demise of Sally Sampson last week, of her brutal murder."

Some people nodded. I heard men's voices and women whispering, too.

"You might have heard the rumor," said Mr. Currie in his auctioneer's voice, "that there was a witness to this dastardly crime."

Some people gasped and their voices grew louder.

Mr. Currie banged his gavel to obtain silence. "Some of you might have heard the rumor that Miss Sally Sampson's serving girl was an Eye Witness to the crime. Or you might have seen the broadsheet in the windows of some local businesses."

As Mr. Currie held up one of these notices, there came another big gasp. The notice read as follows:

SALLY SAMPSON'S MURDERER EXPOSED!

Today at Currie's Auction House at around 2 p.m.
Following the auction of Sally Sampson's goods
An Eye Witness to the Crime will tell Who Done It!

My lawyer & I had dashed off half a dozen that morning and put them in our own windows & anywhere else we thought the suspect might see them. The presence of the Killer showed that our plan had worked.

"Until now," said Mr. Currie in his big auctioneer's voice, "that girl has been in hiding, in fear of her life, but she is now willing to come forward and reveal who committed the dastardly crime."

Everybody said, "Oh!" & all heads turned to the door at the side of the auction room. The Killer looked in that direction, too.

Then all heads swiveled back as I clumped out onto the stage in my oversized shoes. Pretending to be a frightened girl about to expose a Killer was not too hard as a man intent on murder stood only a few feet away. I had assured Martha he would not try anything in a public place but now I was not so sure. I made my knees knock together and pretended to tremble and you can bet I kept my head down.

"Oh!" came a woman's cry. There was a commotion among Big Gussie's girls and a moment later I saw why.

Mrs. Zoe Brown had fainted.

The Killer did not look much better. His face was white as a sheet under the brim of his slouch hat and behind his hook-on beard. I do not think he was expecting to see the Eye Witness of his crime even though he must have come for that very purpose.

Mr. Currie's loud voice came from my right. "Yes," he said, "the courageous girl has appeared at the eleventh hour." He turned to me. "What do you have to tell us, Martha? Who done it?"

I spoke up in a voice as much like Martha's as I could muster. "The killer was a Reb deserter," I said loudly, "name of Deforrest Robards. He froze during a pitch battle and then run off. They are after him."

"Do you see that man in this room?" said Mr. Currie.

I saw the Killer smile behind his beard. He did not know that I recognized his pipe and eyebrows.

I pointed at him. "He is right thar!" I cried. "Under that fake hat and beard!"

There was a clatter as half the Killer's pipe fell to the wooden floor. He had bit the stem in half.

Big Gussie stood near the Killer. "Fake beard?" she cried.

"Why, so it is!" She ripped it off and whipped away his hat, too.

The coward stood frozen, his blond hair and billy goat beard now visible for all to see.

"It was him!" I shouted. "He strangulated Miss Sally!"

Behind me Belle gasped, "Absalom Smith!"

I said, "Yes! He calls himself Absalom Smith but his real name is Deforrest Robards." I repeated it so that everyone could hear. "Dee Forrest Ro-bards! He strangulated Miss Sally and I saw him do it!"

Mr. Absalom Smith stood petrified by fear.

"Miss Sally knows you from Alabamy," I cried. "You killed her 'cause she was gonna tell on you. And on account of she was taunting you." Then I screwed my voice up an octave & cried out, "Flicker, flicker! Yellowhammer!"

"Shut your mouth!" he cried at last.

And then, "Stop saying that!"

And finally, "If I have to go, then by God I'm taking you with me!"

I saw his nostrils flare & his chest heave up & he reached into the pocket of his duster coat & pulled the revolver from his pocket & took aim at me & fired.

Ledger Sheet 49

EVERYTHING HAPPENED REAL QUICK.

Thanks to me seeing his nostrils flare and his chest heave up, I hit the ground.

Behind me a mirror shattered into a thousand pieces & Belle cried out. I had forgot she was standing nearby. All around the room other people hit the floor. Men shouted & women screamed.

"Belle!" cried Isaiah Coffin, and he ran forward as a second shot rang out.

I did not have time to get my gun from the medicine bag beneath my nightdress, so I reached out & grabbed the nearest piece of light furniture & hurled it at the Killer.

It was a kind of tall thin table with three legs & three triangular shelves.

It was a Mahog Whatnot.

It hit Absalom Smith smack dab on his elbow a moment before he pulled the trigger.

Bang! His shot splattered harmlessly into the ceiling.

Within moments another five shots rang out.

Bang!

B'dang!

Bang de bang!

BANG!

Absalom Smith, a.k.a. Deforrest Robards, shrieked & spun around, riddled with bullets from every side.

Everything was confused & wild, but through a cloud of gunsmoke I saw four of my acquaintances brandishing smoking guns.

Langford Farner Peel had got off the first shot with his ivory-gripped Navy.

Big Gussie was holding a smoking pearl-handled Deringer.

William Morris Stewart also held large-bore Texas Deringers. One in each hand. Both of them were smoking, too.

And the Colt's Army had been discharged by Deputy Marshal Jack Williams himself.

My ears were ringing but I heard Langford Farner Peel cock his revolver & address the Killer in his cool English accent. "Drop your piece, Smith," he said.

Despite being riddled with balls, Absalom Smith was still on his feet. Frozen with fear, he stared at Farner Peel.

But only for a moment. Then he showed his true color.

He dropped his gun & turned & staggered for the door, spattering great drops of blood as he did.

Those people still on their feet parted, squealing, before him. Only one man stood firm: my Lawyer, Mr. William Morris Stewart. He stood blocking the doorway & brandishing his Deringers. I observed they were double barreled, so he had a ball left in each.

"Hold, sir!" he said.

Absalom Smith, a.k.a. Deforrest Robards, did not "hold."

Instead, he swerved right & crashed through one of the two big windows, to the accompaniment of more screams and a couple more gunshots.

For a heartbeat or two there was silence.

Then we heard shouts & barking from the street below & everybody in the room ran to the window in order to look out.

I ran, too, but the flapping sole of my shoe tripped me up & I almost fell flat in a pool of Smith's blood. However, I managed to regain my balance & I squeezed between hooped skirts to the window & looked out through the broken panes of glass. I could only see a crowd of people gathered around something down in the street by some wagons, so I followed the crowd downstairs.

Out on B Street I elbowed my way through the gathered populace until I got to the front of the crowd.

There a Terrible Sight met my eyes.

Justice had caught up with the coward Deforrest Robards in the shape of a mule-drawn Quartz Wagon.

When he leapt out the window he must have rolled down

the slanted awning and fallen right in front of the wagon, for he was lying under the wheel. His chest was crushed and there was blood everywhere. But he appeared to be living still. A burly & bearded man in a red flannel shirt was standing there, holding a small dog in his arms. "I didn't even see him," said the teamster. "One moment he warn't there and the next he was. It was as if he fell from the sky."

I went over to Absalom Smith, a.k.a. Deforrest Robards, & scrouched down & looked at him. He squinted back up at me & then his eyes widened in surprise & recognition. "When is a lady's maid not a lady's maid?" he murmured.

"When she is P.K. Pinkerton in disguise," was my answer to his conundrum. "Do you have any last words?"

He nodded weakly, "Do not let them publish my real name. It would kill my mother. Father, too. The shame . . ."

His eyes closed and I thought he was a goner.

Then they opened again. "All I ever wanted to do was be an actor," he said. "I could have been happy here if only she hadn't recognized me." Tears were squeezing out of his eyes & I almost pitied him.

"Do you repent of your Sins?" I said.

"Yes!" he cried. "Oh yes, I repent. May the Lord forgive me!"

I nodded. "I promise I will not let them publish your real name."

"Bless you," said Lieutenant Deforrest Robards, and with that he breathed his last.

HONG WO WASHER 洗

Ledger Sheet 50

WITHIN MOMENTS SOME MEN had pulled the Killer's body out of the road and onto the boardwalk. He lay there, awaiting the undertaker.

I stood gazing down at the corpse.

I wondered if he had made his peace with God or was roasting in the fiery place. His handsome face in repose looked about 10 years younger & almost peaceful, so I guessed maybe it was the former. His tobacco pouch had fallen out of his pocket and I bent down and picked it up. It smelled like Pa Emmet and, together with the sight of his boyish face, made my throat feel tight.

I automatically started to put it in the pocket of my buckskin trowsers, but remembered I was wearing a white nightdress. Instead I tucked it up beneath my night bonnet.

"War is the real criminal," said the husky voice of Big Gussie behind me. "Not all men are cut out to be soldiers."

"And yet every man has the potential to kill," came the deep voice of Mr. William Morris Stewart.

That reminded me about JAG, his three motives for murder.

But Absalom Smith, a.k.a. Deforrest Robards, had not killed because of Jealousy, Anger or Greed. No, he had killed a brave & outspoken Soiled Dove because of cowardice, shame & the desire to be an actor.

I guess you cannot always simplify people.

Suddenly I was gripped by the shoulders & pulled to the fragrant & ruffled bosom of a woman in black.

"Oh, Martha!" said Zoe Brown as she hugged me. "I'm so glad you are safe. I felt so bad after I told you to run and hide somewhere else that night! If anything had happened to you I would never have forgiven myself!"

I reckon she mistook me for Martha but she found out her error when she put a finger under my chin and lifted my face in order to give me a kiss.

"Why, you ain't—" she began, giving me Expression No. 4: Surprise.

I said, "It is me, P.K. Pinkerton. I am personating Martha on account of she was too scared to come."

"Oh no!" cried Zoe Brown. "Is she hurt?"

"Do not worry about Martha," said Mr. William Morris Stewart. "Thanks to P.K., she is safe and sound."

"Where is she?" Zoe asked. "Where is the poor little thing?"

"She is in a Safe Haven," I said. "I can take you to her now."

"Oh yes!" cried Zoe. "Please take me to her and let us not delay a moment longer. I feel so guilty about what I did."

As we walked down to Chinatown, Zoe Brown told us how Martha had come seeking refuge the night of Sally's murder.

"I told her she couldn't stop with me because everybody knew Sally and I were friends and my crib was the first place the Killer would look. I told her she must hide where nobody would find her." Zoe hung her head. "But the real reason I turned her away was that I am a coward. I was afraid he would kill me, too. When I came to my senses, I tried to find her. I felt so bad."

I reckon it was around 3 o'clock in the afternoon when we reached Hong Wo's laundry down in the Chinese quarter of town. There we found Ping, and he took us to see Martha.

She was in fine spirits. She was wearing the pink calico dress and the button-up boots & sitting in her nest of sheets with a little Chinese boy of about two or maybe three years old beside her. They were both eating chow-chow with chop-sticks.

Martha looked up, laughing, but when she saw me with darkened skin & dressed in her nightdress & bonnet she gave a kind of squawk & put down her bowl & clapped her hands.

"Oh my!" she cried. "It is like gazing in a mirror." Then she said, "Look, P.K., Woo is teaching me how to eat chow-chow with chopsticks."

I said, "Woo?"

"This sweet li'l boy here. Ain't he the cutest thang?"

Then Mrs. Zoe Brown came in behind me & Martha gave another squeal.

"Oh, Miz Zoe!" she cried. She leapt up from the sheets & ran to her & threw her arms tight around Zoe's slender waist.

Mrs. Zoe Brown hugged Martha back for a long time & begged her forgiveness for turning her away & said that she was to live with her as long as she liked. Martha could not believe this at first but when it sank in she started crying. That set Mrs. Zoe Brown off weeping and soon Ping's sister and little Woo joined in, too.

Ping looked at me & I looked at him.

He held out his hand. "That will be forty dollar," he said. "For two day."

I fished around in my Medicine bag & gave him two gold coins.

I was almost out of cash. I would have to go down to Wells, Fargo & Co. first thing Monday morning.

I thought, "This Detective business is mighty expensive."

The women & Woo were still crying, so Ping led me out of the maze & back to F Street.

"Thank you, Ping," I said as I turned to go.

He only grunted but I thought I detected the trace of a smile.

On the way back up to B Street, I was getting strange looks & realized I was still in blackface & wearing a thin nightdress and night bonnet. I stopped at a pump & tried to wash the burnt cork off my hands & face.

Plain water had little effect, so I went back to my office & into my back room & took off the shoes & nightdress & sleeping cap. Then I put on my own clothes & went to find a bath house to see if hot water would do the job.

Ma Evangeline had taken me to a bath house once, somewhere outside Salt Lake City, but that had been over two years ago. I had not been to a bath house since, and never by myself.

I headed north on B Street to Selfridge & Bach's Bath House, which was recommended by many local citizens as being one of the nicest.

As I went in, a thin Chinaman carrying crumpled towels came out of a door & before it closed I caught a glimpse of a big steamy room full of naked, hairy & dangling men.

"Negroes got to bathe privately," said a fat man behind a counter.

"A private bath suits me just fine," I said. "How much?"

"Two dollars."

It was only then that I saw a sign behind him. It read:

HOT WATER 25¢

CLEAN HOT WATER 35¢

SOAP 10¢ EXTRA

TOWELS 10¢ EXTRA

CLEAN HOT WATER, SOAP & TOWEL 50¢

PRIVATE BATH $1.00

I pointed at the sign. "It says one dollar for a private bath."

"Negroes is extra," said the man. "Double in fact." Only he did not say it so politely.

I handed him two dollars.

He said, "That will be another four bits if you want soap, towels and clean hot water."

I stared at him for a moment, then fished in my pocket and pulled out a silver half-dollar.

He took it & pointed to a wooden door opposite and said, "In there." Then he shouted, "Hung Lee? Get in here now!"

I went over to the door & opened it slowly, fearful of the sight of more naked men. But it was just a small wood plank room with a galvanized bathtub in the center & a single wooden chair & some wooden pegs on the wall & a small, high window. There was nothing in the tub except a damp white linen sheet plastered to its bottom & sides & hanging over. I was about to go back out and complain that I could not bathe with only a damp sheet when the door opened & the thin Chinese man came in with a steaming bucket. I reckoned he was Hung Lee.

He poured hot water into the bath, then turned and held up three fingers. "You wait," he said. "Three more bucket."

I nodded and waited as he went out & came in three more times until he had finished filling the bath.

When the bath was full of steaming hot water, he went out and I started to unbutton my shirt. I froze as the door opened once more. But it was only Mr. Hung Lee. He was carrying a folded bath sheet & a wash cloth & a small cake of yellow soap.

He placed these on the chair and gave a little bow. "I leave you now. Enjoy."

"Wait," I said & fished in my pocket and gave him two bits.

"Hung Lee thanks you!" he said, smiling & bowing again. He held up a single finger. "One more thing," he said. He hurried out & returned & looked around & quickly emptied a fistful of powder into the bath. "Bath Salt," he announced. "Lavender." Mr. Hung Lee had some trouble saying this final word, but I knew what he meant because of the smell that was filling the room along with the steam.

He brushed his hands together over the steaming bath & bowed. "*Now* I go," he said. On his way out he showed me a small brass hook on the inside of the door so I could lock it.

I used the little brass hook to lock the door. Then I got undressed & hung my pants & shirt & hat & medicine bag on the pegs. Next I climbed into the steaming hot bath & lowered myself slowly in. The gunshot wound in my left arm stung a little at first but then it settled down & I began to relax.

Back in Temperance, Ma Evangeline used to curtain off a part of the cabin and fill a tin tub with hot water for our weekly bath. She always let me go first but the water was never so hot as to require a sheet. Nor did she ever let me indulge in Bath Salts. Also, our tub in Temperance was only half this size.

This bath was a steaming luxury. I felt it was almost worth the princely sum of $2.75 (if you include my tip to the Chinese bath attendant). I could sink right down underwater & blow bubbles up & close my eyes.

When I sank underwater & closed my eyes, I saw an image of Lieutenant Deforrest Robards lying on the boardwalk. It was a sad image so I did what Ma Evangeline always told me to do when I thought of something bad: replace it with something nice. I conjured up the memory of Mrs. Zoe Brown hugging Martha and it made me feel floaty & warm.

When I poked my dripping head back up above the surface of the water, I could hear tinkling piano music leaking in through the small, high window. It was a sentimental song called "Kiss Me Good Night, Mother." That & the bath made me think of Ma Evangeline, who had taught me so much and who had always insisted on kissing me good night despite my protests. Even though I do not like to be touched, I regretted the fact that she would never kiss me good night again.

My cheeks were wet but I never cry, so I guess that was because I had just dipped my head under the water.

I stayed soaking in that bath until the steam dispersed and the water went from hot to warm. Then I reached over to the chair and got the small cake of yellow soap & wash cloth and scrubbed my face & hands.

The black came off pretty easy. A lot of other dirt came off, too, in a very satisfying fashion.

I was just about to get out when I heard the chink of spurs & a voice from the other side of the door.

"He ain't anywhere in there!" the voice was saying. "Ain't you got any other rooms?"

It was a voice that made my blood run cold.

It was a Raspy Voice.

It was the voice of Extra Dub Donahue, my mortal enemy.

He had tracked me down.

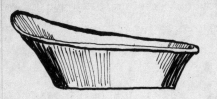

Ledger Sheet 51

THE NOISE OF A FIST pounding on the door filled the small private room in Selfridge & Bach's Bath House.

"Open the door, you galldarn varmint!" rasped Extra Dub. "I know you are in there!"

I was sitting stark naked in a tin bath with nothing to defend myself but a small cake of yellow soap & a wash cloth.

BANG!

The door shook & his spurs jangled as he kicked it from the outside.

BANG!

The door groaned on its hinges. The small brass hook-and-eye lock would not hold much longer.

I leapt out of the bath & lunged for my medicine bag & pulled it off the wooden peg & ran back to the tub & crouched behind it.

CRASH!

The door burst open & there stood Extra Dub. He was wearing his black slouch hat & a biscuit-colored duster coat. In his right hand he brandished a Colt's Navy Revolver. It was cocked and ready for action.

As I peeped up from behind the bathtub my panicky wet fingers were fumbling to open my leather medicine bag.

"There you are, you dam whelp," he rasped. Then he threw down on me.

Bang!

I ducked down just as a loud report filled the room & made the bath shudder & my ears ring. But my slippery fingers had finally opened the leather pouch & I tipped my seven-shooter into my right hand. I cocked it & popped my head up & got some shots back at him.

Pop! said my Smith & Wesson. *Pop! Pop!*

His curse showed that at least one of my shots had not been in vain.

Bang! Bang! said his Colt's Navy.

Pop! I replied.

Something warm ran down my cheek. For an awful moment I thought it was my own blood.

They say that when you are shot you do not always feel it right away.

I reached up and touched my cheek and looked at my fingers.

But it was only bath water.

I had not been shot.

Above the ringing in my ears, I heard Dub's spurs clank as he moved forward to get a better shot at me.

He aimed again and *click!*

Misfire! His cap & ball Navy revolver had let him down.

My Smith & Wesson seemed to have had no effect on him so I tried something else.

Quick as a whip crack I lifted up my end of the tub, sending a cascade of soapy water crashing over the wood plank floor towards his feet.

"Whoa!" he cried and—*Bang!*—his fourth shot hit the ceiling as his legs flew out in front of him & he slammed down on his bottom with a jangling thud.

Extra Dub was sitting and I was now standing, stark naked & using the empty tin bath to shield my Modesty.

For a moment Extra Dub did not move, but sat with his legs straight out & wide apart & his smoking Colt still in his hand. His slouch hat had slipped down over his eyes. He flung the hat away & looked up to see me peeking out from behind the empty tub. I was pointing my seven-shooter right at his heart.

I said, "Drop your piece, you murdering varmint, or I will kill you where you sit. My gun does not misfire like yours."

He sneered at me, "You have hit me twice but your little balls are no more harmful than a mosquito bite." Despite his bold words, he made no move.

I stood firm. "Drop your piece!" I repeated.

His nostrils flared, he cocked his revolver and—

Pop! I shot the gun right out of his hand. But in so doing I had to let the tin bath drop, thus revealing my Modesty.

He stopped cursing in mid-profanity & his eyes opened wide. "Why, you ain't a—"

CLANG!

Mr. Hung Lee brought an empty metal bucket down hard on Extra Dub's bare head. The Desperado remained sitting, but his eyes rolled back & drool dribbled from his mouth. His Colt's Navy lay nearby, but the quick-thinking & helpful attendant kicked out with his wooden clog & sent it spinning across the soapy floor towards me.

I lunged for it & grabbed it & scrouched down behind the tub again & cocked it & threw down on Extra Dub with his own piece.

But he was still groggy and did not protest when Mr. Hung Lee brought the bucket down like a hat, completely covering Dub's head. Next, the quick-thinking Mr. Hung Lee undid the Desperado's own belt and used it to bind his hands behind him.

"There!" said Mr. Hung Lee, brushing his hands together. "Very good. Yes?"

"Yes," I agreed. Apparently he had not noticed my Modesty. I said, "There is a reward for him. Shall we split it fifty-fifty?"

"Yes, please!" said Mr. Hung Lee. He smiled from ear to ear and began to drag the still-seated Desperado back out of the room. "I leave you now," he said. "You get dressed. Then we go collect reward."

He shut the door behind him and although it did not close completely I put down the tin bathtub & toweled myself dry & started to get dressed. As I was fumbling to button my shirt, I noticed that there were three lead balls embedded in the linen sheet still stuck to the inside of the tin bathtub.

When I saw that, my knees began to wobble & I had to sit for a spell & take deep breaths.

By and by I went out of the bath room. Mr. Hung Lee stood beaming & gripping Extra Dub, who was now standing but still wore the tin bucket on his head.

"We go see Marshal?" asked Hung Lee.

I thought about this for a moment and then shook my head. "Might be better to take him to Judge Atwill. The Marshal is still out of town and his Deputy does not like me."

"Judge Atwill good," said the helpful bath attendant. "I know where."

As I turned to follow Hung Lee & our prisoner out the door, I noticed that the fat man behind the counter was staring at me open-eyed & openmouthed. I reckon it was one of the most extreme examples of Expression No. 4 that I had ever seen.

Ledger Sheet 52

EARLY THE NEXT MORNING I came back from a tasty Sunday Morning Pancake Breakfast at the Colombo Restaurant to find Mr. Sam Clemens lurking outside my front door. He had something under his arm. It looked like a large, flat, wooden desk drawer divided up into shallow pigeonholes.

"What is that?" I said.

"Good morning to you, too," he drawled, his speech even slower than usual. "This here is a present for you."

As I unlocked my front door, I scrutinized his face using my Detective skills. His chin was unshaved & the whites of his eyes were red & his dead-critter pipe smoke was mingled with whiskey fumes.

"You have not been to bed yet, have you?" I said, as I went in.

"Your deduction is correct," he said, following me inside. "I have been running with Dan, Joe, et al. Ain't you open for business today?" he asked, seeing that I had not turned the sign in the door window from CLOSED to OPEN.

"Heaven forfend," I said. "Today is the Sabbath. My foster ma and pa taught me to keep the commandments, especially the fourth."

Sam Clemens looked around. "Is today Sunday?" he said, and squinted at the bare shelves, as if something there might provide the answer.

"Yes," I said. "Today is the Sabbath."

He nodded. "That explains why there was nobody from the newspaper over at the Old Corner Saloon."

"Why? Do your fellow newspapermen observe the Sabbath?"

He shook his head. "They observe the Hebrew Sabbath: Saturday. We work on Sunday."

He plunked the thing like the big wooden drawer onto my desk. It was divided up into about 90 small, shallow compartments of varying size. I had seen some of these in the offices of the Territorial Enterprise.

"It is a type tray," he said, taking the pipe from his mouth and knocking it on his heel to dislodge the old tobacco.

I said, "A type tray?"

He nodded. "It is old and got a bit damaged in our recent

move. I thought you could use it for your Tobacco Collection," he added.

As he filled his pipe with fresh Killickinick, I examined the wooden tray. I could put shreds of tobacco or cigar stumps in the compartments & avoid them getting mixed up with each other. This flat tray would greatly aid me in my study and cataloging of tobacco.

I said, "This flat tray will greatly aid me in my study and cataloging of tobacco."

"You are most welcome." Sam Clemens sat in my Client's chair & crossed one leg over the other & struck a match on the heel of the lifted boot. Then he held the lit match to his pipe & got it going.

"Thank you," I said, remembering my manners. "But why did you do this?"

"First of all, to apologize for flinging your tobacco collection to the ground," he drawled. "Second of all, to say thank you."

"You said my Big Tobacco Collection was 'flapdoodle,'" I reminded him.

"That was before I heard how your ability to identify over one hundred kinds of tobacco helped you bring a Criminal to Justice and save the life of a poor serving girl. I am now a convert to the merits of collecting tobacco. You have inspired me!"

"I could use another two or three of these," I said.

The door of my office opened. It was Bee in her bonnet. I observed some of the bounce had gone out of her step.

"Hello, P.K.," she said. "I see you have company so I will not linger."

Sam Clemens twisted around to see who it was. He did not rise from his chair but he touched the brim of his slouch hat. "Morning, miss," said he.

Bee gave him a polite nod, then came forward & placed a parcel about the size of two bricks on my desk. "It is tobacco from Pa's shop," she said. "Samples of thirty brands I do not think you have. They are labeled and everything." She chewed her lower lip & looked at the floor. Then she blurted out, "I feel real bad I didn't help you the one time you asked. I felt sorry for that little girl & would have thought of a way to help if you had not taken me by surprise. That is my way of apologizing," she added.

She looked at Sam Clemens & then she looked back at me. "I will not pester you any more about *you know what*," she said. "If you need help again, please will you give me another chance?"

Before I could respond, she turned & hurried out of the shop.

Sam Clemens turned and watched her go.

I could not read his expression.

He looked at the parcel Bee had left. "Well, ain't you going to open it?"

"Not now," I said. "I will save it for later."

Sam Clemens nodded & pulled a notebook from his pocket. "Then listen to this," he said. "I want to hear your opinion of this article I have just penned about the death of the coward Absalom Smith."

"I promised him we would not reveal his true identity," I said.

"And we shan't," he said. "Nowhere do I mention his real name. Listen." He read, *"About two o'clock Saturday afternoon Justice finally caught up with a Confederate deserter posing as a Music Hall Entertainer. Absalom Smith met his Maker during an auction of goods on B Street. At the inquest it was shown that he was shot several times before leaping from a second-story window and then being crushed by a quartz wagon. After due deliberation, the jury, sad and sober, but with intelligence unblinded by desire for revenge, brought in a verdict of death 'by the visitation of God.' The foreman also made this comment: 'A cowardly deserter and professional punster has met the end he deserved: he was riddled to death.'"*

Sam Clemens guffawed & slapped his thigh with the notebook. "Ain't that bully?" he said. "With this sort of article, I feel I have found a vein I can mine for years."

Here he stood up & leaned over the desk & grasped me by both shoulders.

I winced & wished people would stop grasping me by the shoulders.

"P.K.," he said, "I never had but two powerful ambitions in my life. One was to be a riverboat pilot and the other a millionaire. I accomplished the one but failed miserably in the other, but now I have had a 'Call.'"

"A Call?" I said, trying to squirm out of his grip.

"Yes! A Call!" he cried. "A Call to literature! Not literature of the highest order, you understand, but that of the lowest— i.e., humorous. I confess it is nothing to be proud of, but it is my strongest suit. And it is partly thanks to you!"

He let me go & picked up the cardboard box with the Stone Baby in it. "The boys at the Enterprise were pranking us both with this rock baby," he said. "But it gave me the bulliest idea for my own hoax article. My account of the 'Petrified Man' has been a Wild Success. It is being reprinted in newspapers all over the country. Subscriptions of the *Daily Territorial Enterprise* have gone up ten percent, according to Joe Goodman."

His pipe had gone out so he put down the Stone Baby & struck another match on the sole of his boot & put it to the bowl & puffed. "As a bonus," he said through a cloud of smoke, "I have exacted vengeance on that varmint George Sewall. Even though I misspelled his name in the article, people are writing to him and visiting him by the drove. They are all demanding that he take them to Gravelly Ford to show them the Prodigy. Haw-haw!"

"Why is it all thanks to me?" I said.

"Well, if you had not left that rock baby lying around and made me mad, then I would not have kicked it and got the notion to write my own version," he drawled.

"But the Petrified Man was all a big story, wasn't it?" I said. "You made it up."

He chuckled and puffed his pipe. "Course I made it up," he said. "That makes my vengeance all the sweeter!"

"Vengeance is the Lord's," I said. "Be careful your revenge does not backfire upon you."

"Dang it, Pinky," he puffed, "don't be so sanctimonious. Come on over to the Niagara Music Hall & Billiard Saloon. Let us engage in some jollification. I believe El Dorado

Johnny is still laid out on the Billiard Table there. I will stand you a sarsaparilla and we will see if he is still a good-looking corpse. We will toast my 'Call to Humorous Literature.'" He puffed his pipe some more and added, "No doubt your presence will attract another shooting affray by and by."

"I am sorry," I said. "But I hear the church bells calling the faithful to worship. Are you coming?"

"Not if I can help it," he said.

Ledger Sheet 53

I WALKED DOWN TO D STREET alone to attend my first church service in Satan's Playground. I reckon I was about as clean as I had ever been in my life. I wore my buckskin moccasins and trowsers, my blue woolen coat with the six brass buttons & my black felt hat with the hawk's feather in it. I had sent my faded red (not pink) flannel shirt to be cleaned at Hong Wo's and was wearing a brand-new pink flannel shirt instead. Yes, it was Pink. Not faded red but pink. I like flannel because it is real soft & I had got used to the color pink, too.

It kind of matches my name.

But if anybody says it is a "girly" color I will kick them hard in the shin without counting to ten or quoting Philippians 4:5.

The Methodist Episcopal Church was crammed to the rafters, as they say. I was surprised to see about 20 or 30 Soiled Doves there, along with a couple of Barkeepers and the Coroner for Storey County, Mr. George Sewall, not Sewell. Doc Pinkerton & his wife were there, too, & Isaiah Coffin with Miss Belle Donne on his arm.

(His dash to her side in the presence of a crazed killer had revived their Love.)

My Lawyer, Mr. William Morris Stewart, was also present. He told me he had put my fourteen hundred dollars back in my account and repaid Big Gussie and her Boarding House Girls the six hundred they had raised for my bail.

I sat near the back of the church on the end of a pew so I could make an easy escape if necessary. Sometimes Sunday services make me squirmish and I need to get out in the fresh air. Gussie & the girls all waved at me from the other side of the church. They were got up in their Sunday finest and they looked bully.

Mrs. Zoe Brown was there, too, in her finest mourning dress of black, trimmed with black lace ruffles. Martha stood beside her, wearing the pink calico dress and white boots, but with a brand-new hat on her head. It was straw with little pink flowers that matched her dress.

(I suppose I will have to buy two new calico dresses &

bonnets & pairs of button-up boots. One to replace the ones I had taken from Isaiah Coffin's clothes cupboard & one for my very own Prim Little Girl Disguise. But I do not mind. At least this time I can buy boots that fit.)

The Rev. C.V. Anthony preached a nice sermon on the Grace of God and we sang some hymns that reminded me of Pa Emmet and Ma Evangeline. I always feel closer to God with the sky above me, rather than a church steeple, but this was not too bad.

After the service ended, I stood outside the church in the sunshine, watching the legs & feet of each person who stopped to thank the Reverend.

From a nearby sage bush a quail called out, "Chicago! Chicago!" to remind me of my goal.

I thought, "When I am ready."

When Mrs. Zoe Brown & Martha appeared in the doorway, the Reverend bent his head & prayed for them. Afterwards, they came over to where I stood, beside the Reverend's future rose garden.

"We come to say good-bye," said Mrs. Zoe Brown in her soft Southern accent.

"We's going to Frisco!" said Martha in her strong Southern accent.

"You are leaving Virginia City?" I asked.

"Yes," said Zoe Brown. She slipped her arm around Martha. "We are setting out right now, while the weather is still fine. We will take Sally's rig. When we get to Frisco, I will set up as a milliner with Martha my apprentice."

"Jess like Miz Sal was gonna do," said Martha.

I said, "Are you sure that is the best plan? I have heard it takes about four days to reach Frisco with your own gig. Those steep mountains tire out the horses something awful and then there is the ferry from Sacramento. You and Martha would do better to sell the gig and team and buy passage on a stagecoach."

"No," said Zoe Brown. "I have made up my mind and planned our route: Van Sickles station tonight, Monday in Strawberry Flat, Tuesday in Sacramento, then the ferry to San Francisco. It is my way of honoring poor Sal. Also," she added, "the Reverend has just asked the Lord to bless us with Road Mercies."

"I will add my prayers to his," I said.

"Fortune favors the brave," said Martha.

Zoe Brown opened her little reticule & fished out a gold coin worth $20. She said, "I want to reward you for helping Martha."

I reckoned it was a lot of money for them.

"I don't need that," I said. "I have got plenty of those in my strong box over at Wells, Fargo & Co. You keep it. That reminds me," I added. I reached into my pocket and pulled out Martha's cross & chain and held it out to her. "You should have this. It will remind you of Sally."

Martha looked at me all wide-eyed and then up at Zoe.

Zoe Brown's eyes were swimming with tears and she said to me, "Are you sure?"

"I am sure."

"Oh, P.K.!" whispered Martha. "Thank you!" She took the cross and chain and Zoe Brown helped her put it on right then and there.

"Well, we've got to give you *something*," said Zoe Brown. She looked at Martha & Martha looked at her. Then, before I could stop her, Zoe Brown grasped me by the shoulders & pulled me forward & gave me a kiss on the cheek. Martha giggled & kissed me on the other cheek.

As I scrubbed off the dampness with my coat sleeve, I thought, "What is it about Virginia City?"

"Oh, P.K.!" Zoe Brown had her hands on her hips & was shaking her head. Then she fished in her purse and brought out a striped paper bag. "Have these, too," she said. "Acidulated drops."

"Thank you," I said, taking the candy. "These are much nicer than kisses."

"P.K.," said Mrs. Zoe Brown, "do you ever *not* say exactly what you think?"

I thought about this. Then I said, "Only when I am lying."

Mrs. Zoe Brown laughed. It was the first time I had heard her do such a thing. It made her look real pretty. She said, "If ever you come to Frisco you must promise to look us up."

I put an acidulated drop in my mouth & nodded. "I will."

"Promise?"

"Promise."

They left me & went up to the street and I saw Sissy and Sassy, the two white mares, hitched to Sally's lacquered buggy in front of Big Gussie's Brick House. I watched black-clad Zoe Brown & pink-clad Martha climb up into the shiny black carriage. They both sat in front & Zoe Brown herself gathered up the reins & flicked the whip & Martha waved goodbye with a new handkerchief.

I watched as they clopped right past & then south along D Street & finally out of sight.

Ledger Sheet 54

EVEN THOUGH IT WAS SUNDAY, the Quartz Stamp Mills were pounding out their song & the hoisting works were sending up clouds of steam from their tall chimneys. The mine whistles started to go off. It was noon.

My acidulated drop had almost dissolved when Rev. C.V. Anthony finally came up to me.

"Ready for our excursion?" he said.

"Yes, sir." I decided not to tell him I had briefly suspected him of murder.

"Good. My wife is picnicking with some lady friends. We will have our own picnic."

Ten minutes later I was sitting beside him at the front of a buckboard pulled by a big roan & a gray and we were clipping south along D Street. The road climbed up to merge with C Street and soon we were going over the Divide. It is a kind of hump on the mountainside that separates Virginia from the village of Gold Hill. The Reverend had been talking about the weather & such things but now he grew silent. The road went sharply down now—steep & winding—and I reckoned he wanted to concentrate on his driving. He slowed down to pay a coin at the Toll House and immediately after that we passed between the towering & demonic rocks called Devil's Gate.

We continued down the winding canyon road through Silver City & we saw the stage from Carson City letting off passengers in front of the hotel. I thought we might catch up with Zoe Brown and Martha but we didn't. I guessed they were making good time towards Frisco.

After Silver City, we forked left onto that nice new toll road. It was smooth as silk but as twisty as a snake. It was a hot afternoon, almost like summer, only the Cottonwood trees were golden and trembling, which told you it was autumn. We had both taken off our coats and sat there in just our shirt-sleeves with the breeze on our faces & the smell of horse & sage & the taste of dust in our mouths.

When we finally reached the flat, straight part of the road, the Reverend breathed a sigh & said, "There is a picnic basket behind you with some ham sandwiches and bottles of lemonade. Why don't you bring them out?"

I did so & he looped the reins around his left wrist & we sat eating the ham sandwiches & drinking lemonade as the buckboard clopped south.

We finished our sandwiches & lemonade just as Dayton hove into view. The Reverend picked up the reins & guided the buggy through the town & past the Toll House & across the bridge over the Carson River.

"Tell me," said Rev. C.V. Anthony, "about Absalom Smith."

I said, "His real name was Deforrest Robards. He liked the idea of being a soldier so he gathered together a band of volunteers from among his friends. He became a Confederate Lieutenant. But when he faced the enemy at Shiloh, he froze with terror and then fled, causing a rout of his men and great loss of life. He came here and adopted the false name of Absalom Smith."

"Absalom," said the Reverend. "Perhaps the most heroic coward in the Good Book. 'O Absalom, my son, my son!'" he quoted.

I said, "He went to Topliffe's Theatre on Friday afternoon and they asked him to stand in for Mr. Woodhull, who was ill that evening. Sally knew Robards from Mobile, Alabama. She happened to be at Topliffe's that night. When she saw him, she went to greet him. He had to finish the show but he arranged to meet her later down at her crib. Short Sally loved a brave man but despised a coward. Also, she had a tongue as sharp as an acidulated drop. I reckon he told her what happened, but instead of consoling him, she taunted him. Martha heard her shout 'Flicker, flicker. Yellowhammer!'

That was about the worst thing Short Sally could have said. Deforrest Robards went crazy and throttled her."

"War is a terrible thing," said the Reverend. "It drives some men crazy."

I said, "I should have guessed sooner that he was the killer. He must have followed Martha to my office and used the duel between Farner Peel and Murphy as an opportunity to try to break in. But the door held, so he followed me and struck up a conversation with me in the Fashion Saloon."

"You frequent the Fashion Saloon?"

"Sometimes," I said, and hurried on with my account. "Anyway, Absalom Smith, a.k.a. Robards, froze when El Dorado Johnny challenged him. If I knew how to read people better I'd have known he was petrified with fear."

"You witnessed a gun duel in a saloon?"

"Not that time. Absalom Smith left, but when I went out back to talk to someone, I think he must have been in the other privy. If I was better at conundrums I would have known that."

"Beg pardon?"

"Just before Absalom Smith, a.k.a. Robards, left the Fashion Saloon that day, he posed me a conundrum. He asked me what the difference was between roast beef and pea soup. Before we could answer, he said, 'Anyone can roast beef.'"

The Reverend frowned for a moment, then chuckled. "But not everyone can *pee soup*!"

"Correct," said I. "If I was smarter, I would have known he was going to the privy just like Poker—my friend. The murderer himself was sitting less than a foot away as I discussed my plan to investigate his Crime." I shook my head, amazed at my own stupidity.

"Ironic," said the Reverend.

I was not sure what "ironic" meant but it sounded good so I nodded & continued my account. "I first realized that Absalom Smith was Robards the Killer when I sniffed his tobacco at Sal's crib. I remembered he carried a Confederate revolver. That was also a clew confirming that he was Deforrest Robards, the petrified Lieutenant of Shiloh."

"Brilliant," said the Rev. "Quite brilliant." And to the horses, "Gee up there!"

Another quarter hour's trotting brought us to the tiny hamlet of Temperance out in the hot, sagebrush-dotted desert.

It was the first time I had been back since my foster parents were scalped & murdered there.

Ledger Sheet 55

THE REVEREND HAD GOT a key to my family's cabin from somewhere & he opened the door of the cabin & went in first.

I followed him in. It smelled stale in there but I caught a faint whiff of Bay Rum Tonic & blood.

I tried not to look at the stain on the bare wood floor. I guess they had burned the rug Ma Evangeline loved so much. She had made it from scraps of old calico braided together and then sewed in a big spiral like a squished but colorful snake. It made the place seem bright & cozy. Without that rug, the cabin seemed sad & bare. There were already some cobwebs up on the ceiling near the beam where I had cowered less than two weeks ago.

Someone had packed up the china & cooking things & bedding into wooden tea chests. In one chest were Ma Evangeline's books; I saw the Bible, *Bleak House* & Worcester's Elementary Dictionary lying on top.

"What is this?" The Rev. C.V. Anthony was holding up a flat wooden case with a glass top.

"That is my Bug Collection," I said. "I also have a Button Collection. I like collecting things," I added. "Ma Evangeline said it was one of my Eccentricities."

"Do you want to keep your bed?" said the Reverend, gesturing towards the smaller of the two beds.

"No," I said. "It is too big for my back room. Mr. Bloomfield left me a camp cot and I can sleep on that."

"As you wish," he said. "What about the cabin and the remaining furniture therein? Do you want to keep it or sell it?"

"Sell it," I said. "I will never come back here. If you get any money for it then put it towards the cost of my foster parents' burial, which you paid for. Anything left over can go in the church collection box."

"That is very Christian of you, P.K.," said the Reverend. "You are storing up treasure in heaven."

I nodded to myself. I had donated about $100 of my own funds to help Martha but my share of the reward for Extra Dub had been twice that, for they had doubled his reward money to $400 since his first escape. You cannot outgive God.

We carried the tea chests out of the cabin & put them in the back of the buckboard. I also took my school shoes, a few extra cups, a pitcher & washbasin and a dustpan & broom. But we left the big bed & the small bed & the dresser & the table & chairs & the potbelly stove.

We climbed back up into the buckboard & the Reverend flicked the horses with his whip & we drove back along the dusty desert road & crossed the Carson River & paid the toll & took a left fork at Main Street of Dayton & drove up to the graveyard.

The Rev. C.V. Anthony left the horses by a water trough as there was no shade anywhere. I had never been here before, so I let him lead the way through the dusty gravestones. By the time we stopped in front of one, my throat felt tight and my vision was blurry. I knew it was the grave of Ma and Pa Jones, who had been kind to me & had taken me in & loved me & had died on account of me. The chorus of that song "Kiss Me Good Night, Mother" was going through my head:

Thy tender love, Mother, makes all so bright;
Kiss me good night, Mother, kiss me good night.

I blinked & my vision cleared & I was able to read the inscription on the stone:

EMMET JONES 1818-1862
EVANGELINE WYATT JONES 1822-1862
"I HAVE FINISHED MY COURSE."
R.I.P.

I swallowed hard & took a deep breath & let it out slow. Their race was done & they had gained the Victor's Crown.

I looked around at the barren graveyard on the hill and the sage-dotted mountains around and the blue sky above.

I took another deep breath.

"P.K.?" said the Reverend C.V. Anthony, who stood beside me still.

"Yes, sir?" I replied.

He said, "My wife and I have had a talk. We do not think it right that a twelve-year-old child such as yourself should live alone in a former tobacco store and frequent saloons and pursue such a dangerous occupation as being a Detective. We think you should be fed, clothed, educated in school and also protected."

I did not know what to say, so I kept my eyes fixed on the tombstone & said nothing.

"We intend to start a family soon but we would like you to live with us."

I looked up at him in surprise.

He smiled down at me. "And if it happens that you do not want to live with another Methodist preacher, Doc Pinkerton and his wife said they would be pleased to take you in, too. Tom says you have the makings of a fine doctor. He told me that you are adept, inquisitive and not at all squeamish. So, you see, you have two families vying for you. Which will it be?"

I looked back at the epitaph on my foster parents' tombstone.

Nobody could ever replace Pa Emmet or Ma Evangeline in my affections.

Also, I must confess I like being Boss of Myself. I can

frequent as many Saloons & Music Halls as I like. I can take my meals at the Colombo Restaurant & eat layer cake for breakfast every day, if I so desire. If I want new clothes or shoes, I can just mosey on down to Wells, Fargo & Co., withdraw a few $20 gold coins & buy myself a new outfit at Wasserman's Emporium.

There was also the matter of a certain Secret I did not want anyone to discover.

I said, "I reckon I am fine where I am."

I could see he was downcast by this reply, because he gave a quick nod & looked down & pressed his lips together.

I tried to explain myself in a way that might lift his spirits. "Your offer is very kind. Doc Pinkerton's, too. But I have a Course to Run, just like Ma and Pa Jones. I guess being a Detective is my calling. God gave me a Thorn, but also Sufficient Grace. And He gave me some strange abilities that suit the profession. Where else could I have used my skill at identifying over one hundred types of smoking, chewing and leaf tobacco to bring a criminal to Justice and save the life of a frightened Eye Witness?"

"I admit you did well," said the Rev. C.V. Anthony. "You were inventive in your reasoning and brave in the execution of your plan. But your exploit almost got you killed."

"This earth-life is temporary," I said. "It is only a preparation for the next life, which is Eternal."

"Amen," said he. "But, P.K., are you not lonesome in that little room without anybody to tuck you up at night?"

I said, "No. I like living by myself and being my own boss. Besides, whenever I want people I can just go out my front door and there is the whole World. Even if it is Satan's Playground."

"Bless my soul," he said with a laugh, "you have almost convinced me. I believe you would make a mighty fine preacher. Or Lawyer."

"No," I said. "But one day I just might make a Good Detective."

GLOSSARY

ambrotype—an early form of photograph made directly on glass.

Antietam—The bloodiest single day of the Civil War was a battle that took place near Antietam Creek and Sharpsburg, Maryland, on September 17 1862. More than 23,000 were killed, wounded or missing.

bail—a sum of money deposited to allow a prisoner to go free until they can be tried in court or released. If the prisoner runs away, the money is forfeit.

caliber—the diameter of balls and bullets measured in hundredths of an inch.

Celestial—slang for Chinese, because the imperial court in China was known as the "celestial court."

Comstock—The ledge of silver below Virginia City was known as the Comstock Lode, after one of the original stakeholders. The whole region was sometimes called the Comstock.

Confederate—a supporter of the Southern slave-owning states that were fighting against the Union in the Civil War of 1861–1865.

crib—a square structure like a manger, the framework of a mine or a one-room dwelling.

Daily Territorial Enterprise—the first daily newspaper published in Virginia City, starting in 1860.

Dan De Quille—the pen name of Virginia City journalist William Wright.

Deringer or Derringer—a small one- or two-shot pistol, usually with big caliber bullets.

draw a bead on/draw down on—expressions that meant to point a gun at someone.

hoopskirt—a skirt worn over petticoats with hoops sewn in.

hurdy girls—women who worked in saloons and often played a hand-cranked stringed soundbox called a "hurdy-gurdy."

Lakota (a.k.a. Sioux)—the language and name of a Native American people from South Dakota.

medicine bag—a pouch carried by some Native Americans, usually for magical purposes.

moccasin—a soft slipper or shoe with no heel but a single piece of leather for the sole.

Mount Davidson—The Comstock Lode was in it and Virginia City upon it.

mustang—a type of American wild horse, small but full of stamina.

ore—earth or rock containing valuable metal or mineral.

Paiute—The Northern Paiute were a tribe of Native Americans who lived in Nevada, Oregon and parts of California.

passel—a large group of people or things.

Pinkerton Detective Agency—founded by Allan Pinkerton in Chicago in 1850.

placer mining—a technique in which surface deposits of earth are rinsed with water to reveal gold.

plug—a bowler hat, a piece of chewing tobacco, or an old horse.

privy—a toilet located in a small shed or "outhouse" near another building. The toilet was usually just a wooden seat over a pit.

quartz stamp mill—a machine with pistons that pulverized rock in order to remove the precious metal.

Reb—short for Rebel; a Confederate. Their enemies, the North, or Union, supporters, called Southern soldiers "Johnny Reb."

rolltop desk—a writing desk with a flexible slatted cover, which rolled down from the top.

Sam Clemens (who would soon call himself "Mark Twain")—was a reporter for the *Daily Territorial Enterprise* from 1862 to 1864.

sarsaparilla—syrup made from a root of the same name; nowadays called root beer.

scatter gun—a shotgun that fires small bits of metal or stone.

slouch hat—a soft felt hat with a wide flexible brim, usually in brown or black.

soiled dove—a term used to describe a woman who worked in a saloon or brothel.

spittoon—a metal, glass or ceramic container to catch tobacco chewers' spit.

Stonewall Jackson—a brave and pious Confederate general, who liked to suck lemons.

stovepipe hat—a tall cylindrical hat, famously worn by President Abraham Lincoln.

tableau vivant—a silent group of people posed to represent a famous scene from history, as if frozen in time. (It is French for "living picture.")

teamster—the driver of a team of animals, usually oxen or mules.

telegraph—a method of sending messages almost instantly over great distances by means of making and breaking electrical connections along a wire.

tintype—a form of photograph taken directly on a thin sheet of tin.

Virginia City—a mining town in Nevada that sprang up in 1859, soon after silver was discovered.

Washoe Zephyr—an ironic slang term for the violent wind in Virginia City.

Wells Fargo—Wells, Fargo & Co. was founded in 1848 to transport and bank money, payrolls and gold.

Yank—a supporter of the Union, or Northern states, in the Civil War. Their enemies, the Confederates, called them "Billy Yank."

BUCK UP!

There's more adventure in store for P.K. in
P.K. Pinkerton and the Pistol-Packing Widows.

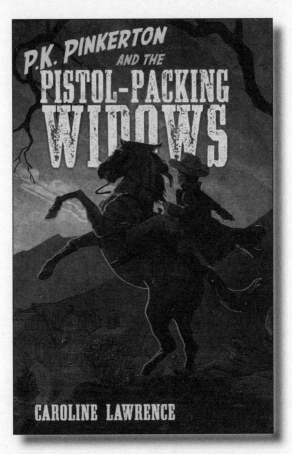

Turn the page to get a sneak peek!

Ledger Sheet 1

MY NAME IS P.K. PINKERTON, Private Eye. I was born in Hard Luck near Mount Disappointment, just over 12 years ago. I reckon that pretty much sums up my short & miserable life, which is anyways soon about to end.

A few months ago, I decided to become a Detective.

That, and my Thorn, is what got me in the Predicament I am in today.

By "Thorn" I mean the fact that people confound me.

By "Predicament" I mean the fact that I am lost in a blizzard somewhere in the Nevada desert.

I have found some shelter, so I will write out my Last Will & Testament before I die of starvation and/or cold:

LAST WILL & TESTAMENT OF ME:
P.K. PINKERTON, PRIVATE EYE

To my business partner, Ping: I leave my office, my
disguises & all the money in my strong box at
Wells, Fargo & Co.

To Miss "Bee" Bloomfield: I leave my Bug Collection,
my Button Collection and my Big Tobacco
Collection.

To Mr. Sam Clemens: I leave my Smith & Wesson's
seven-shooter, which used to be his anyways.

To Mr. Jason Francis Montgomery aka "Poker Face
Jace": I leave my three feet in the Chollar Silver
Mine & also my Indian medicine bag & its
contents (including my original pa's Pinkerton
Railroad Detective button). I leave those things as
a personal memento, even though Jace no longer
cares about me and probably will not want them.

Signed *P.K. Pinkerton, Private Eye*
On this day of our Lord, Sunday December 7th 1862

While I still have the strength to hold my pencil, I reckon
I should also leave an account of what happened, in case they
ever find my frozen body.

It all started last month in Virginia City, when I solved the murder of Miss Sally Sampson and brought her killer to justice. Miss Sally was a Soiled Dove, with a little place on D Street. She was real popular, especially with the miners and volunteer firemen. After I caught her killer & avenged her death, I became real popular, too.

People flocked to my Detective Agency.

Some people asked me to find lost dividends or necklaces or to investigate their partners. But most of the jobs were what I call Romantic Jobs. My clients were mainly miners who wanted me to "shadow" ladies they liked. As there are only two women for every dozen men in these parts, business was brisk.

At first I thought this was good. One day I hope to join my pa, Robert Pinkerton, at the Detective Agency founded by my uncle Allan. Because my pa and uncle have not met me yet, and because I am a half-Sioux misfit, I wanted to become the best detective I can before going to Chicago.

Now I was getting lots of experience.

I was so busy that my Chinese friend, Ping, abandoned a promising apprenticeship with Mr. Isaiah Coffin, the photographer who works next door.

Ping moved into my narrow office and took charge of my desk and made me sit at the back of my store, behind the wooden counter where Sol Bloomfield once sold his many & varied tobacco products.

Every time a client came into my office, Ping would take their details (and a cash money deposit), and then send them on back to me. Ping said I was lucky to have him as a business partner because he was better with money than me.

Ping is right.

I am clever about some things but foolish about others.

For example, I can do any sum in my head, but I am no good at budgeting or bargaining.

I can identify over a hundred types of tobacco, but sometimes I do not recognize a person I met the day before.

I can remember a pack of cards in the order they were dealt, but I have to make up strange pictures in my head to do so.

Then there is my Thorn. I cannot easily tell what people are thinking, though I learned some tricks from my friend Poker Face Jace before he renounced me.

Did I mention my Foibles and Eccentricities?

One of my Foibles is that loud noises hurt my ears but some music entrances me.

One of my Eccentricities is that sometimes I get overwhelmed by people & as a result I need to be on my own.

That was the worst thing about Ping being my pard: he moved in with me. The bedchamber at the back of my office is tiny, with only one window and no door. With Ping there, I hardly had space to breathe.

Even when I was "on a case," I was not alone. Virginia City is getting more & more crowded every day. If a miner hired me to spy on his favorite saloon girl, I had to endure crowded saloons with people shouting & smoking & spitting. If a barkeep asked me to spy on his seamstress lady-love, I got jostled by bankers, miners & mule skinners as I lingered on the boardwalk, waiting to see who might call.

I did not mind the noise so much; I can always plug my

ears with lint. It was the never being on my own that got to me. It was enough to give a person the Mulligrubs.

Why did I not tell Ping to vamoose?

Three reasons:

No. 1—Ping reminded me that we had shook hands on being pards. I was not sure when we had agreed that exactly, but I have a bad memory for some things so I reckoned he was right.

No. 2—Ping was teaching me the "ancient Chinese art of hand-to-hand combat." As far as I could tell, this consisted of bending a finger back or poking an eye. Usually it was my finger that got bent & my eye that got poked, but Ping assured me that I was "making good progress."

No. 3—The Sunday after Ping moved in with me, the Rev. C.V. Anthony preached from the Book of Acts. It was the part where all the disciples share their belongings. The Rev. urged us to be good Christians & do likewise. As the Lord had recently prospered me, I thought it only fair to take those words to heart.

But it was mighty boresome being a Good Christian as well as a Detective. I did not have the opportunity to order my Collections or even read my Bible. I was that busy.

So when two men in heavy overcoats, slouch hats and muffling scarves grabbed me as I was coming out of my office last month, I was almost relieved. They jammed a gag in my mouth & tied it there with a handkerchief & tugged my slouch hat over my eyes & bound me hand & foot. Then they put me in a sack & tossed me into the back of a wagon.

I thought, "I am being abducted. But at least I will have a few moments on my own."

Ledger Sheet 2

IF SOMEONE PULLS your slouch hat over your eyes &
stuffs you into a gunnysack & tosses you into the
back of a cart & then drives you somewhere in a flat
town, you might get confused. But it is hard to lose
your bearings in Virginia City, even when bound &
gagged & in the pitch black.

I was slowly sliding down towards the sound of
hooves. That meant we were going down the mountain. Then I thudded up against some bumpy tur-
nip-smelling things. From that I deduced I was
heading east in a turnip wagon.

Pretty soon the wagon jerked to a stop. I guessed
we had stopped at C Street to wait for a break in the
traffic.

I was wearing my usual attire of blue woolen coat & pink flannel shirt & fringed buckskin trowsers over faded red long underwear. Lying on the hard floor of the wagon, I could feel the bump of my small revolver in my right-hand pocket. My abductors had not bothered to search me. I guess they did not think a 12-year-old kid would be "packing a pistol," as they say in this region.

The cart lurched into motion again. It stayed level crossing C Street but soon tipped forward as it continued downhill. Now I have been tied up before, but never gagged. It was not pleasant. To distract myself, I tried to deduce what type of cloth they had stuffed in my mouth. I guessed it was one of those bags for loose tobacco, as it tasted strongly of tobacco & faintly of maple.

Personally, I do not smoke, sniff or chew. However my office is located in an old Tobacco Emporium. When I first moved in, I acquainted myself with all the tobacco specks & crumbs the proprietor had left behind. Such things fascinate me. In order to learn more about tobacco I started a Big Tobacco Collection. This was useful because sometimes I can now identify culprits by the shreds of tobacco left at the Scene of a Crime.

I know from my Big Tobacco Collection that there are two popular brands of tobacco with maple sugar added.

Mohawk Maple is the cheap brand and Red Leaf is the high-tone label. As I lay jouncing in my sack, I tried to determine which of those my gag had once contained. My tongue figured out that the cloth bag in my mouth once held the more expensive brand of tobacco. I deduced that not only from the taste but also from the texture of the bag, which was fine cotton, not rough burlap. It is hard to get cotton, fine or not, because of the Rebellion going on back east.

I reckoned one of the men who abducted me smoked Red Leaf tobacco.

But I did not know anybody who smoked Red Leaf Tobacco.

I tried coming at the problem from another direction.

I thought, "Who hates me?"

Immediately a Name dropped into my head: former Deputy Marshal Jack Williams.

He hates me because when I arrived in Virginia City there was an increase in shootings, stabbings and murders. He was dismissed & finally he got thrown in jail. But he was not imprisoned on account of an increase in other people's crime. He got those just desserts on account of his own crime, viz: robbing a man at gunpoint.

So how can he blame me for his misfortune?

And yet he does. I know this because he once said, "I blame you, half Injun. Until you arrived in these parts everything was bully."

As I lay gagged & bound in that turnip wagon, I reckoned Jack Williams had got out on bail & decided to get rid of me once and for all.

I thought, "I'll bet he and his accomplice will turn left towards Geiger Grade and toss me into a chasm."

However, Jack Williams and his helper did not turn left.

They carried straight on down the mountain. We crossed D Street and kept on going.

By this time my mouth was full of tobacco-flavored saliva from all the gag-pushing my tongue had been doing. Everybody knows that if you swallow tobacco-tinted spit you will feel sick. That is why there are about ten thousand spittoons all over the city. But I did not have a spittoon and I did not have a choice. So I swallowed.

We crossed E street and kept on going.

Then I thought, "I'll bet they are going to take me down to the Carson River and drown me in the icy water like a bag of unwanted puppies."

Immediately Jack Williams and his accomplice turned left.

Even had I not been counting streets I would have known we were now in Chinatown because I could smell the josh lights & incense & starch & lye soap & hear some women arguing in Chinese. The wagon stopped & jolted & started again & turned & stopped once more.

I felt dizzy & light-headed, probably from all the tobacco juice I had swallowed.

I heard male Chinese voices speaking loudly nearby.

I came west 2½ years ago on a wagon train with a Chinese cook, name of Hang Sung. He taught me about 30 or 40 words of Chinese. Most of those Chinese words were cuss words or words to do with poker.

As strong hands lifted me roughly up & out, I heard some of those Chinese cuss words & also the word for "angry." And then the word for "boss."

It was not Jack Williams and his pard who were abducting me. It was a couple of Celestials.

I thought, "My Detective Skills are still not good enough for me to go to Chicago and work with my pa in the Detective Agency founded by my uncle Allan Pinkerton. I have no clue who is abducting me, or why."

JOIN P.K. ON EVERY
WHIP-CRACKING ADVENTURE!

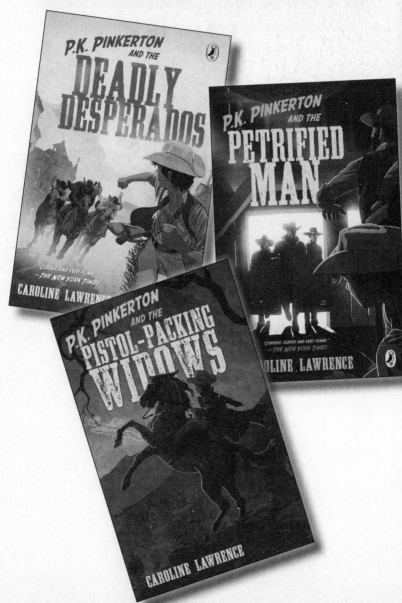